RAVEN

Legends Saga

Book Two

Written by Stacey Rourke

Published by Anchor Group

PO Box 551 Flushing, MI 48433

Anchorgrouppublishing.com

Edited by Melanie Williams

Cover design by Najla Qamber Designs

To my mom,
From a very young age you not only supported my creativity, but encouraged it. You taught me to believe in myself, dream big, and never to quit just because things get hard. For all of this, and countless other things that made me the person I am today, I thank you. I love you.

Prologue

Early in the 1800s

Humming a merry little tune, the old woman sliced the flapping bird from throat to belly. Black feathers broke free as the raven thrashed for freedom, only to have the fight leave its body in a gush of crimson. Scooping up the lifeless bird with her arthritic claw, the woman squeezed it over her cast iron skillet to drain its fluids. With one final shake, she cast its body aside with a casual flick of her wrist.

"There, there," the crone rasped to the cooing baby swaddled in his basket. "It is almost time."

She hobbled to the rickety baker's rack in the corner, the floorboards creaking beneath her bare feet. The tips of her fingers brushed over vials, turning some to find what she needed. Gathering the hem of her apron up like a basket, she dropped in her selected ingredients. Each bottle clinked its welcome to the new additions added. Back at her waist-high work counter, she arranged them one by one in the order she would need them. Popping out the corks, she measured out the necessary drop, dollop, or splash and added them to the skillet. The foreboding smell of sulfur—with its hungry, seething darkness—filled every inch of the tiny cabin. Leaning over the pot, the haggard woman cupped her hand to waft the aroma to her.

"*Hmmm.*" Her hooked nose crinkled in distaste. The quake of her hand steadied only when it closed around the last, and tallest, vial. A slight tip led to a brief roll, sending one newt-sized eyeball bobbing skyward in her mixture. Again, she paused to breathe it in. This time, nodding her pleasure. "Mmmm-hmmm, mmmm-hmmm. Just as it should be."

Slipping her fingers into the handles of her tongs, she plucked the glass pap feeder—that bore a striking resemblance to a sauce bowl upper society would use—from the boiling water in the cauldron hung over the fire within her small stone hearth. Steam swirled from the feeder as she set it down to cool. Reveling in her spare moment, she indulged herself by tiptoeing to the baby's side.

The cherub-faced boy paused from gumming at his tiny fist to peer up at her, his eyes bright with trust and innocence. Clucking her tongue against the roof of her mouth, the old woman wagged her index finger over his head. The infant's arms and legs wriggled out from beneath his swaddling blanket, kicking and wiggling his glee.

"Oh, my handsome boy," the crone sighed, laughter slipping past her lips like frothy bubbles spewing over a pot's edge. "I have such plans for you. Death itself will tremble at the mention of your name."

The baby's cheeks puffed, his pink tongue poking out to blow a raspberry in response.

Her chuckle lingering, she returned to her task. Thumping her fingers against the feeder, she found it adequately cooled. Her frail arm quaked with the strain of lifting the weighty skillet. The sludgy mixture glopped into the waiting feeder, streaking down the pan's edge as if sliced there by the talons of a hell beast. Setting the skillet aside, the old woman gave the concoction a final swirl.

"The time has come," she whispered in equal parts anticipation and disbelief.

Briefly setting the feeder aside, she scuffled over to claim her most valued treasure. One hand cradled his precious head, the other slid under his rump. The very instant she gathered him into the crook of her arm he snuggled in, nuzzling against her sagging breast. Revisiting her hum of that same haunting melody, she collected the feeder with her free hand and juggled them both the eight shuffled paces to her wooden rocking chair. Easing her weary frame to rest, she coaxed the chair in a gentle sway. The soothing rhythm lulled the baby toward sleep's peaceful oblivion. Each of his blinks longer than the last.

"Now, now, Edgar," she rasped, tickling his chin with one calloused fingertip. "There will be time enough to rest. First, let us fill that belly."

The old woman eased the lip of the feeder into his mouth, tipping it just enough to allow one lone drop to test his palate. Instinctively his tiny tongue shoved back against the feeder. His face screwed up in an adorable mask of disgust, long lashes blinking his displeasure. Yet … his lips smacked once, twice, a third time … before his mouth opened to accept more of her carefully formulated brand of love.

"The taste is vile at first," the crone whispered, leaning in to dot a kiss to the top of his velvety soft head. "Even so, it quickly makes you long for it. *That* is the lure of the dark magic."

Leaning back into the chair, she arranged herself with a few careful adjustments so as not to disturb the slurping infant. Back and forth they rocked, the old woman gazing at the precious face of her salvation. *Soon*, another would hear what she heard— see what she saw. Her cursed prison of solitude would come to an end, all thanks to a boy and a raven.

The first bang shook the cabin door on its hinges. The second shattered it into a rain of scraps and kindling, allowing a troop of roughly a dozen soldiers to fill the cramped space. The stomps of their boots drummed an ominous chorus. Each brandished a sword or musket, the business ends all fixed on her.

4

If she found any of this alarming, her stoic façade kept that fact well hidden.

"Shhhh, boys," she shushed, not pausing the sway of the chair, "you'll disturb the baby."

"Secure the child!" the captain, recognizable by the plume of feathers arching up from his pointed hat, commanded.

Emotion finally broke, revealing itself in the frantic scream that contorted her face in primal rage. "*No!*"

Holding tight to the infant, she fought against the officer that attempted to wrestle him from her arms. Cold steel pressing to her throat interrupted their scuffle.

"Let go of the baby!" Freckles dotted the nose of the youthful soldier who pinned her with his sword, adding an odd flare of whimsy to his murderous glare. "Or I'll run you both through."

Vibrating with a potent combination of anger and fear, she relented. Her jaw set tight, nostrils flaring. Hands, which curled into white knuckled claws, loosened enough for her darling treasure to be swept from her grasp without any harm coming to him.

"Officer!" the captain barked, smoothing his hand across his auburn mustache. "We do *not* now, nor shall we ever, make it a habit of harming innocent children."

"I know that well and true, Captain." The lad shrugged with an arrogant smirk. "However, *she* sure did not."

Clasping his hands behind his back, the senior officer nodded his approval. "Very well then, seize her."

Harsh hands closed around her arms, yanking her to her feet with an unnecessary force that instantly bruised her flesh.

"Linker, I want you to ride in the carriage with the baby. He shall be in your care for our voyage. Take him out now before this *witch* can try anything." The Captain's hateful stare fixed on the woman as she struggled to free herself from her captor's grasps.

"No! *No!*" she snarled and spat. "You *cannot* take him! He belongs with me! I am all he has left!"

Sliding his sword from the sheath at his hip, darkness writhed deep in the Captain's eyes. *"You are all he has left because you cut him from his mother's womb!"* The point of his sword jabbed into the wobbly flesh beneath her chin. *"Your own daughter!* For weeks we have been hunting you down like the *beast* you are. A beast capable of atrocities that boggle the mind!"

The woman stilled. Course grey hair brushed her shoulder as she cocked her head, a predatory smile curling across her mouth. "If only you knew the true magnitude behind that claim."

"Insolent wretch!" the Captain spat in her face. His saliva dripped from her nose as he returned his sword to its sheath.

"You will find no judgment or acceptance in the hangman's noose—just a right end."

Turning on the heel of his boot, he clomped back toward the door. His remaining soldiers fell into formation, lining the perimeter of the room and awaiting further orders. "Bind her hands. She can walk behind the horses, far from the baby."

Before his command was finished, a fit of coughs—starting small, but quickly building—rattled the frame of the sinewy woman. Turning her head, she hacked into her shoulder with a violent intensity reserved for the sick and the dying. Tears streamed down her face as she folded in half, her body held up only by the soldiers gripping her. Sudden as the fit started, it stopped. The staged act coming to an abruptly violent halt the second the withered woman lurched forward to clamp her teeth down on the arm of one of her captors. The soldier yelped in pain, pounding the butt of his fist against the back of her skull.

Coppery warmth exploded into her mouth, her head shaking side to side. Dull teeth tore tissue from bone. Eyes, reflecting nothing but madness, trained on the Captain as the woman raised her head and spit the hunk of flesh in his direction. It fell to the ground with a stomach churning squish.

The wounded soldier released his hold to apply pressure to his wound. Blood pulsed from between his fingers, pooling at his feet and seeping between the floorboards. Taking advantage of the moment, the woman lunged for him. Throwing her weight into him, she knocked him off balance. As he teetered back, arms wind-milling, she claimed his sword. Closing her hand around the hilt, the witch spun on her remaining captor and buried the blade in his gut. Gore dripped from the steel that tore straight through him. Not bothering to collect the weapon, she dashed to her workstation. The bitten soldier recovered enough to give chase, his platoon closing in just as he did. Her frantic hands grappled for the tabletop. Her body yanked back by an arm that closed around her neck in a choking hold. Spots danced before her eyes, blackness threatening. Even so, she fought to hold on, to claim her spoils before the shadows rushed in to claim her. Slapping one flailing hand against the table, she felt a squish beneath her palm. Giddy delight invigorated her, strengthened her. Pulling back, she whipped the gutted raven directly at the baby.

Officer Linker, charged with protecting the infant, pivoted on the balls of his feet to shoulder the gore in the infant's place. Unfortunately, his timing fell short. One chubby hand wriggled free from his tight swaddle as the bird flopped down onto the baby's delicate skin. Officer Linker's face crumbled in horror. Shifting the baby's weight, he raised one hand to fling the filth away. Beneath his fingers, ebony wings fluttered. Black, fixed eyes rolled and blinked. Sliced skin knit itself back together. A polished onyx beak snapped and lashed out, slicing the tender flesh of the baby's cheek. As a pained cry tore from little Edgar's chest, the Lazarus bird rose and flapped off into the night.

"You're too late!" the old woman crowed, her victorious chant drowning out her grandson's fusses. "He has been marked! *Darkness owns that boy now!*"

"Get the baby out of here!" the Captain hollered. Stealing a musket from the nearest soldier, he crossed the cabin in three wide strides. Not granting her a pause or hesitation, he trained the barrel on her forehead and fired.

1

Ridley

"I'm just sayin'," Ireland murmured against Noah's earlobe, her chin resting playfully on his shoulder. "We're already here, and I've got that deep, yearning *itch*. Why don't we just go for it?"

Strands of hair, the hue of weathered sand kissed golden by the sun, fell across his forehead as Noah Van Tassel tipped his chin her way. One wandering hand snaked around her waist, tucking into the back pocket of her jeans as he tugged her body closer to his. "Your last tattoo acted as a written invitation for the Headless Horseman to invade your body. Hence our investigatory trip here. That said, as much as I appreciate *all* of your deep yearnings, I'm thinking we skip this particular one and nix further ink."

Ireland's lips screwed to the side, her pert nose crinkling. "As rational points go, that one's hard to argue with."

Spastically flitching at the incessant hum of the tattoo gun, Rip Van Winkle edged up beside them. His watery eyes flicked over the framed sample sheets hanging on the walls while he twirled the end of his beard around his index finger. "I do not care for this place. It feels like a den of debauchery," a wide yawn cut off his sentence, "and not in the fun way. It is making my curse threaten."

Ireland begrudgingly pushed herself away from Noah to clap a hand on Rip's waif-like shoulder. "If you fall asleep here you *will* wake up with a dolphin tramp stamp. I promise you that."

Brow puckered in confusion, Rip looked to Noah for clarification. "What is a 'tramp stamp'?"

"It's a badge of masculine honor," Noah dead-panned.

"Then I have nothing to fear." Rip's narrow chest puffed with bravado. "I shall wear it proudly."

Carrington Love, appearing from the last station on the right, dried her hands on a paper towel she deposited in a stainless trashcan by the counter. Her glossy black locks were curled in a retro pin-up style, accented by a navy bandana. Full sleeve tattoos poked out from beneath the rolled cuffs of her red flannel shirt.

"Hey!" she chirped with recognition the moment she saw Ireland. "How did it heal? Everything okay?"

Ireland bit the inside of her cheek hard enough to taste blood. Call it intuition, but she guessed the artist to be referring to possible healing issues and *not* a mystically force tied to the artwork causing her to kill two people and terrorize a town. Or, did she ..?

"No problems at all." Clearing her throat, Ireland forced a tight smile and turned her forearm skyward for her to see. "Healed great! Ignore the scars and stitches around it. I ... uh…"

Countless words in the English language and she couldn't seem to string *any* of them together to form a believable lie.

"Got attacked by a badger!" Rip interjected on her behalf.

"*A badger*?" Ireland mouthed to him over Carrington's head as the artist encircled her hand around Ireland's wrist to inspect her work.

She turned Ireland's arm first one way, then the other. "Whoa! No shit? That's insane! The ink didn't even get scratched! You got so lucky."

"As lucky as I can be, having been attacked by a creature indigenous to *prairie regions*." Ireland pointedly jabbed the words at Rip as she pulled her arm away from Carrington's intense scrutiny. "This is probably a weird question to ask *after* I have this marred forever into my flesh, but where did you come up with this specific design?"

"I borrowed it from my runaway bride," Carrington giggled, her lip fiddling with its silver post piercing.

"Runaway bride?" Noah asked. Leaning in, his fingers traced circles over the small of Ireland's back. A simple gesture that sent an electric current sparking through her.

"Yeah, this Bear reserved a six hour slot on my day a while back. Came in, paid his reservation fee, and even showed me what he wanted." Her pointy chin jerked towards Ireland's arm. "That's the image he brought. The day of the appointment he showed up sweating buckets. I legit thought he was going to pass out before he got to the chair. Dude even brought his own ink with him, a full collection of unopened bottles of Eternal Ink, which I did *not* turn down because that's good shit. Anyway, while I was getting set up, he asked where the bathroom was. I waved him down the hall and never saw him again. Best I could figure he shimmied his hefty ass out the window and hit the ground running."

Tendrils of venomous suspicion swirled in Ireland's gut. "What made you pick that image for me? I mean, I know I pretty much gave you free creative rein, but why *this* one?"

"I had filed away his stencil," Carrington said, pushing her cat-framed glasses further up the bridge of her nose. "When you came in, you mentioned wanting something feminine, but badass. This was the first design that came to mind because the runner had described it in those *exact* words—I remember because it sounded insanely funny coming from him. I pulled his file and even found the unopened ink bottles. I'd completely forgotten about them. Kinda thought he'd have the balls to come back for them, but he never did. Long story short, you said you liked it, so it was a go. Why? Did someone else get the same image, or something?"

"No, it's definitely—unique," Ireland offered in what felt like the understatement of the century. "What about that ink? Do you still have it?"

Shaking her head, her red-painted lips fell into a frown. "No, sorry. Actually, when I used it on you, it kept clogging my gun. Maybe it thickened up from sitting too long. After that one use I threw it away."

Ireland's hands closed into fists at her sides, her nails digging half-moons into her palms. Her only lead in the mystery of who exactly was behind channeling the Horseman into her, and it seemed to come to a screeching halt here. Focusing to keep her breathing calm and steady, she could feel Noah's worried gaze boring into her skin. Fear that pity would be all he had to offer prevented her from meeting his stare.

"What about the guy's file?" Noah's hand steadied on her back, offering a steadfast support that granted her raging thoughts an iota of peace. "Does it have any contact information for him?"

"I tried to get a hold of him," Carrington shrugged, folding her arms over her chest. "*That was a six hour appointment, and I had people that wanted to get in!* Unfortunately, the only contact info he gave me was his business card from The Richmond Gallery on Fifth. I could never get that wuss to even pick up the phone."

Rip, Noah, and Ireland exchanged matching looks of intrigue.

"How far is that from here?" Even Ireland heard the surge of hope that quaked through her tone, but found herself powerless to squelch it.

"Three streets north, turn right. Then, it's four blocks down."

Without the courtesy of a goodbye, Ireland seized Noah's hand and spun for the door.

Rip, at least, was thoughtful enough to tag on a quick "Thanks," before falling into step behind them.

"If it's any consolation," Carrington called after them, "that design is more your style. That skull was meant for you!"

"Yeah," Ireland grumbled through her teeth, shoving the door open and rousing the chime overhead. "That's what I'm afraid of."

"I have heard things like this happen in New York," Rip yawned, visibly trembling through his onslaught of exhaustion. "I just never expected to find myself subjected to it."

"We've been through way worse than this." Ireland pressed her lips together, her hand curling around Rip's upper arm to keep him standing before his stress-induced narcolepsy stole him from her. "I need you to stay with me, buddy."

"I-I can't!" Rip threw his hands in the air, his fingers coiling into frantic claws. "Look at the horror that surrounds around! *H-h-how could you, Ireland*? *How could you bring me here*?"

Heaving a deep and aggravated sigh, Ireland let her hands fall to her sides with a burden-heavy slap. If for no other reason than to humor him, she spun in a slow circle. Her head cocked as she considered the full spectrum of the art gallery's exhibit. Life-like mannequins were arranged in various situations to make them appear human: waiting for a bus, playing tag with their mini-mannequin kids, showering. Bile rose in her throat at the shocking realism of the bloody car accident, and labor and delivery scene. "I won't be buying the annual pass, I'll give you that."

"This is *not* art!" Rip sniped. "This is a glorified game of dolls! What kind of society have I found myself in that would pass this off as—"

16

Just like that he hit his trigger. Ireland dove to catch him as Rip's sentence trailed off and eyes rolled back.

"I never knew you were such an art snob," Ireland grunted through her teeth as she hoisted up his dead weight. Hooking his gangly arm around her neck, she propped him up *Weekend at Bernie's* style.

"Oh, dear! Is he okay?" The apple-shaped man's silver and black necktie blew to the side, flapping against the sleeve of his burgundy dress shirt in his dart to their quickly sagging side. "I saw him going down and tried to get here in time. You're tougher than you look to have caught him." Immediately taking Rip's other arm, he helped to guide them to a nearby settee.

"Almost to a fault," Ireland mumbled, unceremoniously flopping Rip down on the sage green upholstery.

"Is-is he snoring?" her helper asked, smoothing his tie back into place.

"Sadly," her gaze flicked up to read his Richmond Gallery nametag, "Herb Mallark, he is. In every friendship there are those annoying traits you have to tolerate to keep that person in your life. *This* would be his."

The corners of Herb's crystal blue eyes crinkled with his warm, friendly grin. "Then he must be a cherished friend that you stick by him through it."

17

"Yeah, he's a hoot," Ireland stated dismissively, her almond-shaped eyes narrowing at his oddly familiar face. "I'm sorry, have we met?"

"Well, I'm not sure." Herb pivoted to face her, his sausage link index finger brushing over the strands of his thick mustache. Suddenly, his features brightened. "Broadway in the Park!" He snapped his fingers in recognition. "You understudied *Annie*, didn't you? I worked set design!"

"No," she snorted at *that* mental image and flipped her bangs from her eyes. "That most definitely was *not* me."

Noah picked that moment to round the Family Biking display, his nose wrinkling in poorly concealed distaste. He thumbed his phone off as he neared and dropped it into the breast pocket of his blue flannel shirt.

"Is everything okay?" Ireland nodded in the direction of his phone, anticipating life had officially caught up with her exceedingly wealthy beau that had shunned all his responsibilities to take this impromptu road trip with her.

"Yeah, absolutely," he dismissed, his eyebrows rising at Rip's splayed form. "What happened to him?"

"He is suffering the effects of interpretive art. It seems he is *not* a fan," Ireland explained and turned back to the issue that was nagging at her. "Now, Herb here and I are trying to figure out where we know each other from."

"Ever been to Sleepy Hollow?" Noah hooked his thumbs into his belt loops, the muscles of his forearms flexing.

"Can't say that I have." Herb glanced down at the gold watch fastened on his wrist, his eyes twinkling with an air of mischief. "Although with as steeped as it is in legend, I would love to make the trip."

He's lying. Deep within her a rusted cell door yawned open, releasing a presence as smooth and deadly as the curved blade of a scythe. The spirit of the Horseman that possessed her ... that *owned* her ... had awoke. *See how his stare fixed on yours and held? He thinks he's clever by adopting so bold a strategy. Fortunately, you feel it as well as I. This man is hiding something, and only* you *have the capabilities to draw that truth from him.*

Ireland ran one shaky hand over the back of her neck that was suddenly dotted with sweat. "Actually, the reason we're here is this." Her arm visibly quaked as she stabbed it forward, tattoo up. "Someone here on the staff was going to get this tattoo. Do you have any idea who it was?"

Herb rocked up onto the balls of his feet to lean in and get a better look. "Ah, yes! That would be me. Although now that I see the beauty of it in ink, I regret my cowardice."

The Horseman was right. Ireland's breath caught, anticipating the slew of violent suggestions sure to be his counterpoint. Frantically patting at the pockets of her jeans, she found herself minus the one—and only—tool she had to keep the beast quiet; her iPod cued up to the twangiest country music imaginable. Her chest rose and fell with ragged breaths as the horrifying reality set in. She didn't have it. She was surrounded by innocent people and was at the beast's mercy. Closing her eyes she fought for neutral, taking deep cleansing breathes to fend off that spiral into darkness. Risking a peek through one eyelid, she realized with a shocked appreciation that her paranormal squatter remained noticeably silent.

Seemingly oblivious to her turmoil, Noah latched on to this new slab of information like a hungry Rottweiler. "Then you can tell us where the idea came from, and what was so special about that ink!"

"Goodness, you'd think we were talking about a quest for the Holy Grail!" Herb chuckled, his belly jiggling like a certain jolly ole' elf. "There's really not much to tell. The ink I bought online because I'm a bit of a germ-aphobe and wanted the security of my own bottles. The design I found at an art show held at the home of one of our very best clients." Digging into the pocket of his perfectly pressed grey slacks, he extracted a gold clip holding an assortment of business cards. Shuffling through them, he plucked out one that was stark white with silver lettering and held it up for them to see. "Ridley Peolte, a passionate art lover and stock market Midas, whatever that boy touches turns to gold. And let me tell you, when Ridley invites you to a party, you *go*! It was there, in his loft, that I saw a painting of that sugar skull image. I found it so barbarically common I thought it would be a fantastic tattoo—oh, no offense intended."

"None … taken." Ireland mumbled, her nostrils flaring.

She could hear the pounding rhythm of Herb's heartbeat pulsating through her very core, could feel the tantalizing pull of raw, primal mayhem. This had to be a new ploy of the Horseman, to tempt her with the seduction of savagery. No way could it be her own free will luring her to call forth her sword and unleash a crimson geyser that would paint the walls with scarlet gore.

"Could we keep that card?" Ireland practically panted. Fidgeting and squirming on her feet, she tried to find some comfort in her own skin. None could be found. Every pore of her sizzled and screamed to be sated. "If the guy is a regular client, you could get another, right?"

"Absolutely!" Herb chirped.

Pinching the card between two fingers, his hand brushed hers with a feather light touch. The chill that ripped down her spine shuddered through her frame. A mere blink and intoxicatingly nightmarish images flashed behind her lids. *One hand closing around his wrist, holding him firm as she raised the other. Metal winging through the air, her axe soaring in, end over end, until it settled into her waiting palm. Spinning into a forceful*

21

swing, she widened his smile with the edge of her blade, splattering the floor and herself with a succession of heavy ruby droplets.*

"Are you okay, miss?" Herb's bushy brows puckered in tight with concern. "Your lips are turning ... blue."

Noah's chiseled features swam before her, prompting a naughty little giggle to escape her parted lips. His hazel eyes bulged, instinct causing him to recoil at the visible black veins scrolling and snaking across her face in intricate patterns. Her skin stretched taut over bone, dark shadows swallowing all but the gleam of her irises.

"Time for us to go." Seizing her wrist, Noah yanked Ireland to him, capturing her in a firm reverse bear hug with her arms pinned tight to her sides.

"Mmmm, Van Tassel," she purred in a throaty rasp more demonic than human. "I was wondering how long it would take for you to get rough and bring the kink."

"Ha-ha!" Emitting a sharp bark of shocked laughter, Noah's eyebrows disappeared into his hairline. He addressed the stunned museum curator over Ireland's rolling, writhing shoulders. "There's no pretending ya didn't hear that! She ... uh ... suffers from low blood sugar. It turns her into a slightly demonic nympho. Awkward as it is here, family gatherings are the real bitch."

"C-can I get her anything? Some juice perhaps?" Herb's head cocked, his stare locked on the experiment into the paranormal that was Ireland Crane while Noah scooted her toward the exit.

"Nope, we're good," he lied through a forced smile, before muttering against Ireland's ear, "Do you have your iPod?"

"Check my pockets." Cherry-cola red strands tangled with her lashes as Ireland's head lulled back against his shoulder, the tip of her tongue teasing over his bottom lip. "And dig *deep*."

"Gonna go ahead and take that as a no." Noah glanced back over his shoulder to see how far they were from freedom. He had her talisman in his pocket, but knowing the effects it had on her, chose to keep that as an absolute last resort—for now.

"What about him?" Herb called after them, jabbing a thumb in Rip's direction.

"I'll be back for him!" Noah's hair clung to his head in a fresh sheen of sweat while Ireland nipped and nibbled at his neck. "In the meantime put velvet ropes around him and pass him off as an exhibit. He'll fit right in!"

Out of ideas and quickly losing his hold, Noah bought them a few extra moments the only way he could think to. With an awkward nod to the lingering exhibit attendees, he launched into an off-key rendition of *Desperado* and dragged his hissing, spitting girlfriend the remaining distance to the car.

Ireland flipped the business card between her fingers, making it roll over each digit before catching it with the next. "What do you think came first? The opulent office with white and silver décor or the pretentious business card with the same color scheme?"

Crickets may as well have chirped in response with Noah ignoring her altogether and Rip giving a quick shrug with his lips pressed in a firm line. Not that this was a new development. It had been a *long* and insanely uncomfortable ride to the mysterious Mr. Peolte's high-rise office.

Shifting on the white leather waiting room sofa and shooting a forced smile to the perky receptionist, Ireland crossed her legs at the ankle and braced for the onslaught. "I can't help but think something is bothering both of you."

"*There is!*" Rip erupted in a hushed, but venomous whisper. "I cannot *believe* you two left me behind! I mean, yes, *eventually* you came back for me—and I thank you for that. However, that does *not* change the fact that I woke up to an Asian family taking pictures of me! It is hard to determine who was more traumatized by it, me for waking up with an audience or them for thinking one of the statues *came alive*. From the way their kids screamed, I assure you *they* will never set foot in a museum or gallery again! *I ruined culture for those poor children!*"

Ireland blinked hard, clamping her teeth down on the insides of her cheeks to stifle a threatening snicker at that vividly hysterical mental image. "Again, Rip, couldn't be sorrier." Taking a beat to clear her throat, and drowned the lilt of amusement dripping from her tone, she turned her attention to her visible seething paramour. "What about you, Van Tassel? Is there anything you'd like to share with the class?"

"Oh, are we talking now?" he snipped, his hazel eyes glittering gold with resolute indignation. "Because I didn't think we did that anymore. I thought we were going to ignore the fact that," he glanced around to see if the Barbie doll receptionist was listening before dropping his voice to a barely audible, but clearly pissed off, rant, "you were going full out Horseman in the middle of the day *without* your cloak! Now you're trying to play it off like it was no big deal! What if I hadn't been there, Ireland? *I thought you had a handle on this!*"

"I do, and you were, okay?" she hissed back, matching his muted but urgent tone. "Catastrophe was avoided, and I thank you for that. My iPod is now in my pocket and I learned from my mistake. Can we have a little bit of a learning curve here? *Please*?"

"*A learning curve*?" Pushing himself to the edge of the couch, Noah leaned forward with his elbows on his knees. "You 'slip up' and people *die*!"

Behind her glass and chrome desk, Barbie glanced up. Her perfectly arched eyebrows rose in question.

Noah's chin dropped to his chest, flaxen strands curtaining his face. In the pregnant pause that followed, Ireland watched the muscles of his back expand and contract with a deep, cleansing breath. He allowed himself the moment before he raised his head and met her gaze straight on. "We learned how easy it could happen, and no one got hurt. I'll take that as a win. But I need you to promise me that if you feel yourself slipping again, you'll *tell me*. I can have your back like I did today, or break out your talisman if we're past that point. You know I'm in your corner. *However,* and here's the huge clause in all of this, the whole system we have going here only works if you are *brutally*—hey-Noah-I-wanna-slaughter-everyone-in-the-room—*honest* with me. Deal?"

Dragging her tongue over her top teeth, Ireland tried to wipe away the sour taste left in her mouth by admitting she needed help. Even so, Noah was right. Casting her gaze to the floor in what felt like defeat, she nodded. "Too much is at stake. If I feel myself slipping, I'll tell you."

She caught her tongue before tagging on, *as long as there's time*. Instead that weighty provision hung in the air between them in a rip and pregnant pause.

"He's coming!" the receptionist practically sang in a giddy trill as she pushed her chair from her desk to sashay around it, front and center. Flipping her curtain of blonde waves over her shoulder, she soothed her peach pencil skirt into place and adjusted the plunging neckline of her blouse.

An eager smile dawned on her lovely face the same moment the French doors on the opposite side of the room swung open wide. Sunlight flooded in, haloing his physique in a glowing luminescence. There, framed by the doorway with charisma wafting off of him like the enticing burst of scent from a freshly bloomed rose, stood ... *Ridley Peolte*.

2

EDGAR

Wings, as light as wisps of air, tickled across one round, dimpled cheek. The sweet melody of a child's laugh rose up in a chorus the angels would envy. Plump little fingers moved for the butterfly's orange and black wings just as they fluttered out of reach. On roly-poly toddler legs, little Edgar hobbled after his new friend.

Colors exploded around him like an enchanted fairy land. Trees blooming with bright pink pompons. Every color in the rainbow sprouted from the ground in fluffy bushels. Around each turn a new adventure awaited. Magic grew and evolved in the Poe gardens, all of it just waiting for little Edgar to discover each and every time his mother opened the door and invited him to go play.

Edgar rounded the towering tree that canopied the far corner of the garden with its sweet smelling shade. His tiny white shoes scuffed along the dirt path, laces dragging and flapping behind him. Abruptly, his shuffled steps stopped short. His toffee colored eyes widening the moment his gaze fell upon the blue bird splayed on the path before him. Its head was twisted at the most unnatural of angles. Its black bead eyes fixed in eternity's stare.

"Pretty birdy," the cherub faced lad cooed. Bending into a squat, he waddled closer, leaning his body first one way then the other to maneuver. Baby-fine strands of ebony silk tickled across his forehead with the inquisitive tilt of his head.

"Edgar!" his mother called. "It's time for lunch, my darling."

The toddler didn't respond, but scooted one foot forward. In hopes of rousing the sleeping bird, he poked it gently with the toe of his shoe.

"Edgar? Where have you hidden, my silly boy? I have berries and cream inside for you." Mother's tone was sweeter than the afore mentioned berries, her words slathered in love and adoration.

Edgar turned toward her voice, even started to straighten and go to her, before temptation's curling, coiling finger encircled his chin and lured his attention back to those bright blue feathers.

With each blink his impossibly long lashes brushed the tops of his cheeks. The birds high overhead sang such a lovely tune. More than anything he wanted this fallen vocalist to rejoin their choir.

Extending one finger, stained with dandelion butter and grass, Edgar tenderly stroked the velvety breast of the still creature. To his surprise the bird gave an involuntary jerk beneath his touch. Through the pad of his finger Edgar could feel a soft thump begin to beat a steady rhythm within his winged friend. Warmth chased away the cold's harsh hold. A succession of crackles and pops righted the bird's twisted neck. Black eyes blinked, focused. Feathers ruffled, the once limp form giving a quick hop, and the bird was on its feet. Its head cocked with an avian twitch, considering the boy crouched over it.

"Edgar, what have you done?"

With a hot rush of blood rushing to his cheeks, Edgar whipped around. Mother had *never* spoken a cross word at him, never looked at him with anything except absolute adoration. Yet, in that moment, she stared at him like a lowly stranger.

Behind him, the startled bird's wings beat against the air, lifting it toward its second chance.

"Mama?" Edgar squeaked, his heart thudding against his ribs.

Gathering the billowing fabric of her skirts in her hands, Madame Poe snapped herself from her terrified trance and rushed to her young son's side. With a palm on each of his cheeks, she turned him this way and that in a cursory examination. "W-we must ... we must speak with your father. He will know what must be done. Come now." Seizing him firmly by the wrist, she dragged her confused and frightened tyke inside.

3

Ridley

The very definition of seductive swagger stood before them, one hand slung into the front pants pocket of his tailored navy blue suit. "What have we here, Meegan?" Charm exuded from Ridley Peolte's gleaming white smile. With his free hand he adjusting the knot of his silk taupe, navy, and silver striped tie. One sleek ebony strand broke free from his flawlessly styled hair, casually grazing across his forehead. His eyes, such a deep ocean blue that Ireland could practically see the foam of the white caps swirling in his irises, immediately locked on her.

The receptionist—Meegan, apparently—blushed bright pink clear down her neckline the second her name passed his lips. "They just wanted a moment of your time, Mr. Peolte, in regards to a piece of art. I hope it's okay I had them wait?"

"Again, I must insist you call me Ridley," he corrected, the faintest trace of an accent Ireland couldn't quite place curling through each word. "And, of course, I don't mind. However, you

32

will have to walk with me. I have a platter of California spring rolls calling my name and a meeting I have to rush back for." Waving his hand to the trio in an 'after you' gesture, Ridley shot an over-the-shoulder glance back to Meegan. "Can I bring you back anything, my dear?"

"Surprise me," Meegan murmured. Biting her lower lip, she attempted a coy shrug. "I have a feeling you'd know *exactly* what I'd like."

"I'll take my best guess." He winked, prompting an eruption of girlish giggles Meegan hid behind her hand.

Sliding off the couch flanked by Rip and Noah, Ireland paused to shoot a grimace at their openly flirty interaction.

No sooner did she get to her feet then Ridley dragged one knuckle along her forearm as he sauntered passed. "Come, walk with me."

Watching his occasionally homicidal girlfriend bristle, Noah caught her arm and held her back for a beat. "Easy, girl," he soothed, and tapped the iPod in her back pocket as a none-too-subtle reminder. "The sooner we get the information the sooner we can go … preferably without bloodshed."

Patting his hand, and dipping her chin in an affirmative nod, Ireland fixed on the pursuit that brought them there. "We don't want to take much of your time, Mr. Peolte," she explained, following him into the elevator. The doors slid shut, followed by that familiar stomach-dropping lurch. "I was just wondering if you'd ever seen this."

Turning her arm tattoo up, she held it out before him.

"Mmmm," he muttered in appreciation, one ebony brow hitching with interest. "Your arm? I haven't had the pleasure. But I do hope more parts will follow."

The elevator dinged open, allowing Ridley to stride out without a moment's hesitation.

Rip patted Noah lightly on the shoulder before following. "I am still accumulating myself to modern trends, however am I wrong in assuming that what just happened here was the equivalent to you two ramming antlers?"

"Nah, no worries." Noah's argument to the contrary would have been more convincing had his jaw line not tensed and his octave rose to that of a public speaker. "He doesn't know we're *together*."

"This beautiful siren is yours?" Ridley's gaze flicked back briefly before being averted to an associate across the lobby that he offered a wave and chin-jerk to. "Well, these things change all the time, don't they?"

Noah ran his hand over the back of his neck, sucking air through his teeth. "I may have to borrow your axe."

"*If I can't kill anyone, neither can you.*" Ireland curled her chin to her shoulder to hiss. Then, pushing past their banter, she attempted to steer the conversation back on course. "Actually, I meant the tattoo. Herb Mallark from The Richmond Gallery said he saw this same image at a private exhibit in your loft."

"Mallark?" Ridley snorted a wry laugh, the heels of his expensive leather shoes clicking across the marble floor. "Not the most original of pen names, is it? But I do have a lot of gatherings, so it may very well have been there. Lupé, my housekeeper, insists all cultures be represented in what we showcase and I never argue with her, otherwise she starches my boxers."

"I don't know how to respond to that," Ireland stated, looking to Noah and Rip for behavioral guidance. The best they could offer were awkward shrugs and tight lipped shakes of their heads.

"Jerry, did you watch that game last night?" Ridley rose up on tiptoe mid-stride to catch the security guard's eye over the milling sea of bodies in the ostentatious lobby. "Did I call it, or did I call it?"

"You always do, Mr. Peolte!" The grey haired guard chuckled, brushing the crumbs from his over-sized chocolate chip cookie off the front of his polyester shirt. "I should know better than to bet against you!"

Rip's beard bobbed as he puffed his cheeks and exhaled through pursed lips. "If pompous individuals brought on my curse, I could at least have the good fortune to sleep through this."

Ireland's hands balled into fists at her sides, mostly to suppress the urge to call forth her sword and hilt slap the information out of him. "So this Lupé is the one we need to talk to?"

Ridley spun on his heel and walked backwards, his gaze slowly traveling the length of her before he concealed it behind a pair of designer Ray-Ban sunglasses. "She'll be at my loft at nine a.m. tomorrow. You're more than welcome to stop by and speak with her yourself."

"*All* of us will stop by," she emphasized the first word to make it clear Noah would be playing the part of her rape whistle.

"Splendid!" Ridley threw his arms out wide, another blindingly white smile curling across his strikingly handsome face. Plucking a pen from his inside breast pocket, he clicked it to life and seized Ireland's arm—an act that made her inner beast snarl its outrage. He rotated her sugar skull tattoo skyward to scrawl his address in big, blue letters. The job complete, he dipped his head to blow the ink dry—those raging sea eyes peering up at her over the frames of his lenses.

"Dude, you had business cards in the breast pocket of your shirt." Noah pointed out, turning one exasperated hand palm up. "I can see them from here."

"Where's the fun in that?" Ridley smirked, righting his posture and returning the gold plated pen to his pocket. "Now, you lovely morsel, I must bid you ado. But I shall count the minutes until I'm graced by your magnificence once again." If he noticed her pained grimace or the way she shrank from his touch as he caught her hand and dotted it with a kiss, he chose to ignore it. Then, without so much as a cursory acknowledgement to the other two men, he caught the next revolving door turnstile out of there.

"And goodbye to you less important people as well!" Rip exclaimed in an impressive imitation of the arrogant Mr. Peolte.

Noah and Rip chuckled together, elbowing each other and exchanging verbal jabs at Ridley's expense. Ireland, on the other hand, stood stone still. Every fiber of her being sparking and pulsating with the charge of a yet unseen threat. Through the glass revolving doors, she watched Ridley step out onto the sidewalk. Instinct spurred her forward, charging through those same doors, before she could even question as to why. Overhead, a shadow, like a fast moving storm cloud, eclipsed the bright afternoon sun. That same darkness became a tangible menace, complete with ruffling feathers and powerful gusts that whipped and lashed against the skin of all those caught in its wake. In a violent funnel cloud of fury, what appeared to be an unkindness of ravens descended on one lone target—*Ridley*. Shielding his head with his arms, he cowered beneath the viciously pecking beaks and grappling claws that tore at his clothing and flesh.

Slamming her weight into the turnstile, Ireland urged the slow moving door on, all the while helplessly watching Ridley's entire form disappear beneath the shroud of angry ravens.

Making one final push against the stubborn door, Ireland raised her hand in the air in a silent call to her blade. Gleaming metal winged through the air, settling into her palm the second the revolving door spat her out on the pavement. Two quick slashes was all it took to disband the violent flock. What they left behind was a frazzled mess of the formerly dapper business man. Glasses hanging akimbo from his nose. Expensive suit shredded to ribbons. Hair darting off his head in every possible direction. Blood dripping from his face and hands. With a look in his eye that could only be described as manic, Ridley pushed his broken glasses up the bridge of his nose. One swinging lens popped free and fell to the ground with a soft thump. Jerking his head from the fallen lens, to Ireland, and back again, he expelled a bewildered, "Huh?" before turning on his heel and stumbling into the cab waiting at the curb.

What does a monster do at night when their skin is itching and burning for mayhem? Ireland rolled her neck one way, then the other, unable to think of anything but that particular conundrum. The pull to ride tugged at her, luring her into the darkness … where she belonged. Groaning her frustration, she slammed her forearms against the balcony rail, subsequently rolling her arms down until she clenched it in a white knuckled grasp. The twinkling lights of New York loomed before her. An entire city plagued with life and congestion, making it absolutely the most impractical place for her to sling on her cloak and indulge her inner beast.

It was official. Whether she liked it or not, Sleepy Hollow was now her home. There, Horseman sightings were an exciting testimony to the history of the town. Here, a simple ride to ease the raw longing screaming through her veins could get her chased through the Lincoln Tunnel by a police escort. Rational thought was a cruel, relentless bitch. One whose strict parameters became far more constricting the instant her skin ignited like a struck match. Predicting the cause, she instinctively gazed the two floors down to the parking lot below. Sure enough, Regen's narrow, onyx muzzle emerged from the thick white fog of a steam vent. His mane danced against his powerful neck with each wide stride, summoning her to him like the beckoning curl of a finger. His gleaming saucer eyes found her without fail. They always would. She was his totem. Or maybe he was hers—her true north that anchored her in the sea of chaos that was her curse.

Clucking her tongue against the roof of her mouth, Ireland grinned at the perk of his ears and his guttural whinny in response.

One little ride. What was the worst that could happen?

Behind her, the sliding door shushed across its track. Noah stepped out, his hand raking through hair still wet from the shower.

"There you are." Droplets of water flung from the damp strands. They rained down on his chest, zigzagging across taut muscles. Trailing down, they teased across the V of his hip bones, disappearing inside the waist band of his low-slung cotton pajama pants. "If you're contemplating seeing if the Horseman could survive that jump, I'm going to ask you not to. It's *way* too early in our relationship for you to hear my girly scream."

"No, I was just admiring the view." Curling her face into a Ridley-esque leer, she did her best to adopt his high-class pimp tone, "Which just got a whole lot sweeter."

"*Too* good an impression." Noah's nose crinkled, a wet strand sticking to his brow as he shook his head. "My testicles retreated inside me."

"I'm guessing the suave Mr. Peolte has that effect on a lot of people." Pivoting on the ball of her foot, Ireland leaned her back against the rail. "So, are you okay with this trip taking a couple extra days or is Sleepy Hollow falling to pieces without their prodigal son?"

One pull-up perfected shoulder rose and fell in a casual shrug. "Running the risk of sounding like a pretentious ass, I'll just say I have people handling everything, so I'm good."

"How very Corleone of you," Ireland smirked, then hitched one eyebrow pointedly. "I'm not kissing your ring. I feel that needs to be said."

Closing the space between them, his tongue flicked across his lower lip. With a hand on either side of her and his body molding to hers, he pinned the suddenly breathless Crane against the rail. Cool, damp hair tickled over her feverish skin as his forehead brushed hers, nudging her face up to his. Pillow soft lips teased over hers with the tempting promise of their salty-sweet euphoria. "I can think of much more fun activities for your lips."

Her breath caught, swelling in her chest until it seeped past her lips in a throaty sigh.

"Plus," he murmured against her neck, kissing and nibbling his way down to her shoulder, "I wouldn't miss this show for the world."

"Show? You mean my life?" She wanted to bristle at his words, maybe form some small iota of indignation. Unfortunately, he'd pushed the strap of her black tank top aside and was implementing a masterful technique with his mouth along her collarbone that made coherent thoughts unattainable.

"Actually, I just introduced Rip to *Breaking Bad* and am looking forward to Old English calling everyone bitch," Noah clarified, his voice noticeably low and husky. "But you keep things interesting, too."

With a clearer head Ireland may have been annoyed at his cavalier view of her curse. Right then, she couldn't think beyond her own desire that scorched more white-hot than her blazing skin. Weaving her fingers into his hair, she claimed his mouth with a primal urgency, making the message clear of *exactly* what she wanted.

Lifting her from the cement balcony, the muscles across Noah's back flexed in an impressive masculine display. Ireland's legs snaked around his waist, eliciting a deep animalistic growl that rumbled from his throat. Her fingernails raked down his back, her breath coming in urgent pants as he spun them toward the room. Pressing her back against the stucco wall, its rough surface scrapping her skin and fueling her desire, he freed one hand to fumble with the door. Ireland ground her hips against his, enjoying the swell of his excitement. Her hands traveled the expansive spread of his back, delving beneath his waistband to the seductive rise of his perfectly formed ass. Groaning against her neck, Noah forced the door open and plunged inside. A sheen of sweat glistened from the pair as they collapsed on the bed locked in each other's embrace.

What does a monster do at night? They live.

EDGAR

Edgar slid the gloves over his hands that betrayed him by trembling with the relentless quakes of those inflicted with the fevers. All the while he murmured a silent prayer to get his shaky digits concealed before Father came in to witness his state of unease. Such a display may prompt him to take back his agreement and force Edgar to stay home for yet *another* year of tutoring under the leadership of the dreadful Mrs. Nesbit. Often Edgar amused himself during her long-winded lectures by picturing her stern expression if she ever dared a smile. Such a simple act would surely shatter her firmly puckered face into a million tiny shards.

No sooner did Edgar secure the supple leather of his second glove around his alabaster wrist than John Allen, his adoptive father, strolled in, trailed by his mother, Francis. While her porcelain face remained purposely neutral, her own case of nerves showed itself in the way her index finger brushed her cheek as she twirled one chestnut ringlet. Edgar expected her to rush to his side and fret over him: finger-combing his hair, straightening his collar, smoothing the creases of his tweed coat. He winced in shock when, instead, Father took a knee before him and grasped Edgar's narrow shoulders in his large hands.

"You look well, son. A strong lad well prepared for this endeavor."

Edgar nodded his enthusiasm, a lock of onyx hair falling forward and tangling in his lashes. "Yes, Papa. I am."

Mother stifled a high-pitch yelp of protest behind her hand, causing Father to silence her with a firm scowl before returning his attention to his son. "I know how much you want this, Edgar. Even so, you must consider how difficult it is for your mother and I to let you go. If anyone were to discover your ... *affliction—*"

"They could not possibly, Papa!" Edgar interrupted, his frantic voice rising with the fear of his dream being yanked out from under him. "You have already informed the Dean that I have a skin condition and must wear my gloves at all times. I *promise* I will not take them off! You taught me well, *both* of you. I *know* the power of my touch is an atrocity against God himself. I will *not* use it or let anyone know of it. I beg you, please, *please*, let me go to school with the other boys!"

Mother gathered the billowing fabric of her skirt to drop to her knees beside them. Gently, she cocooned Edgar's hand in both of hers. Pressing his fingers to her cheek, she dotted his palm with a quick kiss. "Edgar, you do *not* have to do this. There are other options. Remember Stanley Lankey from down the street? Ever since he fell off his parents' roof he spends his days home with his mother. They make cookies together. She wheels him out into the garden where he watches her tend to the plants. That sounds nice, does it not? We could do that!"

"Mother, the boy is not an invalid, nor shall we make plans to treat him as one." Father urged in his deep baritone that left no room for argument or discussion. "Edgar is ten years old and is dabbling with all the facets of what it means to be a man. If he claims he is ready for this, we must trust him and support his decision."

Edgar's scrawny chest puffed to emulate the proud stance his father often assumed. "I'm ready. I know it."

"Very good, then." Flecks of gold, that only appeared when he was truly pleased, beamed within the molasses pools of John Allen's eyes. "Mother, please fetch his satchel and umbrella. We will have the carriage driver drop him at the school gate."

Indecision marred Mrs. Allen's elegant perfection with concerned creases that cut between her brows. Pressing her lips together hard enough to cause white lines around her mouth, she rose to her feet, flipped her mane of pin-curls, and—with visible reluctance—strode off on her task.

Only at her exit did Father's brave façade crack. His hands slid down his son's arms until he caught both the boy's wrists. Turning Edgar's hands palm up, he inspected the gloves, searching for any snag or catch that would allow the horrifying truth to seep through. "Whatever happens, do *not* remove your gloves. Promise me that?" His gaze scoured his son's face, encouraging the words he longed to hear to tumble passed his lips.

"Of course! I *promise*, Papa!"

Folding both his hands around his son's, John brought them to his chest as if in prayer. Suddenly, the man that always seemed able to mold the world to his will appeared genuinely vulnerable ... and frightened. "If *anything* happens, Edgar, anything that scares you or that you cannot control, you run straight home without pause. It will not make you a coward, son. It will make you a man aware of the severity of his condition. Do you understand?"

Edgar swallowed hard around the lump of trepidation that had wriggled its way into his throat. "Yes, Papa. I understand. Yet you must know that nothing will happen. Death does not loom on school yards."

Outside the wind lashed and whistled, its powerful gust allowing a nearby tree branch to scratch against the windowpane like bony fingers.

"Edgar Allen," John muttered, staring out at the threatening storm. "I fear wherever you are, death will *always* follow."

Happiness was shoes clumping through busy halls, the hum of constant chatter, and boys stealing one another's caps and playing 'keep away' with them. Edgar watched all this as an outsider not yet initiated into the fold, yet he remained optimistic. More than one of the lads gave him a friendly nod of the head in greeting. A simple gesture that made the heart of Poe, the eternal outsider, sing. To be one of them, to be included. Such an idea was nothing short of pure bliss.

Despite his distaste for Mrs. Nesbit, Edgar did owe her great respect. He was right on track with all his classes, except for mathematics where he was actually a lesson or two ahead. Retrieving his coat from the row of hooks, he prepared to join the other boys for their post-lunch outing to stretch their legs. The heels of his shoes scuffed across the hardwood floor, his hands plunging deep into his pockets. Moving with the crowd toward the door, he kept his gaze cast to the floor. Air, still crisp from the morning rain, swirled around him the moment he stepped into the yard.

Many a time Edgar had stared out his bedroom at the orchard next door and tried to picture what an actual schoolyard would look like. The reality did not disappoint. Under the canopy of a towering oak, a group of boys engaged in a lively debate over a leather bound text. At the picnic table beside them, another group set up dominos in a path that led across the table, down to the bench, and ended with a spiral on the ground. In the center of it all sat the field where a dozen or so lads retrieved cricket equipment from a storage closet and assigned themselves positions for a game. Unsure of where he fit in any of this, Edgar skimmed along the brown stone school. The rough brick snagged his wool jacket as he slid down the wall to watch their game.

"Ayo, ayo, chaps! It looks like we 'ave a new bilge rat in our galley!" A hefty lad with a shock of red hair and forest of freckles flung his cricket bat over his shoulder, shooting a grin to Edgar.

More than anything, Edgar wanted to acknowledge the boy's greeting. Unfortunately, his own painful anxiety allowed him little more than a forced glance, before returning his stare to the top of his shoes.

It was a rodent-faced boy with a crooked smile that came to his aid. "D-d-don't mind H-h-Harold," he stammered. "H-h-he learned of the East India Company hiring C-c-Captain Kidd to combat p-p-piracy in history class t-t-today and n-n-now wants to be just like him."

"Not just like him," Edgar softly advised, brushing the dirt from the tips of his shoes. "He was later tried for treason and hanged."

"Blimey," Harold's face fell, his bat wielding arm dropping limp at his side. "We didn't get that far in the lesson yet."

A plain looking boy with sandy-brown hair hanging in his eyes flung an arm around Harold's broad shoulders. "You cannot let that bit of trivia stop you! Your frame could use a bit of stretching!"

Harold used excessive force to shove the boy away, sending him stumbling back three paces. "To bowler's position with you! If you want to have time for a game at all!"

"I'm Douglas b-b-by the way," the boy with the lopsided grin announced, jabbing a thumb over his shoulder at the other players taking their position. "D-d-do you play?"

Edgar gnawed on his lower lip, his own inadequacy growing into a ravenous monster that threatened to swallow him whole. "I know the theory behind it. That the bowler bowls to the batsman, who then attempts to score runs. Unfortunately, I have never had the opportunity to play … or even watch a game for that matter."

Douglas nodded as if he understood Edgar's very plight. "Watch a g-g-game or two. S-s-soon as you are ready, you can p-p-play substitute."

With an eager nod, Edgar settled back on his heels to watch as the game began. The blond fellow, referred to as Anderson by the other players, seemed quite the bowler. The majority of batters swung and missed at each of his powerful throws. All took turns taunting each other's failed attempts at bat, yet none seemed up to the task of besting Anderson.

Until Harold stepped up.

Ball and bat met in a clap of thunder, wood splintering at the impact. The bat snapped in two, the ball shooting out long behind the hefty redhead.

"What should we call *that* play?" Harold bellowed, leading the boys in a rousing chorus of laughter.

"Land a second one, Harry, and we can name it after you!" Anderson teased, grabbing another ball from the pile beside him and rolling it in his palm.

Harold tossed the half of the bat he still held aside and accepted the new one offered to him by Douglas. "Not a hard feat, considering you throw like my sister!"

"Do we want to speak of sisters?" Anderson smirked, throwing the ball and catching it behind his back. "Because with tits as big as yours you could pass for one!"

"From what I heard you know the curve of your own sister's breast well." Harold took a practice swing, a cat that ate the canary grin curling his thick lips. "Amusing you must be one of the poor girl's chores."

Ignoring their banter, Douglas bent to retrieve the section of shattered bat that had fallen beside Harold's feet. His bent posture prevented him from seeing Anderson, face flushed with aggravation, arch back and whip the ball with all his might. Oblivious to the warning cries of the horrified onlookers—Edgar's own voice among them—Harold instinctively swung just as Douglas's head rose at their shouts.

Many ghoulish things would haunt Edgar Allen Poe all of his days. None more so than the gruesome, hollowed *thunk* of the bat colliding with Douglas's temple, splitting his skull open wide. His head snapped to the side in an inhuman angle, a steady current crimson gore pulsating from the wound. The bat slipped from Harold's guilty fingers, slowing time with each of its rotations before hitting the ground. The entire schoolyard seemed to suck in the same shocked breath. Moving as one body, every boy rose to their feet in fretful panic. The hue of Douglas's skin drained chalk white, his eyes rolling back as he toppled to the ground, stiff as an axed tree. His jaw hit first, driving into the dirt with the unmistakable crunch of bone. Like an enraged mother aching at the pain of her young, life picked that moment to roar back to real time.

Anderson dove to Douglas's side, cradling his friend's lulling head in his lap. Yanking off his blazer, he pressed it firmly against the spurting gash. "Harold, go get the school nurse! *Now!*"

Harold stood rooted to that spot, gaping down at the expanding patch of blood soaked grass stained an inky black. Sweat dampened hair clung to his head as Harold shook his head in denial of the truth staring back at him with fixed eyes.

"Harold? *Go!*" Anderson bellowed.

Seeing how fear had immobilized the larger boy, two of the domino players darted inside to fetch help. A crowd gathered behind Anderson, each boy looking every second of their youth in the face of true travesty.

It could have taken a minute or an eternity for the nurse and two teachers to come spilling out of the school's double doors. They brought with them a flurry of activity: frantic footfalls, fumbling hands assessing wounds, exchanged looks of shock and knowing. Two fingers nestling into the crook of Douglas's neck, just below his slack jawline. And the head shake—that fateful gesture that dashes all hope without a single word being uttered.

Violent sobs shook Harold's hefty frame as the nurse shook out Anderson's blood soaked blazer and used it to cover Douglas's face. Students huddled together, whispering their shock and awe of the unimaginable. All this noise and chaos faded to a dull buzz in the background of Edgar's existence. Staring down at his hands, he pinched the tip of fabric on one gloved finger and peeled the leather away. Alabaster fingers wiggled back at him, daring him, taunting him. Whispering he could be a hero—with a simple touch.

"Dougie, come to dinner," a high-pitched voice mocked from beside him. "Every day at dinner time, as long as I can remember, that is how my mother called to me. The fact that I was on the precipice of manhood made no difference to her. Why would it? She saw me as nothing more than her precious baby boy who only stopped wetting his bed two short years ago."

Eyes bulging, bile rising up the back of his throat, Edgar slowly turned to find a form of Douglas standing beside him. The boy leaned casually against the wall, seemingly oblivious to his gaping head wound or the blood that matted into the hair around it. His jaw hung unhinged on one side, giving his smile the demented twist of death.

"Do you think she will finally call me Douglas at the wake?" The ghoul's smile widened, grey gums visible where his jaw swung slack.

Edgar's chin retreat to his chest, his hands rising to curl around his ears. "Y-y-you're not here, *cannot be real.*"

"L-l-liked my stutter so much you had to steal it, Edgar?" Douglas scoffed, dabbing at his wound with the tips of his fingers, then wiping the ooze on the leg of his pants. "But know, my friend, that I am *very* real. Of course a little *less* real than I would be if you had used that little talent of yours." Douglas's head rolled toward Edgar, his eyes narrowing with malicious intent.

Edgar's nervous gaze flicked around the crowd in front of him. No one was turning their way or tearing their stares from the body still sprawled in the grass. Which meant this little haunt was reserved for him alone.

"I do not know what you are talking about," Edgar whispered, trying not to let his lips move, else he look like the mad loon he was certain he'd become.

Douglas rocked up onto one shoulder to face him. "Oh, yes you do, *Edgar Allen Poe.* We *all* know about you. What you are, what you can do." He leaned in close, his rancid breath making the air around them unbreathable. "Did you think you could hide it from us forever? That darkness within you offers such promise to all of us that have found ourselves in the unfortunate vocation

55

as worm food." His head fell back to guffaw at his own humor, his jaw fully unhinging like a hungry serpent.

Blinking hard, Edgar tried to free himself from what had to be a macabre hallucination. "What do you want from me?" His voice betrayed him by cracking, rising with the bubbling panic he could no longer contain.

A few of the nearby boys glanced his way, sizing him up with judgmental glares.

"What do we want? Well, let us take a moment to ponder that. There is that magic touch of yours that could give any of us a second chance to shimmy back into our meat suits and dance. That is, quite obviously, a hardy handshake we deeply covet. However, there is also the more ... subtle gift of yours. Where, once you find yourself by the location of our demise, you can see us plain as day." Douglas's head dipped, allowing him to glare up at Edgar from under his lowered brow. Blood welled within the whites of his eyes, spilling over the lids in ruby torrents. "And *that* makes us want to play."

Finding himself at sanity's limit, Edgar pushed himself off the wall. His loose glove fluttered to the ground at his feet as he sprinted across the schoolyard.

"Edgar? *Edgar Allen!* Where are you going?" one of the teachers called after him.

Edgar didn't pause to acknowledge him, but slammed into the gate and forced it open with fumbling hands. The heels of his shoes dug deep into the soil with each pounded stride.

Even his own heaving breath huffing in his ears couldn't drown out the chilling echo that pursued him. "See you soon, E-E-Edgar!"

Ridley

"By definition it means 'female dog,' which is why calling someone that is so comical!" Rip gushed, facing the closed door before him.

Ireland cast a sideway glance to Noah, her expression dripping with judgment. "This is your doing. You get to have the *appropriate public conversation topics* talk with him."

"I totally deserve that," Noah admitted, reaching one arm out to knock again. "Peolte said nine a.m., right?"

Before his fist could meet the door for a second rap, it flung open wide. A stout, frazzled looking woman, whose caramel-skin was dotted with beads of sweat, grabbed his arm and yanked him into the apartment with an impressive amount of force.

"I'm so glad you're here," she fretted, both of her quaking hands clinging to Noah's wrist. "I've never seen him like this before! You must help!"

"Uh ... if you called for some kind of assistance, we aren't it," Noah stammered, his confused gaze drifting to the vacant, yet extremely expensive looking, fish tanks that lined both sides of the stark white hallway. "We're here about a piece of artwork—Ireland?"

Ireland caught his hint, knew that to be her cue to thrust her tattooed arm forward for the question and answer portion of their visit. Unfortunately, the perplexing matters of her own cursed existence couldn't break through unexpected fog clouding her mind.

True darkness lurked within those walls. It batted its lashes, curled one taloned finger, and beckoned her closer. Shuffling forward without an actual invitation, Ireland heard nothing but the seductive symphony of her racing heart thumping against her ribs.

"It's like stumbling into the nest of the Skymall core demographic," Noah muttered, taking in the white, leather, and chrome décor. His quippy comment cut off short as his gaze fell on his hypnotized sweetie.

Ireland could feel the heat of his stare boring into her back and wanted to reassure him, but couldn't tear herself from the magnetic pull tethered to her very core.

"Ireland?" Noah ventured. "You okay? You're not in need of that certain special piece of jewelry I'm holding, are you?"

"There's no time!" the woman, Ireland assumed to be Lupé, insisted. Hooking her arm through Ireland's, she herded her in the direction of the open French doors that led out onto the balcony. "He's going to fall! You must help him!"

Feeling her skin was scorching beneath Lupé's touch, Ireland shook herself free. There he stood, the beacon of darkness that had called to her. Perched atop the cement ledge that acted as the balcony rail, his stare cast ten stories straight down. Shocked gasps and whispered plans buzzed around her, annoying as a bothersome fly. Ireland swallowed hard and flicked her tongue over suddenly dry lips. Stepping out on to the balcony, the wind whipping her hair from her face, Ireland gaped in awe at ... *Ridley.*

"A parade of fallen angels. Their sin? A simple step." His chin tipped toward her, allowing her no further acknowledgment than his perfectly carved profile. "I can see them all."

"Has he self-medicated in some fashion?" Rip asked, straddling the balcony threshold to maintain a safe distance from the potential jumper. "I once tried opiates and thought myself to be a barn owl."

"No, sir," Lupé fretted, nervously wringing her hands. "He tried a friend's homemade absinthe once. Made him think he was Spiderman and he got stuck up in the ceiling rafters for three hours. After that he swore he would never do anything like that again."

"He's not on drugs." Though the words slipped from Ireland's lips, their deep gravel tremor belonged to another. "He's cursed."

Ridley's spine straightened in response. Crossing one leg over the other, he slowly turned their way. This simple, yet dangerous move caused Lupé to clamp a hand over her terrified yelp. The man they had met mere hours ago was gone, robbed of his polished perfection. His onyx hair darted out in a disheveled mess. The peaches and cream pallor of his skin had drained ashen. A shadow of stubble had sprouted across his jawline and lip, sharpening his features and giving him an alluring edge of mystery.

"Gliding in on raven's wings, came the father of the notion that the divide between life and death is a vague one." Even with the others pacing anxiously behind her, Ridley's stare locked on Ireland alone. Clouds of emotion rolled into his eyes, swirling and churning in a deep storm blue. "He claimed we're the same, he and I. Took me on a stroll into the horrors of his reality—now passed to me. All that we see—that we so desperately wish to be a dream—yet, the truth was there, waiting for me." Ridley glanced back over his shoulder at the deadly plummet mere inches away. His brow knit together in deep, furrowed creases. "It prompted the question; would my leap of faith end in a rustle of feathers, as his did? Or would it be a free fall into that never-ending night?"

"Mr. Ridley, no!" Lupé pleaded, her trembling hands reaching for him. "Please come down before you slip!"

"You're sure it's a curse? Like yours?" Noah ventured, his hand closing around Lupé's upper arm and guiding her back inside. Not that she blamed him. If Ridley's monster had a blood lust like hers they all needed a football field of distance, immediately.

Ireland cocked her head, considering the specimen before her. His tattered, unbuttoned shirt flapped open in the breeze, revealing a light smattering of hair across his well-defined pecs. "It calls to me," she managed in a throaty rasp.

Noah filled his lungs and exhaled through slightly flared nostrils. "I'm gonna suppress the undeniable urge to be the dick boyfriend about that comment. Instead, I'm going to get the innocent bystanders out of the way so your inner monster can slap the stupid out of his inner monster and get him off the ledge. Sound like a plan? Good. Go Team Horseman."

Ushering Lupé inside, Noah grabbed the back of Rip's collar and steered him in as well. No sooner had the doors met behind her with a soft click than Ireland shifted the satchel slung over her shoulder, repositioning it in front of her.

62

Fighting to keep the paranormal gruffness in her voice as subdued as possible, Ireland unzipped the bag and fished out a corner of the heavy weave fabric of her cloak. "I saw some seriously twisted things when it first happened to me: medieval torture devices being put to use, disemboweled friends, a trunk full of heads. All of it left me wishing a good brain bleaching was a feasible option. But you, sir, are fortunate enough to have something I didn't."

She caught his gaze and held it. Her fingers stroked the fabric. Her breath coming slow and level as the first signs of her change began. The heightened tingles of sensation from the skin of her face pulling taut over bone. Her vision sharpening to a point that made her thankful for the grey, overcast sky. Wetting her lips, she found them cold and clammy—the only clue she needed to *know* they had bloomed a deathly blue.

"You have someone that can guide you through it."

Ridley's jaw fell slack, but not in fear. His chest swelled, each breath coming fast and urgent. One step forward and he landed with a *huff* right in front of her. His hand rose as if to stroke her cheek, yet hesitated and hovered there. Maintaining a veil of energy between them, he let the tips of his fingers trace over the scrolled veins that now decorated her porcelain skin like hand-woven lace. "A maiden of rare beauty that blesses me with the gift of her true face. Death seeping through silken pores, delicate and fatal as the petals of Night-Blooming Jasmine. The strangeness only adding to her exquisiteness."

"So, h-have you heard the hoofbeats yet?" Even Ireland heard how breathless the query sounded, but could do nothing to correct it. Somewhere, in the back of her mind, she knew she *should* take a step back and attempt to break this spell with a bit of much needed space. Regrettably, her legs were less than cooperative. "First time I heard them I thought I was going nuts."

"Insanity is only achieved when the heart has been *truly* touched," he murmured. A simple gesture that caused Ireland to wage a full-out war with herself not to become completely trans-fixed on the soft curve of his lips.

Tucking her cloak back into her bag, she attempted to shake off her physical maladies in hopes of regaining a pinch of control. "As far as I know, there's only *one* Horseman and *one* Rip Van Winkle. I'm not too familiar with any other Washington Irving works." Puffing out her cheeks, she exhaled through pursed lips. Forming coherent thoughts would be *so* much easier if he would stop looking at her like a prime-cut sirloin. "We may have to do some research to find out what infliction you're going to wind up with."

Wordlessly, he shook his head. "We walked streets of graves, tipping our hats to the dead that failed to slumber. Never once along our trek did the man tell me his name." Bowing slightly toward her, Ridley hid his conspiratorial whisper behind the back of his hand. "He didn't have to. I already knew."

Losing the battle to not to close the distance between them, Ireland leaned in. "Who was he?"

In place of an answer, a single black raven landed on the ledge vacated by Ridley just moments before. Filling its narrow chest, it tipped its head and emitted one loan caw into the sky.

Ridley turned an ear to the bird, his posture snapping pencil-straight, as if contemplating the perplexity of its declaration. When he met Ireland's stare once more the emotion had been white-washed from his handsome face. Desire. Angst. Mystery. A fair amount of madness. All gone, leaving behind an empty vessel that blankly stated, "We have to go. She's waiting."

Without further explanation, Ridley ducked around her, bumping Ireland's shoulder as he passed. Her gaze wandered back to the avian messenger that seemed to be studying her with matching interest. A possible answer to this riddle teased at the tip of her tongue, luring the name to slip from her lips.

"Poe?" she muttered in a barely audible whisper.

The raven perched, and sat, and nothing more.

EDGAR

"Sir, your son is here," the file clerk proclaimed, his hands clasped behind his back.

Removing his glasses, John Allen leaned back in his chair and tossed them on his desk. "Send him in please, Phillip."

"Yes, sir." The young man ducked his head in a brief show of respect before stepping back to wave Edgar forward. Breathing through his mouth became mandatory to avoid the pungent stink of alcohol and vomit that permeated from his boss's stumbling son.

Taking in the spectacle that was Edgar as of late, judgment curled the corners of John's mouth. Red rimmed eyes darting around manically. Hair brushed only on one side, as if he'd lost interest mid-task. Stains of the grossly unrecognizable kind covering the front of his shirt like patch-work.

"Phillip, please leave us. Shut the door behind you."

Phillip averted his gaze and dutifully obliged.

Edgar's plight to cross the room and settle into a chair was not unlike watching a foal take its first steps. A great deal of stumbling and bumbling, accompanied by the lingering question of success, right up until the end when Edgar seized the arm rests and lowered himself to sitting. A victorious smile spreading across his dazed face.

"I see your misadventures have already begun for the day," John frowned, his fingers drumming against the edge of his desk.

"On the contrary," Edgar helped himself to the pitcher of ice water on his father's desk, his quaking hand causing it to slosh over the rim as he poured. "This is the remnant of last night's debauchery. I have yet to find my bed, yet am optimistic it is where I left it. Wherever that may be."

John bowed his head and massaged his temples, just below his salt and pepper hairline, where a throbbing headache had sprouted. "And you are happy with this lackluster existence?"

"Happy, Father?" Edgar snorted a humorless laugh. "Why, yes. I am gloriously beside myself that I have been chosen to walk the dreary path of being courted by death."

"There's no need for such dramatics, Edgar," John huffed with an exaggerated eye roll. "Others have suffered ailments far worse than yours."

Ebony brows disappeared into Edgar's bushy hairline. "I cannot imagine even one scenario where that would be true."

The chair squeaked beneath his shifted weight as John leaned forward, folding his hands on his desk. "Son, I—more than anyone—know what you suffer with. I admit every day for you is its own brand of hell ... if you let it be! Your schooling is done, all through home tutoring at your own accord, and you have matured to manhood. It's time for you to find your place in this world and *claim* it. Or, if such a Shangri-La does not exist, then at least find a way to contribute to the world around you. Children fear ghosts and goblins, Edgar. You must no longer entertain such notions."

Edgar's pale lips pressed together in a firm line. His fingers raked into his hair, gathering handfuls in his tight grasp. He could not even pretend to listen. Not after the dapper looking gentleman wafted in through a solid wall, causing the temperature in the room to plummet. Edgar knew he would be there, as he always was at two o'clock every afternoon. Hence the binge Edgar had gone on, beginning the very moment he learned his father wanted to meet with him.

He knew this spirit by name—Benedict Carter. He had been his father's business partner in life. Now his lingering essence showed him for the grisly mess he truly was. A broken and rotting shell, whose shoulders shook with sobs as he crossed the room like a man walking the final mile to the guillotine. His form dissipated around the edges as he wisped on top of John's desk without disturbing a thing.

Edgar fought to keep his expression neutral, nodding along to whatever it was his father happened to be saying. Every bit the attentive, albeit anxious, son that was most definitely *not* watching an apparition fling a noose over the ceiling rafters.

"I gave up everything, *everything*!" Benedict whimpered, fixing the knotted loop around his neck. "Still it is not enough for these blood thirsty vultures!"

"S'okay," Edgar muttered under his breath in a private reassurance that this would all be over soon.

"Such a lackadaisical existence is most definitely not *'okay'*!" His father erupted, slapping his palm down against the desk. "Do you understand *at all* what it means to be a man?"

Benedict scooted to the edge of the desk on tiptoe. Tears zigzagged between craters in his sagging and rotted flesh. "Duty, responsibility, honor," he gasped. One step and the rope was swinging under the full effects of his weight. "This ... is ... my ... reward."

"Hanging from the rafters," Edgar manically snickered, then blanched the moment he realized he'd spoken the words out loud.

Fresh understanding dawned on his father's face. "Give me the flask, Edgar."

Edgar guiltily shifted his gaze, his hand plunging into the inside pocket of his coat to retrieve his silver flask. As if to crow his father's wisdom, he brandished the item high over his head.

"Hand it over." John extended his hand, beckoning him forward with the curl of his fingers.

Benedict's feet twitched and spasmed over the mahogany desk. Wet, choked gasps rattling from his constricted throat.

"Absolutely, Father." Edgar leaned in, stopping abruptly. Forcing a tight smile at his increasingly impatient father, he tried to figure out how to maneuver under the dead man without disrupting him. Finally, he ducked low to the desk and inched the flask across to his father, careful to avoid the flailing tips of Benedict's polished shoes.

Confusion creased his forehead as John Allen accepted the item from his splayed son. Fortunately, experience had taught him not to question Edgar's antics. "Thank you, son. Let this be the last time I have to intervene on your excess of spirits."

"Of course." Edgar's agreement noticeably lacked conviction as he righted himself.

Overhead, the ropes shifted. Benedict dropped to the floor with a heavy thump. "Such a good lad," he gushed, his icy hand clamping down on Edgar's shoulder as he found himself momentarily free of his infinite loop.

"Is that all, Father?" Edgar asked as an involuntary shudder rocked through him.

"Almost." The flask disappeared into the top drawer of John's desk. "There is one more thing. I want you to reconsider my offer for you to join me here at the tobacco company. I have a position in mind for you."

"Father, I do not think it—"

John halted Edgar's argument with one raised hand. "No need to rehash old arguments. I am well aware of your hesitations, which is why I want to show you we can work around them. Tonight I have a dinner planned with a potential client. He is a family man, therefore it would be very beneficial for us to present a united front. You and I can dine with him and his daughter. I believe her name is Lenore. What do you say, my boy? Will you dine with a lovely young Miss as a favor to your dear papa?"

7

Ridley

At some point Ireland's enraptured draw to Ridley had faded to a moderately tolerable level. If she had to guess, she would blame the bus they hopped on, that reeked of body odor and stale beer, for killing the romanticism of encountering someone else cursed as she had been.

"The car was right there," she grumbled, her fingers thumping against her satchel. "Right at the curb. We actually passed it getting into this … rolling house of *funk*."

"That makes it sound bluesy," Noah mused, then immediately raised his hands in retreat at Ireland's murderous glare. "Hey, don't blame me! You saw how fast Ridley darted on here. Our choices were jump on or lose him."

Biting the inside of her cheek hard enough to taste blood, Ireland's narrowed gaze flicked across the aisle to where Ridley sat. A tennis racquet—he'd made the point to grab before darting from the loft—laid across his lap, his finger tracing the lettering on its cover. The pretty, strawberry-blonde seated beside him, with freckles speckled across her pointy nose and the tops of her cheeks, scooted a little closer and crossed her legs in his direction.

"Do you play?" she asked, gesturing toward the racquet. Her full lips puckered in an *obviously* practiced pout as she thrust out her over-worked push-up bra.

Ireland tipped her face toward Noah's shoulder to mumble, "Nope, carries it as a conversation starter."

Noah's chin fell to his chest. The blond strands that fell across his forehead did nothing to muffle his snort of laughter.

A third party, however, was less than amused by the harmless flirting. *Call forth your sword!* the Hessian roared in his beastly tremor from within the confines of Ireland's mind. *Ram it through the strumpet's skull. She is in no way deserving of the dark magnificence that lies within that being!*

Someone has a cruuuush, Ireland thought back, playfully injecting the sing-song inflection.

Silence, you plague on my existence! If I could will your own hands to rip out your innards and rid me of your incessant torment, I would happily oblige.

Running her tongue over her top teeth, Ireland fished into the front pocket of her satchel to dig out her iPod. *Keep talking, sweet-cheeks. It'll make this that much more fun for me.*

Do your worst, you petty wretch! This cage cannot hold me forever!

"Isn't that the Carrie Underwood song about keying some cheating dude's truck?" Noah asked, reading over her shoulder as she thumbed the selection from the menu.

"It is!" Ireland said, her wide smile dripping with mock innocence. "I thought maybe I could work on redirecting my creepy little friend's anger issues."

"Only in this group is vandalism considered an improvement." Rip—seated on Noah's other side—shook his head, his finger twirling and knotting the end of his beard.

Clicking the song on, Ireland settled back into her hard plastic seat. A smug smile curled across her lips. As predicted, the Hessian sneered and grumbled his retreat into the dark oblivion of her mind. Unfortunately, after his departure she could blame no one's interest but her own for her gaze wandering back across the aisle. For a moment she noticed Ridley's agitated stare managed to focus. A bit of his former swagger reappeared as he ogled the ample terrain of the hussy's curves. An appreciative smirk tugged back one corner of his mouth.

"I've always wanted to learn to play tennis." Flipping her hair over her shoulder, the mass transit floozy forced her chest out farther still. A move that was asking an awful lot of her already strained buttons. "But for any sport like that, you really need an expert … *teacher*."

"She's like a walking cautionary tale against VD," Ireland tsked.

Switching the grip on his racquet to the other hand, Ridley's free arm slid across the back of her chair with skillful grace. His head dipped ever so slightly, allowing him to gaze up at her from under his lashes.

"There is no topic in the world more tragically poetic," the smooth words poured from his lips like warm molasses, "than the *death* of a beautiful woman."

Every single person within earshot, Ridley and Floozy included, froze.

"I … uh," her mouth falling slack, Floozy rose from her seat, "… think my stop is coming up. I should just—"

Without another word she scurried to the front of the bus, took a seat right behind the driver, and didn't risk a look back.

Ridley's face crumpled as though the incident hurt more than just his pride. "Your words, not mine," he hissed at the floor. "In my head. *Muttering. Whispering.*"

"Ya, know." Noah cocked his head, his hand rubbing over his chin, "I really expected him to have mad game with the ladies. But if that's the *right* way to pick up chicks, I've been doing it wrong."

"The can of pepper spray she just pulled from her purse says it's not," Ireland pointed out.

"We cannot leave him like this." Rip's lower jaw worked, chewing on the matter at hand. "Ireland was never this bad. It would be cruel to leave him to face this alone. For the time being at least, it seems our little family has a new member."

Ireland filled her lungs and forced the breath out through pursed lips. "I just wanted to know the origins of my tattoo. Maybe get a little insight into who made me the Horseman's bitch—"

"*Heehee*, bitch," Rip giggled, despite the suddenly somber mood.

Purposely, she chose to ignore his amusement over his new favorite word. "But, you're right. We need to keep an eye on him. Find out if he's going to end up caught in some crazy poltergeist time loop like I did. Even if it means following him to what has to be a pretty friggin' crucial tennis match to interrupt his current cloud-o-crazy."

"Uh …" Pinching her chin between his thumb and forefinger, Noah pivoted Ireland's head toward the window. "I don't think we're headed to any kind of country club."

Outside, high rises had been replaced by dilapidated housing. Shiny town cars and taxis had switched out for lowered rides and pounding base.

"It could still be a country club," Ireland argued weakly. "Maybe the membership dues are just *insanely* reasonable."

A scraggly beard wedged itself into the conversation, Rip craning around Noah with his watery eyes widened to goose eggs. "You know all of those horrible stories depicting New York as a terribly scary place? I fear we have found ourselves in the birthplace of that particular reputation."

Brakes squeaked as the bus slowed to yet another stop, and the door hissed open.

"This is it!" Ridley instantly brightened. Bolting from his seat, he flipped his covered racquet over his shoulder.

"Of course it is." Rip yawned, reluctantly rising to his feet to follow his troop from the bus. "The upside is if my sleep curse strikes, I will blend with all the other vagabonds slumbering on the sidewalks."

She couldn't have prevented it if she wanted to. Horns honking. Brakes squealing. Rip, halfway across the street, spinning at their high-pitched screech. Black clouds, reeking of burnt rubber, billowing out from the tires of the fish-tailing full-sized pickup truck.

77

But the ugly truth was, part of her didn't want to prevent it.

Ireland's heart stuttered in her chest. Her breath coming in anxious pants as the bumper slammed into Rip's knees, rolling him over the hood and shattering the windshield. She loved her friend, wished him no harm. Yet she couldn't deny the fiery flush that tingled over her skin, sparking every nerve ending with violent delight. Her mouth watered at the blood that gurgled over his parted lips, staining his beard as it puddled beneath his head.

Her name formed on Noah's lips as he darted between cars. The sound of his call drowned out by the deafening roar of her pulse pounding in her ears. Hooking his forearms under Rip's arms, Noah eased the injured man from the hood and immediately began CPR.

Such a good boy.

Working so hard.

Completely oblivious to the truck door opening, or the hooded figure that emerged. Thick weave fabric, so eerily familiar, brushed against the driver's calves as they rounded the open door.

My cloak, Ireland's muddled mind managed to form the thought only to lose it to the tight fist of fear that constricted her throat.

Her gaze locked, transfixed, on the narrow, female hands that rose to grasp the hood's edge. Vertigo pinched her reality, *stretching it out wide, before snapping it back with dizzying force. The earth itself seemed to buck beneath her, her knees threatening to give.*

The face beneath the hood glaring back at her ... was her own.

"You are death," her doppelgänger purred through blue-kissed lips. The black, scrolled veins visible beneath her skin moving and shifting like living artwork.

"I am not." Ireland's nostrils flared, her palms itching to call for the reassurance of her weapons. "You are the monster."

"You'd love to think that, wouldn't you?" Her darker self turned away, a prowling panther not the least bit concerned by the quaking antelope before it, and sauntered to Noah's side.

Flaxen hair fell into his eyes as he glanced up at her ... and froze. His life saving task all but forgotten. One seductive curl of her finger was all the motivation he needed to raise to his feet. Truly a man bewitched, who refused to allow even a blink to break his enraptured stare.

"You are me, and I you." Curling her fingers around the collar of his shirt, her Hessian counterpart pulled Noah's body against her. Her lips teased over his, causing his entire frame to tremble at her touch. "We are the harbinger of death. Our very touch is as deadly as a blade when wielded properly."

In a blur of speed, she stabbed her arm forward. A choked gasp eked past Noah's slack jaw. His chin dropped to his chest, staring in bewildered astonishment at the hand buried wrist deep in his chest.

"I-Ireland?" he croaked, accusation and confusion gouging deep lines between his brows.

Sticky, wetness beneath her hand yanked Ireland's head down sharp. Her cloak snapped out behind her in the night breeze, its familiar cadence welcoming her home. She had become the beast, Noah's still beating heart pulsating in her grasp. She wanted to loosen her hold, to set him free. Even so, her murderous limb rose, holding the dying muscle up for him to see.

"Nothing to offer, but death." Crimson streaks raced down her fingers, dripping from her palm as she dug her nails in deep ... and squeezed.

"Ireland? The flashing, illuminated man means walk," Noah patiently explained, gesturing to the street sign behind him. "Look, it's even counting down for you! You now have 16 seconds to cross the street before this become a game of *Frogger*."

Ireland came to with a start, finding herself standing on the opposite side of the four lane street from her troop with her frontal lobe throbbing. Blinking hard, she took a quick beat to clear her head before darting across the street like a cat duct taped to a firecracker.

"There she is. See traffic lights are our frie—*whoa*, okay." Noah's glib comment cut off the second Ireland threw herself at him.

Her arms twined around his neck, squeezing tight as she peppered his face with kisses.

"Yes, crossing the street *can* be scary." He patted her back in comfort, shooting Rip a confused cringe. "It was pretty touch-and-go there for a minute, but you totally made it."

Ireland's breath came in stuttered gasps. Reluctantly she pulled away, resting her forehead against his chin. "Just had a moment. Like the library all over again, only without the charming third person perspective."

"Was that code for something?" Noah asked Rip over her head in a barely audible whisper.

"I'll explain later, when she's not shaking like a nervous chihuahua." Craning his neck over Noah's shoulder, Rip invaded Ireland's space with an expectant stare. "While I'm sure this moment is justified by some scarring form of torture the Horseman inflicted upon you, I must point out that Ridley just disappeared around the corner. Perhaps you could put a pin in this particular meltdown until later? We can all watch that movie about iron magnolias and weep over a communal box of tissues."

Centering all the physical and emotional angst from the Hessian's cruel joke into her core, Ireland pushed it down and buried it deep. "No," she said as she steeled her spine and pried herself free from the comfort of Noah's arms. "I'm fine. Let's go get Ridley."

The trio rounded a bend landscaped with mulch and fresh saplings, their strides matched in determination. Immediately, they stopped short. Ridley stood statue still; a display of chiseled—yet slightly insane—beauty, staring eagerly at the charming white bungalow before him.

Blue eyes, wide with hope, flickered her way. His smile spread a touch too wide, crossing the threshold into manic. "*This is it*. The orangutan told me."

While her boys hung back, Ireland approached with cautious steps. "Ridley," she tsked in her most maternal tone, "don't you know not to believe every primate that talks to you?"

Her words stole the smile from his face, forcing on a mask of aghast revulsion. "*This one had a blade!*" he hissed in an urgent whisper.

Grinding the butt of her palms into her temples, Ireland massaged her head in small circles. The base drum headache had swelled into a pounding marching band drumline. "I-I have no idea how to respond to that."

"Neither did I," Ridley shrugged, his stare wandering back to the small house so painstakingly maintained. The covered porch and walkway were framed by meticulously groomed flower gardens. To the right of the stairs, nestled in a bed of burgundy and yellow mums, sat a bronze engraved plaque.

Ireland rocked forward on the balls of her feet. Stretching her neck to see, she read it out loud, "Brooklyn Historical Society; Cottage of Edgar Allen Poe."

Noah bumped Rip's arm with his elbow. "You know anything about this?"

Rip directed his answer to Ireland instead, weariness adding a few more years to his centuries of life. "I have told you before of the cloaked men that gathered a group of us and stressed the urgency of us hiding the truth behind our situations. Those men demanded absolute confidentiality. We were not allowed to tell one another much of anything that may give away what they considered to be 'too much.' However," starting at his mustache, Rip brushed his hand down the length of his beard, "I have since seen pictures of Mr. Poe, and I do believe him to have been the slightly troubled lad that sat directly beside me. I sincerely wish I had more information than that to offer."

Ireland's chin dipped in a brief nod. Beside her, Ridley shifted his weight from one foot to the other and back again. Under his breath he muttered incoherent words in a methodic cadence. A soul lost, searching for answers to questions he couldn't fathom to ask. She knew that feeling well. She'd been there herself, recent enough for the memory to still sting.

Irving.

Poe.

She was right. The pattern was repeating.

"Ridley." His name slipped from her lips in a throaty breath. "Is there something in there you need?"

The once suave businessman nodded. His glossy veneer rubbed away to reveal the frightened, child-like reality beneath.

"Then let's go find it." Flipping her hair from her eyes, and refusing to grant her throbbing head another moments thought, she offered Ridley her hand, "Together."

Tentatively, he laced his sweat-damped hand with hers. His eyes snapping open wide the second their skin touched. Unbridled awe dawned across his face, brightening the shadows that burrowed into the hollows of his features.

"All right," Ireland snipped, fighting off the urge to retract her hand. "Quit looking at me like Heaven opened and angels are singing, and let's get this over with."

Prompting him forward with a light tug, the two strode inside. Side-by-side.

EDGAR

"I could make it all go away. I *long* to make that so." Douglas murmured against Edgar's ear, his rancid breath causing the young man's nose to twitch with disgust. "All you have to do is listen to me—to *us*. Help us, Edgar, in ways we can no longer help ourselves. You do that, and your existence will instantly become far less … *dreary*."

Edgar's head twitched to the side, beads of sweat forming along his hairline. He tried to stay attentive to the dinner conversation, for his father's sake. A task that proved increasingly difficult. Eyeballs rolling in the ice water. Maggots squirming between the tongs of his fork and all through his salad. None of it was real, he knew that. Still, it succeeded in squashing his appetite—as it always did—and made him thirst for a long pull off the freshly purchased flask in his coat.

"Are you well, son?" Father's bushy-bearded business associate, whose name Edgar could not recall, asked between mouthfuls. "You are chasing that lettuce all around the bowl, yet have scarcely managed a bite."

Across the table John Allen's posture went rigid. His jaw tightening in barely concealed disapproval.

"I am, sir," Edgar forced his gaze up to their guest, hoping that—despite how awkward it felt—his attempt at a smile came across even a smidgeon believable. All the while he tried to wade through the murky fog of his mind for a plausible explanation. "I ... *ahem* ... had a rather large lun—"

Distraction picked that moment to blow in on a gust of fresh air and jasmine. Edgar blinked hard, momentarily convinced only he could see this yellow-haired seraph before him. The low scoop neck of her emerald green gown hinting at the supple curves beneath the layers of flowing fabric.

"Ah! There you are, my darling." Mr. Reynolds dabbed the corners of his mouth with his cloth napkin before pushing his chair back from the table. "Gentlemen, I'd like you to meet my daughter—"

"Lenore." The name the angels themselves must have dubbed this enchanting vision slipped free from Edgar's lip before he could think to filter it. He slowly rose from the table on wobbly legs that threatened to fold beneath him.

Her head cocked with interest, she turned his way. A soft smile lifted the corner of her luscious lips as she peered at him with eyes the exquisite violet shade of impending twilight. "That's right," a lilt of laughter bubbled through her tone. "And you are?"

His mouth opened to answer when a sudden rush of awareness seized in his throat in a constricting vice grip.

Stillness. All around. Douglas's unsettling presence, along with his maddening tricks and illusions, were … *gone*. No longer did the shadows across the ground elongate into disfigured ghouls shrieking his name and pawing at him with decaying fingers. Tranquility had followed this mesmerizing beauty. Peace and serenity had a name—more beautiful than any other.

"Lenore," Edgar whispered a second time.

"Well, that will make it easy to remember." Lenore giggled, gracing him with the full wattage of her beaming smile. "However it will be *dreadfully* confusing at gatherings of any sort."

"Edgar," his father injected, wiping his face before standing in greeting. "His name, which seems to have eluded him, is Edgar Allen. And I am his father, John."

"The pleasure is mine, Monsieur Allen." Lenore offered him her hand, dipping in a slight curtsey. John dotted it with a quick kiss, then caught Edgar's eye to silently encourage him to do the same.

A hot flush rushed to Edgar's round face. His trembling hands racked over his unruly hair, suddenly wishing he had taken a bit more time to tame it. It probably jotted off his head like a plethora of carrot sprouts. Even so, he eagerly anticipated the offering of her hand … which failed to come. Instead, she momentarily stuck a blade into his heart by taking a step back toward the door she entered.

The blow was softened the moment she spoke. "I passed the loveliest garden off the foyer. Edgar, would you mind showing it to me? I am enamored with flowers of any sort."

Before Edgar could trumpet his ready acceptance, Mr. Reynolds intervened. His plump chest expanding in a huff. "Lenore, you know this to be a *business* dinner. Such flights of fancy are *highly* inappropriate."

She waved his bothersome words away with a flick of her delicate hand. "Yes, and I know that Edgar and I were only brought here to make you both appear to be upstanding family-men deserving of each other's trust and association."

Silence fell across the room. Each shifted foot blaring like a train-whistle. Both men in question pointedly cast their stares anywhere but at Lenore or each other.

Biting her bottom lip to stifle a grin, Lenore attempted another tactic.

"Of course, Father, you know as a female I haven't the sense for business." Lenore innocently widened her eyes, her impossibly long lashes brushing her brow. Catching one cascading lock of her hair, she twirled it around her index finger. "Saddle Edgar with the task of occupying my simple mind with the lovely blooms of their garden, and I will spend the time regaling him with stories of what a kind and doting papa you are."

Instantly, her father's features softened. Like so many men, he was putty to be molded by the whims of his little girl. "Of course, my dear," he grinned, leaning in he brushed a quick peck to the tip of her nose. "Our talks will be frightfully dull for you. This is, by far, the preferable option."

Over her father's shoulder, Edgar watched Lenore's expression of mock innocence sharpen with sly victory as she shot him a conspiratorial wink.

For years the vindictive spirits had denied Edgar the beauty of the garden, making it appear to him as nothing more than a rotted and barren wasteland. In Lenore's presence the floral paradise had returned to him. Unable to contain his enthusiasm, Edgar released the arm linked with hers and rushed to the giant pompon puffs of the pink and blue hydrangeas. Gathering them in gentle hands, he tipped his face to inhale their sweet, but light, fragrance.

"Heaven to the senses, yet so fleeting," Edgar murmured. Out of the corner of his eye, he spied the long pink and white petals of the stargazer lilies. Dirt and rock kicked up from under his shoes as he darted the distance to the beckoning blooms. Eagerly, he filled his lungs with their aroma. "*Mmm*, you could scour the world over and would be hard pressed to find a sweeter, more intoxicating, smell."

Behind him, Lenore folded her hands in front of her. A small smile tugged at her glistening lips. "Monsieur Poe, I had expected *you* to show *me* the garden, not the other way around. You do realize it is in *your* backyard? This beauty is always here for you to enjoy."

Edgar righted his posture, yet could do nothing about the wide smile that made his cheeks ache. "Apologies, miss. The last time I frequented the gardens all I saw was ..." unable to think of a suitable description he opted for the blatant truth, "... death."

Dandelion-yellow brows disappeared into her hairline. "Such a dreary description for the winter months! Surely, you can see some beauty in their death though?"

His heart pounding a happy rhyme against his ribs, Edgar turned his head one way then the other, not wanting to miss one leaf of his enchanted garden restored. "In theory, I know the passing of each withered petal allows for fresh growth to take its place. Even so, I have come eye to eye with death more times than I care to admit. I shall not grant it the mercy to say beauty lies there. It only corrupts what once had been."

Waving locks brushed her shoulder as Lenore cocked her head, her violet eyes narrowing. "I suddenly feel the conversation has shifted away from foliage."

His cheeks blooming a matching pink to the roses beside him, Edgar cast his stare to the dirt path beneath his feet. "My apologies, Miss. Caught in the moment, I lamented."

"Please, do not apologize." Lenore crossed to him, her flowing skirts shushing across the ground with each step. "By the spark in your eye I see that it is a topic you hold great passion for. We should never apologize for *anything* that invokes a response of true passion. On the other hand, perhaps I could offer a fresh perspective?"

At this close proximity, where he could see the flecks of silver swirling in the violet pools of her eyes and the swell of her cleavage with each breath, Edgar predicted he would agree to anything she required of him. "It would be my honor to hear it." The words came out with a raspy edge. His mouth suddenly arid.

"If I were to drop dead on this spot right this moment, how would you remember me?" Lenore tipped her face up toward his. Her heart shaped lips stretching into a playful smile.

Trepidation threatened to clamp his throat shut, denying any possible answer from escaping. Swallowing hard, Edgar forced those bothersome doubts down and seized his fleeting moment of sanity. "I would remember you as a maiden of the rarest beauty; all light and smiles that no painting or sculpture could ever compare. That your violet eyes terrified my very heart, for I knew their color to represent the purest of magic as that is what I felt whenever I had the good fortune that they be cast my way. And, of course," he grinned, pleased with himself for the rosy flush that ascended up her slender neck at his brazen words, "I would recall that you were an expert manipulator. At least when it came to your own father."

"See? You have made my point for me!" The trill of her laugh would have made the sweetest of songbirds envious. "In death even our flaws are raised up on golden pedestals. They are remembered as delightfully charming in our absence. All that is left is the beauty of the memory."

Lenore knew nothing of Edgar's curse, yet the pure goodness that radiated from her had chased it away. As the truth of her message resonated through him, Edgar was struck by an awareness as real as the very breath in his lungs. This angelic beauty was the elixir to his particular ailment. For that, he would be her slave ... *forevermore.*

9

Ridley

An opulent display of riches belonging to the reigning king of macabre was not to be found inside Poe Cottage. Instead, Ireland was pleasantly surprised to find a cozy nest that offered the serenity and comfort needed to allow a brilliant creative mind to wander. The hardwood floors appeared newly refinished and polished to a glossy sheen. The smell of fresh paint lingered in the air, undoubtedly from the impeccably maintained walls and trim work. The rooms were small, meant to meet needs without the excess of extravagance.

"Hello, hello!" A white-haired woman blew into the room like a sparking storm of energy. Her vibrant red and yellow scarf, which perfectly matched her bauble earrings, flapped behind her with each of her wide, exuberant strides. "Welcome to Poe Cottage!"

"You look like my Nana." Ridley cocked his head to consider her, his voice flat and monotone. "*Before* she came back from the dead to tell me I used to spend too much time with the bathroom door locked."

The woman—whose nametag read Lois—blinked rapidly. Her freshly glossed red lips parting, only to clamp back shut in a firm, disapproving line.

"Ha! Field trip day from the home!" Noah graced Lois with his most charming grin. His arm wound around Ridley's neck in a gesture of brotherly affection that tightened into almost a headlock. "Ridley here has a problem with the rules of normal social conduct. You'll have to excuse him."

"No problem at all," Lois dismissed with a light-hearted chuckle that, thankfully, broke the palpable tension. If she passed any judgment, her practiced mask of graceful neutrality gave no indication. "And what can I do for you today? Are you here for the tour?"

"For the tour," Ireland parroted, her stare fixed on Ridley as he strode past Lois into the main living area like he'd been there a million times before.

Lois folded her hands in front of her, her practiced smile fixed. "Fantastic! We start promptly at the top of the hour." Over the guide's shoulder, Ireland watched Ridley yank the tennis racquet cover off ... revealing a splitting axe beneath.

Beside her, Rip pressed the knuckles of his fist to his lips to suppress his shocked yelp of alarm. Ireland wanted to see his contained freak out and raise him a full-blown hissy fit, yet she fought to keep her expression neutral.

"We give any last minute stragglers until then before we begin," Lois continued, seemingly oblivious to their plight. "In the meantime feel free to make yourself at home. We only ask that you respect the velvet ropes and remain behind them."

"Respecting those ropes is our biggest concern right now!" Ireland exclaimed, her voice coming out a high-pitched octave that would make dogs flinch. With her foot tapping an anxious beat against the floor, she watched the certifiable lunatic—that shouldn't be trusted with a *stapler*—flip the axe from one hand to the other.

"If you'll excuse me I have a few matters to attend to until then." Lois's cordial façade faltered, their hodgepodge band of weirdoes having effectively used up all her niceness. Granting them a brief nod, she disappeared back down the hall.

Ireland's fingers curled around the sleeve of Rip's button-down shirt as she forcefully yanked him into whispering distance. "Follow her! Do *not* let her come back out here until we get the axe away from him!"

Rip flinched as if she'd slapped him, his hands rising in confusion. "What am I supposed to do? As a caretaker here she has full wandering rights!"

"You're always grossing me out by bragging about what a ladies man you used to be. Now, you get back there and woo the crap out of her!"

Glancing in the direction Lois had disappeared, his nose crinkled in disgust. "She's a bit *old* for my taste."

"You're like four hundred!" Ireland hissed. *"Go!"*

"Yes, ma'am." Rip saluted, then pivoted on the ball of his foot to chase after the tour guide.

The moment she watched his scraggly grey hair disappear around the corner, Ireland spun in the direction of the far more alarming issue. *Ridley.*

Noah was squatted down between the darkly stained wood rocking chair and the sky blue painted fireplace with his forearms resting on his knees. "Ridley, you seem ... really busy," He chose his words carefully, so as not to upset Ridley who was shuffling around the room on his hands and knees, sporadically stopping to press his ear to the floor boards. "Maybe while you do ... *that* ... you could just slide over that axe?"

If Ridley heard him, he seemed far more interested in what the floorboards had to say.

Ireland pressed the back of her fingers to her lips, lightly drumming as she tried to come up with a plan. "Any idea what he's doing?"

"Listening to the vital wisdom of the oak flooring?" Noah craned his neck her way; tension sharpened the edges of his smirk and deprived it of its usual cavalier authenticity.

Further conversation was cut off by Ridley leaping to his feet. Grasping the axe handle in a tight two-handed grip, he arched back, every inch of his well-muscled frame twitching in eager expectation.

"*No, no, no!*" Ireland and Noah chorused in urgent whispers.

Bounding for the interception, Noah swiped for the handle but caught only air. Putting his weight behind it, Ridley drove the axe down hard. Wood cracked. Splinters flew. The floor beneath their feet trembled at the impact.

Her eyes widened to softball size, all Ireland could do was shake her head. "No way did that just happen."

"Fun time with destruction of property is over," Noah muttered through his teeth. Stepping forward, he caught hold of the axe handle before Ridley could let his second swing fly. "I'll take that now, brother."

Night had fallen in Ridley's eyes. All light snuffed out by the heavy storm clouds of maddening mystery that had blown in. Desperation forced his stare not to Noah, but to Ireland, the only other person on the planet that could understand his plight.

"I have to know," every pore of him pleaded. "*Please?*"

Ireland swallowed hard. She knew the desperation scrawled across his face … intimately. It stared back at her in the mirror daily. "Noah, let him go."

Noah's head whipped her way, tousled strands falling forward to frame his eyes. "This place is a historical landmark, and he's reducing it to kindling. This is an act you want to support?"

"He'll pay for the damages. Just … let him swing."

Noah hesitated, his moral compass searching for true north. Filling his lungs with a deep, cleansing breath, he let go and stepped away. His shoulder bumped Ireland's, his fingers automatically twining with hers, as the two watched Ridley unleash holy hell on the wood flooring.

"*What in tarnation?*" Lois exclaimed, darting back into the room with her lipstick smeared and her hair mussed.

Rip trailed her, held up by tucking his shirt back in. "I tell you, my dearest, there's nothing of concern—"

His words came to the same abrupt halt as his body did with his toes teetering on the edge of the ever-growing hole in the floor.

"You've got lipstick on your neck, dude," Noah offered in place of an explanation and raised his hand for a congratulatory fist bump.

Tipping his head in a paltry attempt to hide his triumphant smirk, Rip returned the bump and blew it up just as Noah had taught him.

"*This is a piece of agricultural history!*" Lois raged, her face morphing from red to purple.

"I understand that and promise we will make this right," Ireland said in her most calm, even tone. Holding out one arm, she blocked the enraged tour guide's advance. "But right now there is an emotionally unstable man wielding an axe and I need you to stay a good distance from it."

"*We just had that floor refinished!*" Lois screamed, the tendons of her neck bulging her frustration.

"If it makes you feel any better, they did really quality work," Noah offered, bending to pick up a chunk of wood Ridley had cast aside. "Look at that! Battered with an axe and it's still shiny."

"That does *not* make it better," the miffed guide snapped, her nostrils flaring.

Shirt soaked through with sweat, Ridley finally paused. "You may want to stand back," he panted to no one in particular, his chest rising and falling as he fought to reclaim his breath. Offering no further explanation, he hopped down waist-deep into the hole he'd made and immediately dropped to his knees. Like an industrious mole, he busied himself delving into the dirt. A cloud of dust billowed up around him, growing with each slung handful—until he encountered an ominous *thunk*.

"Th-there's something buried down there," Lois muttered, suddenly inching closer to Ireland's side.

The earth itself seemed to answer her, shuddering beneath their feet. A low, animalistic groan seeped from the hole—followed by a slow, but steady, drumming beat that grew louder, louder, louder still.

"Any chance that's the house settling?" Ireland asked, even though the prickling sensation along the back of her neck confirmed to the contrary.

"I have walked these floors a million times and have never heard anything like that before." Leaning in, with deep creases etched between her brows, Lois stammered, "D-did it sound angry to you?"

"Been down there too long, my sweet flower." While Ireland watched the words slip from Ridley's lips, the low tone of the unearthly reverberation could in no way be mistaken for his own. A man possessed with purpose—or something more untoward—Ridley climbed from the hole, dropped to his belly, and shimmied what appeared to be a handmade coffin lid from the soil it had rested in for ages. A ghostly sigh seeped from the yawning cavern he unearthed.

Not one body in the room moved.

Not one blinked.

Silence seeped and swirled around them, giddily taunting them with the disclaimer its presence would be fleeting.

That same fickle silence was chased away by a rumble beneath their feet. A shift in the very structure of the house sent them all stumbling. Before the stunned onlookers could regain their footing, a yellow-haired creature exploded from the ground like a demented daisy. Dirt and rock showered the living room, bits of it catching in the matted hair that fell to the being's waist.

"I-it's a girl." Lois gasped, taking in the ankle-length lace nightgown worn through with holes.

Those simple words snapped the ghoul's head up. The whites of her eyes were stained black, glowing purple irises glaring from their core. Grey lips curled back to reveal rotted teeth. A demonic hiss quaked up from her narrow chest, shuddering the hole in her cheek were the flesh had rotted straight through. One of her eyelids was split, like a snake's forked tongue. A flaw that gave each blink a flutter effect. An ear-piercing shriek was the only warning she gave before launching herself from her earthly prison. Her venomous glare locked on Lois.

Instinctively, Ireland shoved Lois behind her. Her hand rose to summon her sword. Experience had taught her it took a second for her weapons to respond, and that was one second she knew she didn't have as the ghoul bent to charge.

"Get down!" Ireland screamed, her fingers curled into the fabric of Lois's blouse and tossed her to the ground just as one cold, clammy arm slammed into her head hard enough to cause spots to dance in her vision.

Their salvation came in the form of the Hessian's late arriving sword that burst through the front door, tempting the long-dead blonde with a glimpse of what she wanted most ... *freedom*. She lumbered out with four sets of eyes staring after her in abject terror—Rip's eyes rolled back as his curse claimed him.

"*That was a scary bitch!*" Ireland squawked, easily snagging the hilt of her sword as it winged a tight circle around her.

"So are you!" Noah hollered. Catching Rip's snoring frame, he eased him to the ground. "*Go after her!*"

10

EDGAR

"Tell me what you've learned of the Stourbridge Lion." Edgar leaned back in his chair, his fingers steepled beneath his chin in an imitation of the posture his father often assumed.

"Great excitement is building around it!" Phillip, the file clerk that had recently been reassigned to Edgar's service, practically bounced in his seat with excitement. "The first steam engine built in the United States is *quite* the ordeal. A new age is upon us and the general populous is beside itself in anticipation."

"Excellent," Edgar nodded. "With all that attention, we *need* our product on its maiden voyage. Contact our buyers along the route and find out if they would be willing to receive their tobacco order via a different distribution option. If any hesitate offer them a discount, *only* if they hesitate."

Phillip pressed his lips together in a firm line, fighting off a grin that would have bordered on patronizing. "Very good, sir.

Your father could not have commanded such a dealing better himself."

Leaning forward, Edgar pressed his forearms to the edge of the desk. "Careful to speak such things about John Allen in this building," he whispered. "It borders on blasphemy."

"I'll keep that in mind, Monsieur Poe," the younger man said with a curt nod.

"Were there any further matters we needed to discuss?" A potent chill shivered down Edgar's spine, a familiar affliction that hounded him whenever an ominous presence neared. Stretching his neck first one way, then the other, he attempted to ease the spasming muscles that betrayed him.

"There is one more small matter, sir," Phillip said.

Leaning across Edgar's desk, he grasped the sterling silver letter opener. Before Edgar could think to question it, Phillip seized his own tongue in a closed fist and plunged the letter opener straight through it. Blood sprayed as he moved the blade up and down, sawing through tissue and raining fat droplets of splatter across the desk.

The moment the dull edged blade broke through the other side, Phillip slapped the still wriggling muscle down on Edgar's desk next to his daily planner. A free flowing spigot of crimson gushed from the wound, pouring down the file clerk's chin and dousing his shirt with gore. "Mith Lenow wanth meh tah reminn you of yahr lunth date."

"How could I forget such a thing?" Edgar fought to keep his expression neutral, despite the twitch under his right eye and vomit rising in his throat.

"If there is nothing else, sir, I shall leave you to it." Phillip rose with a bow, any traces of his momentary self-mutilation gone without a trace.

The door no sooner clicked shut behind Phillip than Douglas shimmered into being wearing a cat that ate the canary grin. "Not even a squeal? I feel I might be losing my touch, and that bothers me more than I care to admit, E-E-Edgar. Need I try harder?"

Time had not been kind to the specter. His otherworldly form had been ravaged by decomposition just as his flesh buried in the ground must have. Patches of grey skin had been lost to decay, revealing the skull or bone that lay beneath.

Edgar straightened the papers on his desk, breathing deeply to steady his shaking hands.

"Still ignoring me?" Douglas flopped down in the chair opposite him, his split and oozing lower lip protruding in a pout. "You cannot keep doing this, Edgar. I fear eventually my good nature will run out and things will get *ugly* for you."

Checking the time on the pendulum clock that maintained its incessant chorus in the corner, Edgar rose from his chair. He paused only to brush the wrinkles from the front of his slacks before rounding the desk and striding out with his head held high.

"Oh, come now, Edgar!" Douglas called after him. "That tongue debacle was truly i-i-inspired! How could you possibly ignore that?"

"Because bouts of hell are far more tolerable when mingled with moments of pure Heaven," Edgar muttered under his breath and shut the door on the seething ghoul.

He strode through the factory, giving a brief nod of greeting to the crew boxing up product. Their new Bull Jack machine belched and grinded away, filling muslin bags with loose tobacco in an efficient manner that would vastly improve their production times.

Sensing movement to his right, Edgar felt that nagging shudder claim him. Reflex screamed for him to spin toward it and acknowledge the pulley system that had materialized, the edges waving with flickering transparency before solidifying into a full-blown vision. Instead, Edgar steeled his spine and quickened his pace. Looking wasn't necessary. He knew from multiple horrifying viewings that a man in a brown shirt and dirty overalls would appear, guiding and directing a large pane of glass that was being raised to the waiting frame in the ceiling.

Edgar cringed at the first snap, well aware it meant the rope had begun to unravel. The glass dropped a few inches before it caught with a sudden jerk. The heels of his shoes clicked against the floor ever faster, urging him to run, to bolt for the door before that braided rope shredded. Its fibers hissed and snapped their ominous warning. The door was mere feet away when he heard that final pop and the whistling wind of the pane's final plummet, end over end, toward the ground.

With his hand on the door knob, and freedom from this ghoulish prison only a push away, Edgar leaned his shoulder in to give the heavy door a forceful shove. The angled position put him at the precise vantage point to see the ghostly apparition throw his hands up to shield his head. His effort being to no avail as the deathly sharp edge halved him from neck to hip, easy as slicing softened butter.

Pinching his eyes shut at the grisly remains that convulsed on the ground, Edgar threw himself against the door and its promise of escape. The midday sun that had beckoned from his office window was not to be found in *this* world—nor was any hope of retreat from his chilling existence. Grey clouds of smoke and ash formed a blockade that smothered the sun's buoying rays.

Baltimore, with its quant storefronts and factories eructing puffs of smoke toward the heavens, faded around him. An echo lost over a valley too vast. All around him wisps of energy morphed into soldiers locked mid-battle. Canon fire shook the earth beneath his feet, sending his heart rocketing into his throat. His nose and lungs aching from the gunpowder heavy in the air; Edgar shielded his nose and mouth in the crook of his elbow. Debris, and severed body parts, thumped down around him in a horrifying shower.

Muskets fired. Men shoved and jostled past him in their search for cover. Gravel pelted against his skin with enough force to leave welts on contact. A mushroom cloud of smoke and dust erupted in front of him from yet another canon blast. As the throat scorching haze it created dissipated, a face still blessed with youth's tender touch appeared before him. The boy could not have been more than ten or eleven years old, though he wore the full military garb of a soldier.

Wide, frightened eyes, the color of ripe hickory nuts, locked on Edgar's face. The boy's slight frame trembling with spastic surges. "I want to go home," he pleaded in a hoarse whisper. "Please, sir, t-take me home."

Smoke tendrils curled back, a black curtain revealing the gut-wrenching crescendo of this scene. The boy sat propped against a cast aside barrel of gunpowder, his lower extremities shredded to ribbons of meat and gore. Life gushed from him into an ever-growing puddle that stained the earth around him crimson.

The weight of his own ineptitude sagged Edgar's shoulders. "I am so very, very sorry."

"Edgar? Are you okay?" His head—drooping with sorrow—rose at the sound of Lenore's voice.

Yellow hair danced across her shoulders. Ivory fabric billowed out with each step. To him she became the embodiment of an angel of mercy as she crossed the battle scene. Her very presence parted the clouds, allowing the sun to shine through. Violence and chaos vanished in her wake, allowing beauty and color back into the dreary darkness he called life.

The light brush of her velvet soft skin against his sweat-dampened cheek tethered him back to a world where happiness yet remained. "Did you have another episode, my pet? Is there anything I can do?"

Damning the restraints of proper decorum, and the judgmental stares of those who passed by, Edgar gathered Lenore in his arms. Breathing in the scent of her sunshine-warmed skin, he attempted to steady his racing heart with a few cleansing breaths. "Yes, there is one thing," he muttered against her silky tresses.

Tipping her face to his, she allowed him the pleasure of plunging into the adoration that sparkled from the deep violet tarns of her eyes. "Speak it, dearest, and if it lies within my power it shall be yours."

Gathering both her hands in his, he brushed his lips across the back of one then the other. "Before you came into my life I breathed an atmosphere of sorrow. I stood, lost deep in darkness. Wondering, fearing, doubting I would ever escape. Then, suddenly, a corner was turned and there you stood, a blaze of hopeful light before me. My love for you is more than love."

"As is mine for you," Lenore assured him, her voice heady with emotion.

"If my present existence with you is but a dream, it is one I never wish to rouse from." Gulping in a breath like a man about to dive to the depths, Edgar dropped down on both knees. Completely at the mercy of she who owned his heart. "Be mine, my flower. Marry me. Let bells toll and my very spirit sing at our blessed union."

The ring he dug from his pocket was far from extravagant. Even so, it gleamed with eternity's spark.

Resolute devotion warmed the face of his beloved. Extending her hand, she allowed him to slip that uniting band on her finger. Before he could pull back, she caught his hand and pressed it over her heart. "Can you feel that? With every beat I love you more than the last."

And he could feel it. That joyful telltale beating growing louder, louder, louder still every blissful moment.

11

Ridley

Having never changed midday before, Ireland battled the awkwardness of the situation by puffing her cheeks and casting her stare to the steps beneath her feet. She was painfully aware that people were walking on the sidewalk not twenty feet from where she fastened the coarse wool cloak around her neck and drew her hood, but couldn't let their presence deter her.

Madness tipped its hat—as it always did—during the sensory extravaganza of her change. Ripe, prickling nerves alive with agonizing bliss over their heightened sensitivity. The hellish roar of the beast within rumbling through her as it stirred. Hoofbeats clapped against the pavement a moment before Regen made his regal entrance, skidding to a stop in front of her. His wide nostrils began expanding and contracting in eager expectation. Metal winged through the air, churning up the mingling scents of sunshine, horse, and leather, before she caught her circling axe and holstered it at her hip. Ireland treated the beautiful stallion to a soft muzzle scratching before she slid her scuffed black boot into the stirrup and hoisted herself astride. Threading the well-worn leather reins into the grooves of her waiting grasp, Ireland gently nudged Regen with her heels.

"This could be your weirdest ride yet, buddy," she warned, blowing her bangs from her eyes. "Is there an equestrian term for conspicuous? Because we could really—*whoa*!"

Immediately, the stallion stopped short. An abrupt act that almost sent Ireland flying over his head.

"No, not you! Keep going," Ireland urged, her voice morphing into a high-pitched squawk as she turned her hand one way then the other in front of her. Like an analog TV losing signal, her skin—along with all her other parts, accessories, and even the formidable stallion beneath her—turned to static then faded before her wide, unblinking eyes. Flipping her wrist, she wriggled her fingers. They were there, she could feel them. Be that as it may, not a flutter of motion could be detected.

"Are you doing this, or am I?" Ireland muttered, her head shaking in disbelief. "You know what, Reg? It doesn't matter. Just when I think things can't get any creepier ..."

The ebony stallion's sides quaked with a whiny; his not so subtle cue that he was still seeking a little direction.

"Sorry, bud," Ireland said, the leather saddle creaking as she adjusted her position. "Back on track. Let's go flat-line Gozer The Destructor so I can return to my joyously corporeal state. Turns out invisibility makes me queasy."

Cueing him on, she experienced the familiar, but always exhilarating, rush of his muscles contracting beneath her. The pull-back right before the jarring launch, that whisked them head long into adventure, stole the very breath from her lungs.

Ireland leaned into his strides, his hooves cracking a sharp chorus against the pavement. Turning the corner, they found the street bustling with activity. A fact that made that *particular* ride even more invigorating. *The thrill of the forbidden.* Ireland's head spun, a smile teasing across her sapphire lips, as she watched a man chase his newspaper that the forceful gust of their passing ripped from his grasp. With expert precision Regen dodged and weaved, winding himself between bewildered pedestrians that were bumped and jostled without a clue of what caused it. When the congestion of milling bodies on the sidewalk became too constricting, Regen veered into the street. His gait opened up, full gallop toward a taxi stopped for a red light. Ireland's breath caught as they went airborne. Metal creaked, buckling the hood in a perfect horseshoe formation. A split second before they slammed into the windshield Regen tucked his front legs, catapulting them in high arc over the cab and its bewildered driver. Ireland couldn't have stifled her giddy peel of laughter if she wanted to—and she had no desire to do anything of the sort.

Her momentary elation was squashed by a chorus of screams and gasps up ahead. Standing up in her stirrups, Ireland craned her neck to see over the gathered crowd. A flash of dandelion yellow set her jaw firm, her palms itching for her weapons. Distance being the cruel bitch it was, Ireland could do nothing but watch a well-meaning man approach the ghoul with his hands raised to steady her.

"Now if not sooner, Reg," Ireland urgently clucked just as the nightgown clad undead grabbed the man by both shoulders and frisbeed him onto the hood of a passing car.

Cowering at the screeching brakes and panicked screams that followed, the violet-eyed ghoul disappeared down the alleyway behind her. A spray of loose gravel kicked up under Regen's hooves as he skidded to a stop at that same alley entrance, his unseen form blocking anyone else from entering. Kicking her leg over his head, Ireland dismounted. Her knees bent to absorb the impact. The second the soles of her boots hit the cement, her corporeal form rushed back. Toes to head in one broad sweep.

"Huh? Guess it was you." Ireland gave credit where it was due, in this case to her still invisible horse.

Any frightened animal, with their hackles raised and lip curled in a menacing snarl, still couldn't hide the fear boiling deep in the reflective pools of their gaze. The same could be said for the creature pacing before her. In life the girl must have been quite the hottie; with her delicate features, supple shape, and ethereal violet eyes. Unfortunately, no amount of skin cream or Botox could wipe away the tread marks where merciless time had stomped across her face in iron-spiked boots.

We could take our time with this one, the Hessian purred from the dark recesses of Ireland's mind, his demonic tremor husky with longing. *Imagine, playing with it here in the open. No one would say a word to stop us. Hell, girl, they may label us a hero for ridding the world of its existence.*

Ireland filled her lungs to capacity and exhaled slowly, snuffing out the desire that flared at his suggestion. The fluttering twitch beneath her left eye made the strain of her internal struggle visible. Still, she squared her shoulders and overcame it.

"You don't fit the monster stereotype," Ireland pointed out, her fingers drumming against the hilt of her sword. "Maybe it's the quiet contemplation angle you're working. Although, I'm guessing the guy you flung into traffic would disagree."

Full lips, cracked and weathered by the abrasive sands of the hourglass, parted. The ghoul's tongue struggled to force words passed her desiccated throat, "P-p-p." Long, matted locks

117

Raven

slapped against her cheeks as she shook her head in frustration and tried again, "P-p-Poe!" Victory brightened her eyes with bursts of silver sparks.

"As in Edgar Allen?"

Dipping her head, the ghoul nodded in a way that would've appeared demure if not contradicted by her morbid appearance. Again, she paced. Mostly likely feeling the need to move after centuries trapped in a coffin. Her bare feet cracked at the wear, brown ooze seeping from the wounds.

Ireland widened her stance, a foreboding chill prickling down her spine. "And you would be—?"

The bewildered ghoul cocked her head, as if mystified by the question. "L-l-Len-o-ore," she managed.

"Lenore? You're not quite as fictional as American Literature would have us believe." Running her tongue over her top teeth, Ireland chose her next words very carefully. "I *really* hate to tell you this—especially since you seem to be having the mother of all bad centuries—but Edgar Allen Poe died over a hundred years ago."

Lenore's indigo eyes narrowed, her hands curling into claws at her sides.

"Easy, blondie," Ireland warned. One hand rose to halt the ghoul's threatening advance, the other closing around the hilt of

118

her sword. "Just to be clear, I had nothing to do with his death. Alcoholism was rumored to have played a part."

An animalistic roar tore from Lenore's throat as she charged with death steaming from her glare.

"I guess talk time is over." Unsheathing her blade, Ireland flipped it over the back of her hand before allowing it to nestle into her waiting palm. "Any way I can get you to reconsider this? We had a good thing going on here. We're practically girlfriends."

In place of a response, Lenore swiped at Ireland's core with yellow dagger-like nails.

A spinning side-step landed Ireland safely out of the way, yet also invited in the red haze of malevolence that clouded the edges of her vision. "Look, I get you're pissed," she snarled through her teeth. "You've been in a box! But as far as New York real estate goes, it was surprisingly roomy."

At the second vicious swing that winged passed her face, Ireland arched back Matrix-style to avoid getting her nose pierced in the most unsanitary way. Black tendrils of madness crept up the back of her neck, urging her to give in and unleash the salivating beast just beneath the surface.

A pause.

A breath, as she waited for her conscious to weigh in with the moral implications. Only to hear ... silence. The fingertip hold of control she clung to slipped away, that red veil descending before her eyes.

"Ireland is ever the diplomat. Always talking, seeking the nonviolent methods." While it was her own throat that reverberated with the menacing growl, the booming voice belonged to another. The Hessian raised the sword before him, turning the blade to admire how it gleamed in the sunlight. *"But you're not dealing with Ireland anymore."*

Leaning to the side, he kicked Lenore away with a well-executed boot to the mid-section. She stumbled back maybe four feet. Her nostrils flared, a deadly hiss seeped from her blackened teeth.

The very definition of casual nonchalance, the Horseman flipped the blade over the back of his hand and caught it in the other with a liquid fluidity. *"Let's have it then, beastie,"* he snarled, crouching into a battle ready stance.

A sly smile curled across Lenore's time ravaged face, her chin rising with a haughty indignation one wouldn't expect a corpse to possess. She closed the distance between them with two wide, determined strides. Before the Hessian could plunge his blade, her hand closed around it. If she noticed the deep valleys that it sliced into her putrefied flesh, it failed to register. Instead, she yanked it free from his grasp, as if confiscating the favorite toy from a naughty toddler. His upper body spun for the axe, only to be caught by Lenore's unrelenting grip to his throat. One hand, its flexing tendons visible through decomposing flesh, was all she needed to raise him high over her head.

"*No manners,*" she rasped and spiked him to the ground with bone rattling force.

Ireland's head cracked against the unyielding pavement, jarring the Horseman's essence into retreat. White starbursts danced before her eyes, hot, sticky warmth trickled from the back of her head and soaked her hood. Blinking hard, she fought for sight in a suddenly blurry, warped world—a seemingly simple act that made her wince in agony. Instinctively, she raised one trembling hand. The axe shifted at her hip. Wiggling free, it winged from its holster—only to be intercepted by the hand of her hovering enemy.

"*Tsk, tsk, tsk,*" Lenore taunted, waving the lethal edge back and forth before Ireland's tearing eyes.

"Well, shit," Ireland mumbled weakly and let her hand fall limp to her side.

Wind whistled passed the axe blade as Lenore offhandedly flung it through the air, the strength behind her effort embedding it deep into the wall of the brick building beside them.

Ireland knew enough to know she *should* be bothered by this—or at the very least, vaguely concerned. However, as her world spun like a carnival ride around her, she couldn't seem to muster the strength. She found her lone focus on a shimmer of silver that appeared overhead. A lone star visible in the impending darkness.

As she watched with hazy vision, that same star plummeted to the earth in a shower of twinkling lights, tearing through her core and pinning her to the ground. Electric shocks of pain shuddered and nipped through every nerve ending in her body. Choking on the gush of coppery warmth that bubbled up her throat and foamed over her lips, Ireland forced her heavy head from the ground to tip her chin to her chest. To her shock she found her own sword jutting from her gut. Regal and proud it stood, like the proverbial sword in the stone, with Lenore's bony hand possessively clasped around the hilt. The new power. *Victorious.*

A jumble of thoughts and emotions slammed into Ireland all at once. Every pivotal experience of her twenty-four years taking its final bow. Pushing all of them aside, she gasped one final warning to the world, "*Horseman … won't … die.*"

Violet eyes, brilliant as a neon marquee, swam over her. The once stunning corpse smiled warmly, impossibly long lashes coquettishly brushing the tops of her grey pallor cheeks.

"*He* is life." The head trauma could've been to blame, or perhaps the veil between life and death was retracting. Whatever the reason, Ireland suddenly had no problem understanding

Lenore's triumphant trill. "*You* are death. An unholy union that shall *never* be."

Grinding the blade in deeper with a vicious twist of her wrist, Lenore severed the world's tether to Ireland Crane.

12

EDGAR

"The torture is unbearable," Edgar breathlessly gasped. "I beg you, my flower, if the love you have for me is true, please do not withhold relief a moment longer."

"Regretfully, I cannot." Lenore giggled, her head tipping with pity. "I will not end your life, no matter how much you beg. This is a lesson you must learn on your own. That at a wedding cake tasting you *sample* each with a bite, *not* by devouring six full pieces of decadence."

"If our time together has taught you nothing else, you should know self-control is *not* one of my stronger attributes." Edgar offered her a playful wink that quickly morphed into a pained grimace.

"I'm sorry, love. Here I am making light of your misery whilst you suffer. Shall I take you home and rub your belly like a mother would her constipated toddler?" Lenore hid her smirk by turning her shoulders to acknowledging the carriage driver with a polite nod as he hopped down from his seat to wrench the side door open for them.

"You tease, m'lady. However I find that idea quite appealing," Edgar jibed. Tucking his hand under his arm, he stepped from the mahogany stained carriage. "I may even be able to put my pride aside—"

His thought abruptly trailed off, distracted by the ominous sight across the street.

The branches of a tall maple rooted and roosted—an impossible feat they were somehow managing. Green leaves, that ought to be dancing in the day's light breeze, were blocked out by bluish-black feathers. Every branch, every limb, every twig was occupied by regal breasted ravens. Countless black, marble eyes watching ... waiting. Edgar rubbed is hands over his arms to chase away the goose pimples that suddenly dotted his skin.

The avian gathering wasn't found bothersome by him alone. A young man, with his shirtsleeves rolled up his forearms, stood at the base of the tree. With wild swings of a broom handle over his head, he attempted to dislodge the settled congregation. Not one feather ruffled for his efforts.

"That's not how you scare birds away!" a toothless old man rasped, stomping out of the neighboring apothecary shop. His hunched shoulders curled in, as if hugging the musket gripped tight in his arthritic hands. "Out of the way, boy!" he hollered, shoving the lanky lad aside. Pressing the butt of the musket tight to his shoulder, he aimed it straight up into the tree.

Edgar's gaze flicked up to the body of life that was the birds. A chill skittered down his spine at the recollection of the call names of this particular grouping, a *conspiracy* or *unkindness* of ravens. Without tearing his stare away, his hand closed around Lenore's as she eased her foot onto the first step descending the carriage.

"Lenore, wai—"

One lone shot cut-off his warning and shattered their peaceful serenity. The birds rose as a single entity, moving in a malicious cloud of black that swirled and churned in search of direction. They should have gone up, seeking altitude's sanctuary. For unexplainable reasons that went against the very laws of nature, they did *not*. Instead, the ebony wave crested above the tree, banking hard to the right in a rip current that then dove straight to the ground—right in front of their carriage horses.

The frightened geldings backpedaled, nostrils flaring, ears pinned back. Their frantic heads jerking one way and the other in search of shelter from the noise and chaos. Lenore hesitantly pulled her foot back, only to have Edgar's grip tighten on her delicate hand. A protective flame burned in his eyes as he pulled her from the carriage and into the safety of his arms.

126

"Easy now." The carriage driver's attempt to soothe the frantic horses fell on deaf ears the moment the flock looped around for a second swoop.

Edgar and Lenore pulled apart, shielding their faces with their arms to ward off the funnel cloud of wings that lashed against them. The palomino gave two warning hops on his front hooves before arching back in a mighty rear. The chestnut brindle quickly mirrored the act, his front legs pawing viciously at the attacking sky. Their primal need to flee won out over the hushed whispers of their caretaker. Both of the agitated horses launched themselves toward the left side of the carriage, flipping their heads and fighting for freedom against the harnesses that held them tight.

Time slowed.

The carriage rocked on its narrow wheels.

Urgent whinnies accompanied the stomps of frenzied hooves.

The carriage driver backed from Edgar's side, his eyes wide.

Edgar's hand closed around Lenore's upper arm, tugging her back ... just as the carriage tipped.

Her graceful hand was ripped from his grasp, lost in a wash of snapping boards, airborne cargo, and flying kindling. Those violet eyes he treasured locked with his as she sank beneath the weight. Edgar scrambled for a hold, his deficient fingers catching nothing but the whisper of where she had been. Yellow hair fanned around her face, giving her the appearance of a surfaced mermaid swan diving back to the depths. The toppling beast of a carriage stole the very breath from Lenore's lungs in its crash, pinning her beneath its weight.

"Help me!" Edgar screamed over his shoulder at the carriage driver, his fingers grappling under the rumble for a corner he could seize. "We must lift it off of her!"

"S-sir," the maddeningly still driver stammered, "the ... blood."

Edgar refused to acknowledge the growing crimson pool around his feet, would not entertain where it was coming from. *No.* Such things were of little consequence. All that matter was freeing his bride-to-be.

"That matters not!" Edgar bellowed, the pounding of his heart resonating in his temples. *"Help me, damn it!"*

"Edgar," his trapped angel whispered, without the slightest inkling of fear. "Be still, my love."

Abandoning his mission, he fell to his knees at her side. Quaking fingers he scarcely recognized as his own brushed strands of hair from her paling face. "I am here. Right here. Stay with me. We will get a team of men, if need be, to—"

"*Shhhh*. Let me look upon thy face," her full lips, which death so selfishly robbed of color, barely moved at her faint declaration. "So fair ... and debonair ..."

Locked with the desperate stare of her lover, Lenore took her last lingering gaze.

"Lenore? *Lenore*?" Edgar's fingers clasped the fabric of her sleeves in a white knuckled grasp, the realization slowly seeping in that this beautiful temple that once held the essence of his beloved was noticeably, irreversibly vacant.

He rose on jelly legs that threatened to fold beneath him. His place in the world snatched from him with the sigh of Lenore's last breath. All around him darkness descended. Spirits slunk from the shadows, wringing their hands with devilish delight. Edgar stumbled over his own feet in a scramble to escape the cold, demanding hands of the dead that clawed at him. Caught in the flurry, he found himself spun in a dizzying waltz of the past and present. Being jostled from one entity to the next. A jumble of faces swirled before him. Some marred by death and tittering with glee; others folded in concern, the spark of life still burning within their eyes. None belonged to the only person that truly mattered. Even so, she *had* to be there. Seeing her one last time would finally give him reason to thank God for his affliction. It would give purpose to his curse if it granted him the chance to say a proper goodbye.

"*Lenore! Lenore!*" Breaking free, Edgar dashed up and down the street like a madman, screaming her name all the while until his throat grew raw and parched. His urgency reached its peak when the flurry of faces began to duplicate with no sight of her. A choked sob caught in his constricted throat that threatened to rip his very soul to ribbons if he accepted the nightmarish reality before him.

His beloved Lenore, the flower that brought beauty back to his dismal existence, would be his ... *nevermore*.

13

Ridley

Desolate, barren land comprised only of varying hues of grey. Arid earth cracked in patchy scales as far as the eye could see. The only vegetation thriving in such a wasteland was a thick trunked tree that grew roots up. Its thin, twining appendages stretched to the heavens, praying for a sip of life giving water. In this world of death and despair, Ireland Crane was queen. Her crown a braided grapevine decorated by a spray of raven feathers. Sand, caught in harsh gusts of relentless wind, lashed against the bare skin of her arms. The constricting bodice and flowing skirt of her ebony gown caught several of the airborne granules. They clung to the fabric, reflecting light like precious jewels inlaid in the layers of silk and taffeta.

Her loyal subjects knelt before her. Their chests bare. Their hands clasped behind their backs, while they tipped their faces to her in admiration. The first two in line were Victor Van Tassel and

Mason Van Brunt, her first two victims after becoming inflicted by the Hessian's curse. Neither man's vigor had been plucked by the sling of her blade, but had flourished in it. Victor's youth had been restored; his thick gut and thinning hair replaced by luxurious locks and a barrel chest. Mason had claimed his manhood; the sharp lines of his handsome face having chased away youth's last remaining traces. Each man omitted a low, throaty groan of pleasure the second she placed a palm aside each of their faces. The energy that animated them pulsed through her, lighting her skin with an ethereal luminescence. As their pallor paled, Ireland bloomed. The eyes of both men rolled back. Their bodies shuddering as the throes of euphoria consumed them. Like the harsh landscape around them, the vitality of their skin drained to ash. The next passing breeze exploded them both into puffed clouds that swirled around her waist in one final farewell before they fluttered off wherever the wind would take them.

Lifting her skirt enough to allow herself movement, Ireland ventured further down the line to those patiently awaiting her attention. Her breath caught, the next two faces turning to her like flower petals meeting the rays of the sun. Rip Van Winkle, not the decrepit shell of himself she knew but the man he had once been, knelt before her. Strong, strapping, and staring up at her with a level of trust and admiration that made a flush of guilt stain her cheeks. Forcing her troubled gaze to travel farther still, she found her heart seized in desire's iron fist.

His name escaped her parted lips in a breathless sigh, "Noah."

A crooked smile meant just for her curled the corners of his lips. "You know what we want and why we're here ..." his words trailed off as he tipped his head, offering her his throat.

Beside him, Rip matched the gesture.

Ireland stumbled, her heel tangling in the hem of her skirt. "No! I-I could never hurt you! You know that! You know me!"

Catching her hand, Noah reeled her body back to him. One strong arm hooked around the rise of her hips and pinned her to him. "Your gift is beautiful. Don't ever doubt that." Turning the inside of her arm skyward, his mouth teased the tender flesh of her wrist. The heat of his breath and delicate caress of each dotted kiss sent waves of desire coursing through her. Hazel eyes, warmed to molten gold by palpable desire, locked with her own and refused to falter. "Please, don't deny me."

The adoration in his gaze, and the seduction of his touch made Ireland feel like the most beautiful being on the planet ... until she caught sight of Rip out of the corner of her eye. He was wearing that matching mask of longing. It wasn't her they wanted—it never had been—but a taste of what she could do. To be near death, and delve into the darkness. Their own twisted yearning to thumb their nose at mortality led them to follow her.

Clamping her eyes on the wash of tears that threatened, Ireland ignored the wailing of her heart … and laid a palm to each of their cheeks. One lone tear snuck between her lashes at the cascade of tingles seeping up her arms.

"You can't blame them for not understanding," a familiar voice drawled behind her.

She spun as he neared, leaving Rip and Noah wheezing for breath—or, more likely, completion of her task.

Techno-colored flowers bloomed in a colorless world each time the sole of Ridley's shoes met the earth. The crisp cut of his white, tailored suit was accented by a burst of color from the button-down shirt beneath that changed in hue to match the species of flowers that sprung to life. Hydrangeas blue. Orchid purple. Lily fuchsia. Rose coral. As he neared, Ireland noticed his eyes morphed to match as well. The result hypnotic.

His haggard and troubled façade was a thing of the past. The man before her exuded confidence and a zest for life from every pore. The draw of which was so magnetic Ireland had to fight to keep her feet planted while her body insisted she close the distance between them.

"To them this is a thrill, a game of chicken against the Reaper himself." Ridley paused beside her, his shoulder skimming hers. Even then he didn't grace her with a glance, his attention fixed on Rip and Noah. Tipping his head toward her, the warmth of his breath teased over her breast bone. "For us, it's destiny."

The moment he stepped away from her, the chill of solitude lashed at Ireland's soul and cut deep. Bending eye-level with her withering subjects, Ridley pursed his rose petal lips to blow a soft, healing breath over both of them. Wan complexions of the dying were ripened to plump apricot. Both men blinked away their disappointment before dipping in a low bow— foreheads to the ground in a show of respect.

"No need for that, boys." Ridley smoothed the front of his suit coat, a self-depreciating chuckle playing over his lips.

Neither humbled servant budged.

"You're like me?" Pacing in a slow circle around him, Ireland's eyes narrowed.

He matched her steps, leading them in an intimate waltz normally reserved for predators—or lovers.

"Like you?" He tsked. "Oh no, my darling flower. There is no other like you. Our only similarity is being pawns in a game that began centuries before either of our fathers got an amorous gleam in their eyes."

Ireland's gaze lingered over the soft curve of his mouth, wondering if his lips could possibly taste as delectable as they looked. "How do we play?"

Curling one finger into a ruffled tuft of her skirt, Ridley pulled her to him. Bowing his head, he brushed his cheek over the delicate curve of her collarbone. "The game is already in motion," he murmured. "The rule sheet not meant for our eyes. All we can do now is stay alive."

Ireland weaved her fingers into his hair, yanking his head back with a passion driven force that bordered on violent. "I've taken lives. I'm a monster," she snarled against his lips, tormenting them both with the agonizing veil of energy that denied their touch.

His hand snaked up her arm to find her fingers and loosen her grasp. Palm to palm. Fingers entwined with fingers. "Does granting it make me any better?"

Ridley didn't give her time to answer. With one hand pressed to the small of her back he crushed her to him. Their lips met with a desperate urgency that caused Heaven and Earth to quake in nervous anticipation of what was coming ...

A soft chorus of beeps roused Ireland from what was turning out to be a disturbingly hot dream. Fighting against medicinally weighted down eyelids, she struggled to reclaim her consciousness. Her head lulled to the side, the pillow beneath rustling like sandpaper, in search of the warm and delicate touch that cocooned her right hand. She expected Noah to be the cause as he diligently hovered by her bedside. A dry rasp, that sounded a little too much like a groan, escaped her parched throat before she could stifle it. The cause? Ridley, staring down at her while clutching her hand in both of his. Behind him was a backdrop of medical supplies and contraptions.

A plethora of questions pirouetted through her mind, *Why are you touching me? Where are we? Did I make sex noises in my sleep? What the hell happened? Are you really that good a kisser?* Thankfully, the one that snuck past her chapped lips was, "Where's Noah?"

Ridley rubbed the rough stumble of his chin against his shoulder to scratch it instead of releasing his hold on her suddenly sweaty palm. "Rip watched them insert your I.V. and hit the floor like a chopped tree. A flurry of activity followed. It seems to the medical community a black out like that is a cause for concern. Noah followed them out, screaming at them that using a defibrillator on a narcoleptic would make matters far worse. I'm sure he'll be back soon."

The simple act of swallowing awoke what seemed to be shimming razor blades lining Ireland's throat. "You're surprisingly articulate for a guy that admitted to conversing with an invisible orangutan a few hours ago." Wincing and adjusting her position, she attempted to retract her hand from his. "Can I have that back, please?"

"No!" he barked, then immediately attempted a softer approach at her wide-eyed reaction. "I'll explain, I promise. Just, please, don't let go yet."

As odd and uncomfortable as it was to endure physical contact of any kind with the guy she just dream cheated with, Ireland couldn't bring herself to deny his desperately pleading eyes. "Okay, easy." Her free hand rose, the heart monitor waving off her pointer finger, to halt his freak out. "Take a breath and maybe loosen your grip a little. I'd like to be able to feel those fingers again when you're done with them."

"Sorry. It's just …" His scruffy chin fell to his chest. His pause dragging on in his hunt for the right words, "Right after the birds, everything changed. I started hearing … voices."

Feeling her eyebrows raise, Ireland struggled to maintain a neutral façade and prayed her expression came across as even remotely casual. "What kind of voices? More *'Come play with us, Danny'* or *'If you build it, they will come'*?"

"Horrible ones, saying ghastly things."

"The Stephen King variety then. Never a good omen. Can you hand me that water?" Ireland rasped, lifting one finger to point at the tray behind him.

Ridley released her hand with *one* of his. The wheeled stool beneath him squealed its protest as he pivoted to retrieve the Styrofoam cup. Positioning it beneath her chin, he guided the bendy straw to her lips. "The visions started soon after that. Awful, horrible things that would make every scary movie ever made look like a Pixar fairytale. I felt myself on the verge, about to break. Then, at the cottage, I realized there is one thing that can make it all go away—*your touch*. The moment you took my hand, you hushed all their ghostly shouts and scared away their rotted forms."

Cringing at the pain that jolted through her contracted her muscles from tipping her head, Ireland eased herself back down on to the pillow. "We're really going to have the 'I see dead people' talk?"

"I guess you could say that," he huffed with an almost smile. "Only they were well aware they had died and were ten degrees of pissed off about it. Like when the EMTs first wheeled you in here, two men appeared in the hallway charred to black smoldering briquettes. They were gang members burned alive in front of their rivals as sport. Can you imagine anyone doing something like that in jest?"

Her mind drifting to the Horseman living inside of her and all the atrocities he committed, Ireland shifted her gaze away guiltily and merely nodded her head.

After setting the cup back down, Ridley leaned his forearms against the edge of her hospital bed. His index finger traced the edges of her sugar skull tattoo. An intimate gesture Ireland bristled at, however considering that he was pouring his heart out she refrained from clubbing him with her I. V. pole—for now.

"One spirit in particular warned me that there was more to this than the voices and apparitions. He claimed," Ridley's tongue flicked out to wet his lips before he pressed on, "that my touch could ... resurrect the dead."

A fresh rush of panic launched Ireland's palpating heart into her throat and lodged it there. "I was stabbed ... *oh, God*. But ... that's not ... you didn't bring *me* back did you?"

The terms of her curse were quite simple; the Horseman is unending. Ireland's death would not stop it. Instead, the end of her mortal life would allow the beast to run free without the limitations of her humanity to keep it in check. Her hand fluttered nervously to her neck, wishing the talisman, which kept her other half at bay, there.

"No. *No*," He reiterated for emphasis. "Your wound—severe as it is—miraculously missed anything vital. Before we arrived here at the hospital the EMTS already had you stabilized."

Puffing her cheeks, Ireland exhaled a relieved sigh through pursed lips.

Ridley bowed his head sheepishly. His gaze cast to the flimsy blanket that covered her, he found a fuzz ball and plucked it free. "Even if you hadn't been, I couldn't have attempted it. Not after what the spirit told me."

Whether she believed his story or not—and really, she was the *last* person that should *ever* accuse an idea of being too far-fetched—there was no denying that Ridley was a broken version of the man he'd been just yesterday. Gone was the chiseled heartthrob. Hours in his haunted hell had cut heavy bags under his eyes. Turmoil had sharpened his features, drained his complexion to a sickly yellow.

That alone was all the reason she needed to hear him out. "What did he tell you?"

"That if I touch someone like that, they come back … wrong. That's why he led me to her. He wanted me to see for myself. A lesson I could've learned without the help of that terrifying visual aid, by the way."

"So, she was real?" Pinching her eyes shut, Ireland raised her free hand to massage her temples. "I get some pretty messed up visions of my own and I was *really* hoping she was one of them."

"Nope, she's very much real and very much still out there somewhere."

"Well, aren't you a sunbeam of happy news," Ireland grumbled mostly to herself just as the pink curtain, spotted with yellow diamonds, that surrounded her bed hissed across the bar.

"Look who's awake!" The doctor's eyes crinkled at the corner, the rest of his smile hidden beneath a surgical mask. His thick apple shape strained against the fabric of his light blue scrubs. "You gave us all quite a scare. It's not every day we get a patient in here with a broad sword injury, of all things."

"Well, that's me." Ireland stared at the drop ceiling overhead, blinking hard in a paltry attempt to distract from the sharp ache drilling through her core. Whatever they had given her for pain was clearly wearing off. "Always thriving to be different."

"Maybe next time just try an outlandish hair color." Hooking his hand underneath the edge of the bedside tray, the doctor wheeled it around to the edge of the bed and stopped it in front of him. From one scrub pocket he pulled a packaged syringe, from the other a small vial. "Now, it's medication time. Which, unfortunately, means your boyfriend is going to have to step out for a minute."

"I'm not her boyfriend."

"He's not my boyfriend" Ireland and Ridley clarified in unison before exchanging matching offended sneers at each other's disgusted tones.

"No offense intended." Amusement drew the doctor's eyebrows up to his surgical cap as he gripped each side of the syringe packaging in a gloved hand and tore it open. "I saw the hand holding and took a guess."

"He's just really needy." Ireland's dry snort of laughter quickly morphed into a pained cringe.

"I hope that hurt." Ridley glared out of the corner of his eye, his mouth twisting up to the side.

Turning the vial top down, the physician rolled it between his palms. "Friend, brother, neighbor, distant cousin—doesn't really matter. You two can work that out between you, *after* I administer the medication. But for now, out ya go!"

For a brief moment, Ridley had almost returned to himself. His over-confident Casanova gleam warmed his ocean blue eyes like the tropical sun coaxing lapping waves onto a white sandy shore. Yet all it took to turn those blue seas stormy was the mention of him extracting himself from her touch.

"I-I can look away," he stammered in his building dismay. "But you have to understand after the scare she gave us, I hate to leave."

The doctor's head cocked in sympathy. "I can respect that. Truly, I can. Even so, it's hospital policy and my hands are tied. I'm sure you can understand that."

Something in the physician's comforting tone sparked a memory that skirted along the dark corners of Ireland's mind, refusing to step into the light. She was snapped from this momentary reverie by Ridley's hands tightening around hers in a vise grip that threatened to reduce bones to splinters.

"Hey," her voice sounded weak even to her, but she fought for some semblance of assertiveness, "It's only for a minute. You'll be—" Her stare flicked to the doctor for a quick check that he hadn't caught that very blatant slip up, "—*I'll* be fine. Then you can come right back in here and be the creepy guy watching me sleep, if you need to."

His dutiful smile failed to make it to his eyes. "Only for a minute," he mimicked quietly.

Ireland placed a comforting hand over his, her face a mask of mock sincerity. "Ridley, for someone that seemed disgusted by the idea of being my boyfriend you're coming off as really codependent in front of the good doctor."

The doctor stifled a snort of laughter behind his meaty hand, playing it off as a sudden coughing fit.

Her ill-timed jab succeeded in releasing a bit of the tension from Ridley's shoulders. "Point taken. I'll be right outside, but rest assured the second he's done I *will* be back."

"I'll be counting the seconds." She couldn't have blocked the snark from that rebuttal if she tried.

144

Filling his lungs, as if the last remaining passenger going down with the Titanic, Ridley released his hold and bolted from the room, the curtain waving after his rather rash exit.

Injecting the syringe needle into the vial, the doctor pulled back the plunger and drew it back slowly. "I know it's none of my business, but I think you're wise to stay platonic with that one."

There it was again. Something in that considerate tone that tickled at a particular memory. Ireland's eyes narrowed. "I'm sorry, have we met?"

His gaze immediately snapped to her face. Was that alarm creasing his brow, or professional concentration? Whatever it was vanished before she could pin a label on it. "I have been tending to you since you came in, perhaps you weren't quite as out of it as we believed?"

A low-lying fog was setting in from her injuries, clouding her already hazy mind. "No, it's not from here."

"Another life, maybe?" He chuckled. Holding the syringe up, he tapped the bubbles from it as he approached her bedside. The liquid inside looked more mystical than medicinal. Its bright purple hue swirling with iridescent shades of blue and pink.

She opened her mouth to ask what it was, when her sleep-weary gaze traveled to his face. The memory slammed into her, pinning her back against the bed. An extreme case of vertigo spun the room around her allowing only one image to catch and hold. *Those eyes*. Crystal blue, almost clear. She *had* seen them before.

"I remember," she gasped, just as he injected his odd looking concoction into her I.V. port.

"What's that, dear?" His tone was light, as if playing along to a delusional ranting. Even so, Ireland detected the sharp, tense edge that snuck into it.

The medication worked fast, surging an icy blast through her veins and coating her tongue with the taste of metal. Her lids grew heavy, each blink becoming a fight to maintain consciousness. "You came to my house when I first moved to the Hollow," she slurred. "You were a cop."

"A cop and a doctor? I've been very busy." Reaching one hand to the opposite ear he released his surgical mask, letting it flutter to the floor. Resting a hand on the bed rails on either side of her, he leaned in and stared her straight in the face to watch the realization seep through her dulled senses. "Haven't I?"

"The museum … Mr. Mallark?" She forced the words out through what felt like a mouthful of molasses. "Wha-what do you want from me?"

His thick moustache twitched as a slow smile curled across his round face. "You will soon see, my dearly treasured Hessian," he whispered.

146

14

EDGAR

Blades of a windmill suffered the onslaught of ferocious gusts, whirring ever faster. The hum of their rotations drowned out all other sounds around them. Edgar's pulse drummed that same tune in his ears, detaching him from this life he no longer recognized as his own. All around him activity flapped and fluttered, just as those murderous ravens had.

Flowered donations were carted in and positioned around the casket.

Sorrow filled faces offered hushed condolences.

Bent knee prayers were whispered beside Lenore's mahogany pedestal.

Gleeful ghouls wrung their eager hands at the prize they had claimed.

And the whispers—all muttered from behind backs of hands.

"They were to be married."

"Coming from a dress fitting, is what I heard."

"He ran up and down the street shouting her name, while she lay alone and heaved her last breath."

"She is one of us now, Eddie boy," Douglas sneered, tap-tap-tapping one grey, bony finger against the edge of her coffin. "If you loved her enough you could see her. Yet, woefully, it seems even in death you were not deserving of that b-b-beauty."

Through all this Edgar sat. His stare fixed on the profile of the sleeping princess nestled against her white silk pillow.

His father's face swam before him—stern and intense. "You are *not* to be alone with the body under any circumstances. Do you understand me, Edgar? I *know* what you are thinking. Quite honestly, if I were in your position, capable of what you are, I would be tempted as well. However, as your father, I cannot and will not allow it. I *will* save you from yourself, if that is what is required of me."

Edgar simply peered back, his face a chalkboard wiped clear of all markings of expression. "Yet, you are not truly my father at all."

He had not meant that as an insult, had injected no malice behind it. Even so, he watched as his father's face ripened from red to purple. With an indignant snort, the normally poised John Allen spun on his heel and stomped off.

Moments later—or perhaps it was hours—his mother eased herself into the chair beside him, gathering his gloved hands in hers. "Your father and I are worried, Edgar. You have suffered one of the greatest losses a heart can endure."

Edgar's head cocked. His wide and manic eyes scoured her face, searching for signs that she genuinely understood his anguish. Slumping in resignation, he realized meat molded into a mask of mourning was all that stared back at him.

"You must remember, my sweet boy," Francis leaned in close, her breath—smelling of strawberries and honey—warmed his cheek as she whispered, "your ailment is not to be exploited. It is an affront against God. One your soul would burn for if you dared dabble with. You mustn't bring her back, son. If you truly loved Lenore, let her go. Grant her peace."

Edgar blinked. Once. Again.

Mother's gentle palm pressed to his cheek, perhaps under the misconception her message had gotten through. Then she was gone, lost in the sea of mourners coming in going in an incessant ebb and flow.

At some point the crowd dispersed.

At some point the casket, situated in the parlor of the Allen estate, was closed.

149

At some point the lamps were extinguished.

Only then did servants come to collect Edgar. Wrapping his limp arms around their necks, they escorted him to his room and tucked him in like an exhausted child. The vacuum tube light fixture clicked off a moment before they eased the door shut behind them, their steps fading down the hall.

Edgar lay there, staring into the darkness. His muscles rigid beneath the blanket drawn to his chin. There he waited until the entire house settled for the night. Sure he had heard the last of the scuffs and shuffles, he rose on legs made steady with conviction and slid the gloves from his hands. For her that now so lowly lies, he would return the light within her eyes.

The casket opened with little more than a creak. The spirits lingering around him sank silently into the shadows, their rotting lips curling with malicious eagerness. There she lay, his beautifully broken porcelain doll. The side of his hand gently brushed her dandelion yellow hair from her face, revealing the stitches that ran from the corner of her mouth to her cheekbone. A deeply bruised gash zigzagged over one of her closed lids. Both were remnants of injuries from the crash that had been covered by an excess of powder and carefully arranged hair. He would treasure those scars, because they were a part of her now and would forever act as a reminder that even death's harsh hand could not extinguish the flame of their love.

Catching a lock of her hair between his fingers, Edgar's hand slid down the silky length of it. All the while envisioning the moment of her awakening, the same kind of pivotal romantic eloquence found in classic fables where the prince awakens the sleeping princess with a loving touch. Her eyes would flutter open to gaze adoringly upon her rescuer. Finding her legs too weak to stand, he would cradle her in his arms and carry her forth into their future of limitless bliss.

The tips of his fingers, tingling in anticipation, hovered over her skin. Heaven awaited, and it would be brought forth by a simple touch.

"Edgar, do not do this," a hushed, yet urgent, voice directed from behind him.

Guilty hands slapped to his sides. Edgar spun to find his mother in the doorway, a cup of tea cradled in her grasp.

"Mother, I—"

"Extend me the courtesy of not lying to me, Edgar Allen," her tone turned icy as she placed her cup down on a neighboring table. Standing ramrod straight, Francis folded her hands in front of her. An indignant flare lifted her chin. "Step away from the casket, *immediately*."

His trembling hands rose, palms out. "This is not as it appears, I assure you."

"Oh, I know *exactly* what this is, which is why I insist you step away from her, *now*. Keep in mind that I *will* alert your father and the entire staff if need be."

The idea of attempting a fabrication taxed Edgar's already weary soul, forcing his chin to his chest. For lack of a better alternative, he opted for the painfully ugly truth. "I-I cannot walk this earth without her. Cannot fill my constricted lungs knowing she is gone. My serenity has been stolen, casting me to the very bowels of hell. Even if she were to come back … *changed*, she would be here and she would be mine once more." Tears he fought to keep at bay slipped over his lids, streaking down his cheeks.

Her stony exterior chipped away to reveal hints of the compassionate pity that lay beneath. "Edgar, I know of your pain and more than anything in the world I wish I could take it from you and shoulder it myself. However, deep inside you have to know this is not the way. The road you are on leads only to further anguish."

Francis took one step forward, driving Edgar back protectively to the side of the casket. "We will go away together," his words tumbled from his lips in a hurried pant. "I give you my word. Far from here, where—if there be any issues—they will not befall you or father."

Tipping her chin to her shoulder, Francis shouted up the stairs, "*John*! Can you come down here, please?" She turned back to Edgar with her lips pursed, regret creasing her brow. "We asked too much of you holding the wake here. We will remove the casket immediately. Until then, you should retire for the night."

"Francis?" The stairs creaked beneath his father's heavy footfalls. "Did you call for me?"

"How I wish you had trusted me," Edgar quietly stated. Knowing his time had run out, he spun to face his fallen angel.

John Allen rounded the corner the same instant Edgar gulped down his trepidation and plunged his hand into the silk lined casket.

"*Edgar! No!*"

His father's shouts pinged off of him, as if mere pebbles being tossed at a thundering steam engine. Fingers tips brushed cold nothingness; stroking, petting, encouraging life's vital warmth to seep into that beautiful vacant shell. Edgar's heart convulsed in a joyous stutter beat the instant a guttural groan seeped past the rouge painted petals of her lips.

Snatching the oil lamp from the side table, John brandished it defensively before him. With his free arm he shoved

Francis behind him. "Step away from the coffin, son. Walk to me, *quickly!*"

"She needs me," was the only argument Edgar offered.

His *own* pressing need for her became visible in the adoration that radiated off of him as he watched Lenore's impossibly long lashes flutter open. The bruised curtains of her lids drew back to unveil those enchanting lavender eyes eternity had attempted to confiscate.

"There now," he cooed, reaching both hands in to coax his betrothed from her premature tomb. "Steady, my flower."

Slowly, her head turned to find his face, her lips moving to form his name in an inaudible whisper.

"*John! What is it? What has he done?*" Francis shrieked, her clawed hands seizing handfuls of her husband's nightshirt.

Lenore's lips curled from her teeth at the abrasive racket, her clammy hand closing around Edgar's wrist in an unrelenting vise grip. The earth vanished beneath Edgar's feet in a jarring swoop. Lenore had sprung from her casket, toting him along like a cherished rag doll. In mid-air she flung him over her shoulder. Then, hit the ground in a low-crouch to snarl through her teeth at his astonished parents.

"Unarguably an unexpected turn of events!" Edgar proclaimed, his voice muffled as his face bounced off her rump.

Throwing her head back, Lenore unleashed an unearthly screech that quaked the paintings hanging on the walls. A three stride head start was all she needed to launch herself through the parlor's stained-glass window.   Shards of multi-colored glass tinkled to the ground as she spirited off into the night with a powerless Edgar in tow.

15

Ridley

The monstrosity had eyes for only Ridley. Its gleaming red stare locked on him from its perch beside the emergency room's bed three. Ridley tried to play it cool, as if he hadn't noticed its seething pants directed at him alone. He had even gone so far as to pick up a copy of *Field & Stream* from the table beside him to pantomime being engrossed and oblivious to its presence. The tall, shadowy form faded in and out, like a camera lens trying to focus. Possessively it hunched over the age shriveled body of the man lying in the bed. Ridley guessed that body to be its own. The heart monitor beside the bed tracked a rhythm so faint one missed beat would cause it to shriek its flatline alarm. Panicked desperation vined and licked around the sinister spirit in a tangible black fog of despair.

Rotted teeth parted, freeing a malicious hiss. "I'm not ready. Put me back."

Ridley shifted in his seat, making a point not to glance up despite his trembling hands.

"You hear me, boy?" the specter snarled, deadly darts of accusation shooting from the inhuman crimson orbs of its eyes. "Undo it! I *know* you can!"

Swallowing hard, Ridley gave up on the magazine and tossed it aside. The curtain to Ireland's room was directly in front of him. The very second he saw the doctor's hand begin to draw that fabric divider back he was prepared to sprint in there like a Kenyan at the Olympics.

"*Don't you ignore me, you ungrateful prick!*" the apparition bellowed and charged straight for him. Its jaw unhinged and swung out in a wide yawn—like a hungry python set on swallowing its prey whole.

"Be gone, ghoul!" A hand, as if from nowhere, plunged into the specter's core and dissipated it into a cloud of churning energy.

Standing framed by the dissolving wisps was the man that appeared to Ridley numerous times to guide him since this all began. His dark, hair held a harsh wave that made it appear on the border of disheveled. Heavy bags sagged beneath his soulful eyes. His carefully trimmed mustache twitched as he attempted a comforting smile that landed closer to a grimace. Turning to

Ridley, the heels of his shoes clicked together with the precision of his pivot.

"You seem less manic than before." The man's hands smoothed any threatening wrinkles from his suit coat before he eased himself into the chair beside Ridley. "Perhaps you are taking to your curse better than I did?"

Ridley scanned the room for anyone that may be listening. Finding the people around him too preoccupied to notice, he muttered out of the corner of his mouth, "Not likely."

"I meant it as a compliment." For a spirit, the man looked surprisingly dapper. Death seemed to smile on him, marking him as a favorite with a palette of alabaster skin, peach cheeks, and rosy lips instead of the doldrums greys of decay. "I suppose it is a bit early in the transition for you to see it as such. Kind words for another day, perhaps?"

Ridley's bulging eyes stared hard at Ireland's curtain, as if trying to will it open with his mind.

"Not much for conversation today, I see. Very well, let us move on to the reason for my visit." In a movement that appeared reflex, the man patted at the interior breast pocket of his coat, smiling to himself at what he did—or didn't find there. "You did as I requested and freed Lenore. My sincerest gratitude for that, good sir. However in doing so I assume you have learned why it is crucial you use your ability only under the most dire of circumstances?"

"Or never at all!" Ridley snapped, causing the mother and child across the waiting room from him to glance up questioningly. Turning his upper body away from their stares, he hid his mouth behind his hand. "That *thing* is a monster. If that's what happens every time, I'll pass on playing patty-cake with the dead. Thanks."

The man's lips screwed to the side with disappointment. "I had hoped she would fare better. Unfortunately, it seems my greatest fears have been justified. The time 'neath the earth has enraged the seething beast that walks in her shell. The spirits are whispering that she has already killed. A young man I believe, ripped his arms off and beat him with them. He will not be the last." His expectant stare swiveled to Ridley. "It falls to you, my boy. You must do what I could not. *You* have to stop her."

Dropping his hand, Ridley seethed at the man he was well aware only *he* could see. "And how the hell am I supposed to do that? You throw me into this, giving me cryptic clues that tell me exactly dick!"

A few more heads turned his way. This time he found it practically impossible to care.

The man rose from his chair and tugged down the front hem of his black suit coat to straighten out the creases. "You are life. She is death," he casually stated. "Together, you have all that you need."

"She? As in the undead beast? Call me crazy, but she doesn't strike me as a team player."

Once more the man answered with a conversational side-step and a wry smile cast over his shoulder. "And what of the item I charged you to retrieve from her tomb?"

Noticing a curly haired nurse talking to a security guard and gesturing his way, Ridley murmured his response to the vinyl flooring. "Yeah, I got them. Dare I ask how you knew they were there?"

Even as the man dipped his head in a brief nod of acknowledgement, his form began to fade around the edges. Turning his back to Ridley, he strode toward the solid wall before him.

A rush of panic reddened Ridley's face, his heart instantly hammering in his chest at the prospect of being left alone again ... with *them*. "Wait! How did you know?" Grasping at straws, he tested his growing theory by calling out a single name, *"Poe!"*

The man paused mid-stride, confirming Ridley's suspicions of his identity with a knowing smile cast over his shoulder. "Have you not yet figured it out? I knew ... because I was the one that put her there."

With those as his parting words, Edgar faded into oblivion.

160

"Hey, Ridley. You okay, man?" Noah asked, eliciting a rather unmanly squeal from Ridley as his arms and legs drew up tight into a defensive tuck.

"He weaves an intricate tale for a *dead guy!*" Ridley shouted at nothing, and then shot Noah an apologetic look.

"Maybe not the best thing to yell around critical patients," Rip muttered, wiggling his fingers in a polite wave at the glaring nurse behind the counter.

"Fine—I'm fine," Ridley chanted, mostly to himself.

"Didn't ask, but good to know." Hooking his hand under Ridley's arm, Noah used a bit more force than necessary to guide him to his feet. "They just brought a man into the ER that died on the way here. Damnedest thing, his girlfriend claims he was beaten to death by a zombie missing half her face." Noah's nostrils flared as he forced the words through gritted teeth. "Sound like anyone you know?"

"She beat him with his own arms," Ridley helpfully added, then winced at the rush of barely concealed rage that expanded Noah's broad.

"Yes, she did." Leaning menacingly close, Noah dropped his voice to a stern whisper. "Remind me again, who set her free?"

"Is there a problem over there?" Nurse Resting-Bitch-Face asked, her arms crossed under her ample bosom.

"Apparently there was a mix-up over who was supposed to bring the get-well flowers," Rip's head cocked as he graced her with a grin that had probably been charming two centuries, and one scraggly beard ago. "Your hair is lovely, by the way. How do you get it so ... crunchy?"

Noah jerked as if the hairy, little hobo had slapped him, his infuriation diminishing as the prospect of getting tossed from the hospital grew. "Let's remove ourselves from the nurse's death glare and go check on Ireland. Then, we need to go find Ridley's little pet."

The curtain was being shushed across its hanging bar before Ridley could form his warning that the doctor may not be finished yet. Words in general failed him as he caught a parting glance of the rotund physician winding his wristwatch and disappearing in a clicking production of silver fog and blue sparks.

"*What the hell*?" Noah yelped. Dashing to her side he immediately checked her pulse. Satisfied with what he found there, he picked up one of her limp hands, turned it over to inspect it, then dropped it to the mattress and checked the other. Finding nothing there, he lifted the paper-thin blanket to peek at her wound. His lips moved in an almost inaudible whisper, his face draining ashen. "*Look*."

Heavy lids, that appeared pale and bruised, fluttered open just as Noah tossed Ireland's blanket aside. Maneuvering her hospital gown to maintain as much modesty as possible, he exposed her flawlessly flat stomach—noticeably absent of any stab wounds.

"I know we haven't really been together long enough to have had this conversation," Ireland slurred, sleep making her words drawl out slow and heavy. "But I'm not really open to this level of public sharing."

"Sorry," Noah huffed with a laugh that held more shock than humor. "I normally wouldn't be this forward with my girlfriend's body. But discovering you're an alien from Krypton stunned basic social conduct right out of my head."

Ireland's heavy lashes drew back down to the tops of her cheeks. Blinking hard, she attempted to chase away fatigue's stronghold. "Maybe it's the meds talking, but that made exactly no sense."

"Perhaps it's a Horseman thing?" Rip offered, scratching a hand over the back of his scruffy neck. "Although she's never healed particularly fast before."

"Healed fast?" Ireland rasped, her face a question mark. "She cored me like an apple."

"See, but that's the thing ..." Instead of attempting to explain, Noah used the push button to ease the head of Ireland's bed just enough for her to see for herself. "You are a shish-kabob no more."

"*Wha-? How is that possible?*" The shocking revelation flipped Ireland's alert and alarmed switch. Franticly she riffled with the fabric of her gown, moving it this way and that in search of the wound that—by all laws of nature—*should* have still been there. Finding nothing but yoga-toned abs, which Ridley found quite impressive, her head snapped up. Her gaze darted around the room, from one of the men to the next, as she toed the line of full-blown hysterics. "It-it had to be the doctor! Only he wasn't really a doctor, and *he knows what I am*. Did you see him? He injected me with—something. I don't know! But we have to find him! I can bitch-slap him with the hilt of my sword until he talks, if that's what it takes!"

Ridley hid his smirk behind his fist, happy to see someone else in the group taking the role of the crazy one for a change.

"We *could* go after the guy that miraculously healed you," Noah soothed, his tone calm and steady. Easing the tape free from her arm, he pulled out her I.V. port. "*Or,* we could make that step two after we stop the stab-happy dead chick that put you here in the first place and has since developed a taste for blood and violence. Personally, I'd rather send the mystery guy a fruit basket. But, ya know, your call. Either way, we need to get you out of here before the medical staff starts asking questions we can't answer."

More conversation followed as Noah eased Ireland to sitting and Rip went in search of her clothes. Unfortunately, Ridley could only half-listen to their further exchange. From the dark corners of the room a spirit he had never encountered emerged. Its presence, and the depraved power emanating off of it, chilled him to the very marrow of his bones.

"There is still time to pick our side, R-R-Ridley," the freckle-faced ghoul stammered through blackened teeth. Matted hair, the color of a rotted tangerine, stabbed off his head like a wicked armor of horns. His attempt at a smile made gruesome by his severely dislocated jaw that swung loose as if on a rusted hinge. "Your part in this is could be huge. An army of loyal subjects could be yours to lead if you only listened to the line of people *dying* to meet you."

Ridley's eye twitched at the grating cackle that resonated off the walls. His skin crawled as the shadows all around him elongated, writhing and thrashing into forms more demon than human. Inhaling a deep, shaky breath, he shut his eyes and tried to retreat into himself even as the cold, wisps of their claws raked over the skin on the back of his neck ...

A soft, but firm, grip tightened around his wrist, pulling him back from that dark precipice. His eyes snapped open to find Ireland staring back at him with iron-clad resolve. The yellow, flickering fluorescent lights overhead illuminated her like a poor-man's archangel.

With her free hand she finished thumbing the buttons closed on the flannel shirt Noah had loaned her. "We're all leaving here, *together*," she assured him.

Breathing in her gift of peaceful serenity, Ridley laced his fingers with hers. The compassion she showed solidified one nagging thought as truth:

Wherever this journey took them, he would be with her until the bitter end.

16

EDGAR

"Dearest heart?" Edgar's arms dangled over his purple face, slapping against the back of Lenore's legs with each of her galloped strides. "Could we pause for a minute? Perhaps put me down and allow the blood to return to my head? My consciousness has waned thrice now and these moments of black are getting noticeably longer each time."

The sticks and leaves that snapped beneath her feet acted as his only response.

Blinking hard in a paltry attempt to clear the black spots that frolicked before his eyes, Edgar tried again. "Lenore, please," he softly pleaded. "I brought you back, love. I will not flee or harm you. Your soul is an extension of my own and I would give my very life to protect it. Now, can we ple—"

His proclamation trailed off as oblivion claimed him once more.

Edgar had no way of knowing how much time had passed when the curtain of black finally rescinded. The face of his dark angel blurred in and out of focus before him, life's second chance having altered her violet eyes to a bright ethereal purple. The whites that once enveloped them now stained the inky black of a moonless night. Concern creased her porcelain brow as she gazed down at him.

"Where are we?" Edgar eased himself to sitting, gripping the grass with both hands when the world spun around him.

Lenore struggled to force out a rough stammer, "T-t-tracks." Grinding her teeth in frustration, she settled for jabbing a thumb over her left shoulder.

Overhead an owl hooted. Lenore's entire body tensed, her head whipping around for the culprit.

"Be still," he soothed, reaching for her. "Tis nothing more than a bird."

Flinching from his hand, Lenore sprang to her feet and forced a valley of distance between them.

Edgar eased himself up onto still wobbly legs, his lips pressed in a firm line of confusion. Every cell of his being was singing out to touch her. To pull her body to his and rejoice in the sensation of touch that had momentarily been stripped from him. His own longing aside, her taut muscles and nervous twitches shouted that such behavior would not be well received.

"Lenore?" the name of his angel slipped softly from his lips.

Yellow hair, made wild by the wind, lashed against her face as she glanced his way.

"Are you well, my flower?"

Tears welled in her eyes, washing away streaks of funeral powder as they fell. Her nostrils flared like a nervous colt, yet still she managed a brief nod.

As believable responses went, hers fell far from convincing. Even so, Edgar knew enough not to push the matter. He, too, had witnessed true horrors. They knew him by name and fed on his sanity.

Offering her the courtesy of space, he investigated their surroundings by craning his neck to see around the sporadic trees that peppered the field surrounding them. "We appear to be north of town, which is a very good thing. I had been saving money to buy us a home after we wed. After your ... accident ... I gathered it all. It is not much, however it will buy us a fresh start far from anyone that knows of what happened to you."

She cast her gaze to the ground. The salt of her tears watering the earth.

"Lenore?"

Swallowing hard, she forced herself to meet his stare.

What kind of solace could one tortured soul offer another, but hope of a better tomorrow?

"You have done well," he assured her, with a smile he knew didn't reach his eyes. "You secured us a nice head start against those that may be searching for us. We shall continue to travel north until the tracks lead us to the next depot. If you are tired from—hauling me," undoubtedly one of the oddest sentences he had ever said to a woman, "I could find us horses at a nearby farm."

Unbridled panic widened her eyes, her breath coming shallow and ragged as she urgently flicked her head side to side.

Instinct urged him forward a step, his palms out to steady her. "Easy, my angel. No horses. I suppose after the carriage you *would* have a natural aversion. My apologies for suggesting it. Instead, we shall embark on this journey with the means of travel the Lord blessed us with; our own legs. When the tracks lead us to a station I will buy us two tickets to New York and our fresh start together. Come now, if we walk through the night we may be able to catch the first train of the morn."

If his optimistic propaganda had influenced her at all, Edgar couldn't tell. Lenore's troubled frown persisted. The only thing he could think to do was to prove his resolve by trudging on toward his stated goal. He made it five paces, the last three with genuine concern she wouldn't follow, when she broke her silence.

Her voice, the rough grate of sandpaper over metal, still caressed and enchanted him because it belonged to *her*. "E-Edgar? The dead walking ... anguished spirits calling out ... i-is this hell?"

Edgar's head spun at the question, realization's icy chill seeping through his veins. How had he missed it before? The spastic jerks of her head. The ceaseless grinding of her teeth. Those bulging manic eyes that scoured the landscape, seemingly transfixed on the unseen. He knew that look all too well, because he had worn it himself for years. Blame whispered his name as the villain before plunging its blade deep into his heart, finishing him with a vicious twist.

A gasp escaped his parted lips, the weight of his actions and their repercussions plunging him to the deepest depths of *Dante's inferno*. With Lenore's return he could no longer see or hear the ghouls that lingered ... *because he passed his cursed sight on to her.*

17

Ridley

A city under siege. Fire hydrants ripped from their bases, spraying geysers of water into the smoke clouded sky. Cars overturned, their wheels still spinning like *Hot Wheels* cars. The wail of sirens in the distance drowned out by frantic voices calling for their loved ones. People running, jostling through the crowds in search of safety and answers. A pungent odor, like burning oil, stung Ireland's nostrils, making her lungs ache with each breath.

"Where's my cloak?" She turned to Noah to ask.

He slapped the side of her satchel, slung over his shoulder, in response.

"Good." She nodded, gulping down her rising trepidation. Turns out shaking off a near death experience wasn't nearly as easy as she thought it would be. "Keep it close. I don't think tracking her down is going to be quite as hard as we thought."

"One ghoul did all this?" Rip gasped, his bulging eyes scanning the destruction.

"That or Godzilla." Noah's mouth screwed to the side. Shifting the satchel in front of him, he fumbled with the buckle. "Maybe you should call on your weapons? Get them out of police impound, out of the hands of some punk kids, or wherever they landed? Just in case."

Ireland puffed her cheeks and exhaled through pursed lips just as a fire truck and sheriff's car went zipping by, their flashing lights and screaming sirens clearing them a path through the wayward bodies filling the street. "And *that* is why I can't arm up. The mere sight of weapons in this crowd will start a riot."

But imagine the fun, the Hessian tittered in the back of her mind.

"I've told you before, needlessly slaughtering innocent people is *not* my idea of a good time." The day's events had left Ireland so flustered her filter failed her, making her rebuttal audible.

"Who is she talking to?" Ridley winced, pulling away but keeping his pinkie hooked with hers.

Then why does your pulse race at the very idea of it, girl? You cannot lie to yourself forever, the beast soothed in a throaty growl.

173

"The Headless Horseman," Rip stated in no uncertain terms. "He lives inside her."

"And that's why she goes all veiny," Ridley's free hand waved in front of his face as if drawing her markings, "and Day of the Dead?"

Wordlessly—because, really, what further explanation was there?—Rip and Noah both nodded.

"I'm *not* lying to myself." A flush filled Ireland's cheeks, her argument with the undead growing heated. "The only killer instinct in me is *yours*."

"One final question," Ridley held up one finger, then pressed it to his lips in contemplation. "Is that how crazy I look when the spirits start talking to me?"

Again the other two men nod, with more adamant enthusiasm this time.

Ridley's chiseled features crumbled into a scowl. "Well that's simply inexcusable. She looks like a raving lunatic."

"What?" Ireland snapped. Shaking her head, she dismissed their words before they could even form them. "Never mind, we need to get moving. Follow the destruction to our Queen of the Damned before she burns New York to the ground."

"I thought that was your title?" Falling into step behind his slightly manic gal, Noah snorted at his own joke. Her steps stopped short when she paused to shoot him a death glare over her shoulder. "But clearly I am mistaken. You are *lovely*."

Ireland resumed her purposeful strides, dragging Ridley along behind her, unaware that Noah's attention had been diverted.

"Ire, stop! There's a boy!" Noah yelled, before throwing himself into the sea of bodies. He shoved people aside, dodging and weaving through the crowd, while clearing a quickly disappearing path that his friends took advantage of as they hustled to push after him. On the opposite side of the street, balanced on the curb, stood a young boy no more than six years old. Tears streamed down his soot-covered face as he screamed a shrill cry for this mother at the top of his lungs.

Noah took a knee beside him, his flaxen hair falling over his sweat-dampened forehead. "Hey, buddy. Are you lost?"

"Our car had an accident," the little boy hiccupped, wiping his nose on a blood-covered sleeve. "I climbed out, b-but I can't find my mommy."

"What does she look like?" Ireland asked as she grabbed hold of a light pole and stepped up onto its concrete base for a better vantage point.

"She has brown hair and her name is Megan," he answered, his saucer eyes glistening with a fresh wash of threatening tears.

"And what's your name?" Noah asked, his gaze scanning the boy in a cursory inspection for where the blood could have come from.

"Cameron Michael," the boy mumbled, his lower lip trembling.

"Well, Cameron, you are being very brave right now. My friends and I are going to do everything we can to get you back to your mom, okay?" Noah paused and waited for Cameron to nod. "But we also have to make sure you're all right. Does anything hurt from the accident?"

"My arm," Cameron squeaked and pushed his shirt sleeve up his forearm. A gash, about four inches long, sliced his skin in a lightning bolt shape.

"Here, use this to wrap the wound." Rip shook a handkerchief free from his back pocket and offered it to Noah.

"Thanks," Noah nodded in appreciation. "Help Ireland find Megan."

"Have we given thought to the fact that his mother may not have made it out of the car?" Ridley whispered out of the corner of his mouth, his gaze scouring the crowd while his hand stayed locked with Ireland's.

"No!" Ireland barked, then took a deep breath and attempted to soften her harsh tone. "After ... *everything* ... we need something good. So, she has to be okay."

"Fair enough." Ridley's chin fell to his chest in a nod of acceptance meant for him alone. "In that case we need to know for sure."

Without further explanation, Ridley retracted his hand from hers and stepped back out of arms distance. His eyes closed just as the swell of spastic jerks and twitches hit him. His brows knit in tight at the unspeakable horrors he had willingly handed himself over to ... all to help Ireland.

Rip's face brightened as if the last piece of a puzzle had materialized before him. "*Ah*, so he has been holding on to you because it is keeping the spirits at bay?"

"Yeah, he figured that little nuance out at the cottage," Ireland said, turning her focus back to the crowd.

"Actually answers a lingering question I had, too!" Noah called without looking over. Cameron's wound dressed, he made the boy smile by booping his nose.

"They are both noble men," Rip mused, his index finger twirling the end of his beard. "I would not have thought so of Ridley, yet it *is* true. It really is quite fortunate that you committed yourself to one of them before meeting the other. What a predicament that could have been, attempting to decide between the two. Not that monogamy ever worked for me." He punctuated his rambling with a wry huff.

Ireland wet her lips and stared at the concrete beneath her feet for a ten count. "I don't ever want to talk about my love life with you. More than that, I don't ever want to talk about *your* love life with you. 'Kay?"

"Afraid you might learn a thing or two?" Rip mumbled under his breath as he rose up on tip-toe to search the crowd.

Ridley stumbled forward, seeking Ireland's touch the second his eyes snapped open. "She's not dead," he panted, his entire body vibrating in fear. "I don't know where she is, but she *is* alive."

"All I needed to know." Noah gathered Cameron in his arms and hauled him over his head to sit on his shoulder. "You see your mom, you shout. Okay, bud?"

"Let's do this!" Cameron's nose crinkled as his hand curled into a tiny fist.

Keeping a careful hold on his cargo, Noah eased out into the street. Ireland assumed his target to be the dead center of the road, where anyone on the block could see them.

They were nearing that spot when a frantic shriek rose up above the chaotic hum of mayhem, "Cameron! *Cameron*!"

Arms waved, belonging to a brunette woman fighting her way through the crowd.

A slow smile spread across Ireland's face as Cameron jabbed a finger in his mother's direction, wriggling in delight.

Noah removed him from his perch and happily handed him over to a very relieved Megan, who embraced her son first then latched on to Noah for a very grateful group hug. Her lips were forming the words thank you for about the millionth time when the ground shuddered beneath their feet. People stumbled, bracing themselves against strangers to keep their footing. Tremors rattled cars and building fixtures, knocking Ireland from her light pole. Ridley caught her and held her tight against his chest as the earth itself rolled in another ominous wave. To the north of them a mushroom cloud of smoke and debris exploded, setting off car alarms for miles around.

"We need to go," Ireland said, her jaw clenched to the point of pain. "As calling cards go, Lenore seems to have found a pretty direct one."

"I've found that subtlety is a lost art on the dead." Ridley's eyes flared as he fell in step beside her.

18

Ridley

"How can there be no trace of her?" Ireland turned in a half-circle, one hand combing through her hair in frustration. "She somehow sparks one tank at an LP filling station only to ignite a colossal domino effect of ground trembling booms, then— nothing. Doesn't make sense."

"Perhaps she got her anger under control?" Rip's lips worked like a cow chewing cud. His beard bobbing with each rotation of his jaw. "I watched a fascinating documentary about a scientist that was inadvertently struck with a substance known as 'gamma radiation.' The result of which turned him into a reptilian colored ogre with *horrible* coping mechanisms. Only by calming himself could he revert back to his true form. It is possible the same type of technique worked for her."

"Not a documentary, bud," Noah corrected. His hands were balled in tight fists at his sides. His stare wandered up and down the empty street beside them where all other bodies seemed to have sought shelter. "And I don't think we're lucky enough that she just gave up and went back to her cozy little hole in the floor."

"You seem tense, friend." One corner of Ridley's mouth curled in a sardonic grin. "Perhaps what you need is the *touch* of a good woman?" At the word 'touch' he raised Ireland's hand to his face. Brushing the backs of her fingers across his cheek, he playfully wiggled his eyebrows.

Ireland extracted her hand and yanked it out of his reach. "Why? Why would you taunt him like that?"

"I've been trapped in a virtual hell for two days." Ridley shrugged without an iota of regret and reached for her hand once more. "Genuine amusement is really the only excuse I have, and I think it's a worthwhile one."

"Go ahead and take his hand." Noah jerked his chin in Ireland's direction at her obvious hesitation to do just that. "Annoying as he is, at least he isn't whimpering and wetting himself that way."

"I never wet myself." Ridley raised one long, slender finger in clarification. "The whimpering I will openly admit to."

"Two men bickering over a deranged killer." Rip bumped Ireland's arm with his and huffed a wry laugh. "In my day we would drill a hole in your skull to release the demons instead of trying to court you."

Ireland's chin pulled back in indignation, her free palm raised skyward. "*Hey!*"

"Apologies," he said, pressing his lips together in a thin line. "An *occasional* deranged killer."

"Oh, much better," Ireland dead panned. The rattle of a discarded plastic bag tumbling across the abandoned street behind her whipped her head around. Her lean muscles on full alert. "Something is off here. We checked every possible route from that last intersection where she tore down the lamppost and impaled the ice cream truck. And still no sign of her."

"In her defense that grinning clown sign atop it *was* terrifying," Rip interjected.

If she heard Rip's barb she ignored him. Shaking her head, Ireland gnawed on her lower lip. "Maybe we should go back? See if there's anything we missed?"

Noah stopped short and spun on his heel, a mischievous glint adding golden sparks to his hazel eyes. "There's another way. Spirits want to whisper all sorts of nasty things in *his* ear." He nodded in Ridley's direction. "Turn him loose, see if he can *scare* us up any leads."

Ridley stepped well inside Ireland's personal bubble. Catching a lock of her hair, he gave a gentle tug before running two fingers down the length of it. "Anything to get my hands off her, huh? *Tsk, tsk, tsk.* Not a shred of confidence in the sacred bond of your relationship. What a pity."

"You wanna keep that hand?" Ireland muttered, casting a pointed look from him to his wandering digits and back again.

Hooking his thumbs in his belt loops, Noah puffed his chest in full male bravado. "I have complete confidence in us *and* the fact that you are exactly the kind of d-bag she hates."

Running his tongue over his teeth, Ridley made no attempts to hide the glee that crinkled the corners of his striking blue eyes. "And yet, she and I share a deeper, more tragically uniting bond than you two ever will. Seems that knowledge would sting a bit."

Truth be told, their posturing barely pinged Ireland's annoyance radar in light of everything else they were facing. There were far bigger issues at hand than boys and their delicate egos. That made it all the more surprising when their voices faded, as if tumbling down a long infinite tunnel, drowned out by the demonic cackle of her beast within.

In any previous transformation, Ireland found herself at the mercy of a rising wave of darkness that would eagerly consume her unless she clung to the steadfast buoys that kept the storming essence of the Hessian at bay.

This time was different.

The ground of sanity crumbled beneath her feet, sending her freefalling into the realms of madness. Her pulse drummed a hypnotic beat in her temples, hushing her to bite back the pain and be still as the beast ripped his way out. No time to cry out. No chance to stop it. The Hessian birthed forth in the tightening of her skin stretching taut over bone. Her lips ripened, plump berries ready to be plucked. Veins bulged, weaving intricate patterns that framed her eyes with a wicked twist. Metal winged around the bend, slicing the air with a foreboding whistle. Sunlight caught the blade, illuminating it with a halo of divinity. Turning her wrist to receive it, Ireland allowed the hilt to nestle into her waiting palm.

"What the—" Noah's question cut off the second he glanced over and caught the full magnitude of their suddenly dire situation. His hand plunged into the front pocket of his jeans as he locked stares with Ridley. "Dude, step away from her. *Now.*"

A man thrown in a pit of sleeping lions, Ridley attempted to extract himself as quickly and quietly as possibly—only to feel her unrelenting grasp tighten.

Her head turned on her struggling captor. Peering at him from under her lowered brow, venom radiated from her glare. "This is Poe's little stooge?"

Ridley's free hand rose and fell to his side with an exasperated slap. "Is there an answer I can give here that will make you drop the sword?"

"Not likely," she hissed and lunged for him.

A flick of her hand and flawless steel whipped in a wide circle at her hip. Ridley backpedaled as far back as her bear trap grasp would allow, only to get tangled in his own feet. A malicious smile twisted across her face as she followed him down, pinning him to the pavement. The edge of her blade pressed to his throat, bobbing with his deep gulp.

"The spirits whisper that you're some sort of messiah," the Hessian murmured through Ireland, his fleshy vehicle. "I wonder if your touch could set me free? Release me from this hellish prison?"

Ireland's pointy-pink tongue dragged across Ridley's top lip, despite his best efforts to pull away. The pressure of her blade kept the threat of death unmistakably real.

"*Mmmmm.*" She relished the taste of him as if contemplating a fine wine. "Not what I hoped for, but possibly something even better."

Taking advantage of the distraction, Noah caught Ireland in headlock with one arm and used the opposite hand to press the talisman flat against her forehead. Even as the skin sizzled and an anguish wail tore from her throat, he held firm. The whites of her eyes grew, rolling back in her head. Noah grunted and shifted his restricted arm to around her torso as her body fell slack, giving Ridley the opportunity to stumble free.

"That was … invigorating," Ridley's chest rose and fell with each panted gasp, "and somewhat arousing in an incredibly confusing way."

"That pretty much describes every day spent with Ireland Crane," Noah admitted with a subtle cock of his head. Easing her sleeping form to the ground, he brushed a lock of hair from her face and watched the Hessian's hold slowly relent. The peachy hue returned to her lips. Dark, scrolling veins were hidden by life, plumping her skin. The black, bruise-like circles around her eyes faded, leaving no trace behind they had ever been.

She came to with a start, bolting upright with her body quaking in fear. "*What happened*? Did I hurt anyone?"

"No." Noah gently caught her chin with his hooked index finger and tipped her face to his. "Everyone is fine."

Her eyes sparkled with a flood of tears she tried, unsuccessfully, to blink away. "I lost control so fast. I couldn't even—"

"Hey, that's why I'm here with that nifty piece of jewelry, remember?" The chain rippled from the side of his palm before the talisman caught and swung from Noah's pinched fingers. "Consider this you adding purpose to my life."

Her own self-loathing took the form of a steady pounding between her eyes, forcing Ireland to press the heel of her palm to forehead. "And Ridley thought hanging with me was the safer option than the voices and visions."

"Ah, he was being an arrogant prick." Pocketing the talisman, Noah offered her a hand and hoisted her to her feet. "Maybe this was a learning experience for him."

The minute the treads of her boots hit the ground a thought jolted through her, snapping her spine straight and clenching both her hands on Noah's forearm. "That man in the hospital! Whatever he injected me with could be responsible for me losing control! I mean, I couldn't even *attempt* to stop it! What if next time—"

"*Ireland*!" Noah barked in stern interruption, despite the deep creases between his brows that mirrored her own concern. "We have enough life-and-death crap to deal with right now without playing 'I think we might have another problem.'"

"I hate to interrupt," Rip called, his hand tentatively rose to get their attention. "However, I think we might have another problem."

"It's like I'm talking to myself," Noah mumbled, throwing his palms skyward as he turned.

The new issue wasn't hard to spot. Ridley stood statue still, his unblinking eyes drained milky white. The petals of his lips moving in an inaudible chant.

Ireland puffed her cheeks and scratched at the back of her head. "Some couples order Chinese food and watch movies on the couch."

"And us?" Noah smirked in expectation of her answer.

"We go see what the catatonic stock broker is mumbling about."

The trio inched closer, turning an ear toward him. Their cautious steps pausing only when the hushed syllables began to make sense.

"*Moonlight comes with dark intent.*

Caution sinners, ye must repent."

Ireland's head spun in Rip's direction, her cherry-cola colored bangs falling in her eyes. "Is that..?"

"Eleanora," he finished for her. His expression rivaling her own on the stupefaction meter.

The long dead witch, easily recognizable by her habit of only speaking in rhymes, had helped Ireland once before. However to utilize her services on that occasion they had to perform an intricate summoning spell inside a crypt. This time she found her *own* doorway in. The questions of how and why sent a tingle of unease skittering down Ireland's spine.

"*A curse released with a raven's flap,*" the spirit continued in her chilling death rattle.

"*Now the mortal coil threatens to snap.*

An infamous love, destined nevermore,

for death could not claim the enchanting Lenore.

She walks the earth, a plague on mankind,

searching for he her rotted heart doth pine.

Combine the forces of dark and light

to overcome this monstrous plight.

Yet, ye be warned, as the raven doth fly,

for the rest to live … one must die."

"You know what I didn't miss having in my life?" Ireland said, her fingers combing through her hair to push her bangs behind her ear. "Cryptic rhymes."

"The last part of the message was quite clear, and not the least bit uplifting." Rip cringed and stifled a yawn behind his hand.

Ridley lurched forward a step, the motion appearing more mechanical than human. "*A tool gifted by the dead, revealing the path you must be led.*"

Noah, Rip, and Ireland all matched his advance with wide steps back.

"Like a supernatural compass?" Ireland's uneasy tone rose to a breathless squeak. "That could be helpful, right?"

One hand fumbled in his pants pocket as Ridley's form was stiffly forced forward another step. *"A lone being, split to two. Only one will lead to the devilish shrew."*

"Okay, that one I didn't get at al—*whoa!*" Ireland's statement was cut-off by Ridley forcefully shoving her into Noah in his dive at Rip. All the air left the shocked old man's chest in a wheeze as Ridley's forearms hit him mid-chest and rode him straight into the sidewalk.

"Get off me you crazy nit!" Rip slapped at Ridley's hands, which had caught his bearded cheeks and pinched his mouth into fish lips.

Noah steadied Ireland on her feet then stepped around her, intent on breaking up the tousling twosome. Her one step to follow instantly jerked his arm, blocking her path. "No way. You stay out of this. Turn around, meditate, whatever; just stay nice and Zen. Your involvement would turn this birthday candle event into an erupting volcano."

"Good analogy." She nodded her approval and jabbed a thumb over her shoulder. "I'll be over there."

"All right, little buddy," Noah said through gritted teeth. One hand grasped Ridley's collar, the other looping around his belt to hoist him off Rip—whose eyes were beginning to roll with the threat of an impending snooze. "Off ya go!"

A second before being yanked out of arm's reach, Ridley scrambled with whatever it was he had dug from his pocket and forcefully shoved it between Rip's puckered lips. The shock of the intrusion set Rip over the edge, his body sagging as sleep claimed him ... with the mysterious item still lodged in his mouth.

Ireland's head pulled back in a disgusted cringe, while conflicting gross interest inched her closer a couple paces. "What the heck did he put in his mouth?"

Sparing the delicate touch, Noah dropped Ridley to the ground with a heavy *thump*. "*Really* trying not to think about that just yet."

"They're teeth," Ridley's own voice filtered up, muffled by the concrete sidewalk his face was mashed into. Rolling to his side, he sat up, still blinking away the effects of his spiritual overtaking.

Every level of confusion swirled across Noah's chiseled features, his mouth opening and shutting like a land-bound cod. "*Wha ... how ... whe..?*"

"Start with why," Ireland suggested. Crouching beside her snoring friend, she pulled his top lip up to take a peek. "Why you would ever put what looks like antique dentures into another person's mouth?"

"An incredibly demanding spirit was insisting on it." Ridley rubbed the side of his cheek where the pavement had kissed it to

191

a bright pink. "I tried to fight her, but the psychotic witch commandeered my body!"

"She actually *was* a witch, we've met." With one finger Ireland attempted to wiggle the teeth, only to find them locked firm despite Rip's slack jaw. "He's going to go on a full-blown tizzy tirade when he wakes up, because these babies aren't moving. Where did you even get them?" she posed the question over her shoulder to Ridley.

"They were in the box ..." Ridley gulped, forcing the words out as if purging razor blades, "... with Lenore."

Three sets of eyes slowly turned in Rip's direction. A stream of drool streaked down his cheek and dripped to the ground.

"So, you found them on a shelf in the cottage you say?" Noah prompted.

Ridley flinched, his head slowly shaking in confusion. "No. Poe appeared to me and told me to fish them out right after she exploded from the floor boards. They were down by her feet in the coffin."

Still crouched down, Ireland rested one arm on her knee as she explained, "I believe what Noah is asking is if when Rip wakes, is he going to find out he has teeth stuck in his mouth that are laced with a couple centuries worth of decomposing feet tissue, *or* the slightly less gag worthy dust from sitting on a shelf for display purposes only."

For a beat Ridley merely stared. "I misunderstood," he finally nodded, "they were most definitely on a shelf."

Two quick blasts from a police siren preempted a silver and blue patrol car gliding up beside them with the fluid nonchalance of a post-meal shark. The passenger-side window slid down three-quarters of the way, revealing a shadowed silhouette hidden behind reflective sunglasses.

"Everything okay here?" the officer called out. "Does that man need an EMT?"

In an instant the air around Ireland came alive, sparking with energy and a tangible threat. She rose to her feet. Tendrils of darkness twined up her spine, veiling the edges of her vision with thick clouds of red that churned with burning embers. It was *him*. Officer Granger from Sleepy Hollow. Mr. Mallark from the library. The doctor that injected her with God only knows what. He'd shaved off his moustache and hidden those unmistakable eyes. Even so, every fiber of her being *screamed* it was him.

"Everything is fine, officer," Noah said with a forced smile. "Truth is, our friend here suffers from stress induced narcolepsy. He thought he saw that zombie-chick everyone is talking about and hit the ground."

Ireland didn't tear her murderous gaze away, her hope being to magically bore holes in his stupid, lying, serum-injecting face. If he noticed, he kept his expression at a practiced neutral. He did, however, shift in his seat. Sticky vinyl could've been to blame, but Ireland chose to take credit anyway.

"Your friend has reason for concern. There is a perp out here tonight that is said to be armed and dangerous." The officer shoved his glasses further up the bridge of his nose with one sausage link finger. "I'd advise you all to get off the streets for your own safety. There's a subway tunnel terminal one block up and three blocks east of here. That will take you where you want to go."

"Where *we* want to go, or where *you* want us to go?" Ireland vehemently snarled.

The officer huffed a humorless laugh, as if contemplating introducing her to his baton.

"*Ireland, what are you doing*?" Noah hissed out of the corner of his mouth.

Ridley raised one hand, craning his neck to be seen around Noah. "I'm not with them and am far too pretty to go to jail."

Officer Fake-Identity casually adjusted the brim of his hat. "No worries of that, son. She is just a confused, frightened girl speaking her mind about matters she doesn't understand." Tilting his chin, he fixed his stare on Ireland. In spite of those reflective

194

lenses she could feel his piercing eyes peering into her, exposing all her sins and truths. "You have many choices before you, my dear. Many of which will be paved with regret. I can tell you with the utmost certainty the tunnel is the *least* of many possible evils."

Without the courtesy of further explanation, he gave a brief nod and pulled away from the curb.

19

EDGAR

Six months' worth of changes, not all of them welcome. If Edgar's parents had searched for them, their efforts had been fruitless. Not a day went by that he didn't think of them. Despite what he had done, would they—could they—ever be proud of the life he had forged for himself and Lenore? The bungalow he had found them was a modest one. It consisted of little more than four rooms and a water closet, yet Edgar had put great care into restoring it. That, along with lovely view of the pond out the back windows, made it quite the cozy abode.

The beginning, however, wasn't all comfortable bedspreads and afternoon tea. It was overcoming one agonizing obstacle, only to be struck by another without the luxury of a pause to exhale. Lenore couldn't rest for more than a few minutes at time. Each time she dozed it ended with her bolting upright in bed, trembling and shrieking to the heavens. Edgar watched her while she slept, at her insistence, so that the very moment she woke in her fit of terrors he could gather her in his arms and shush her quietly while they rocked. His lips would nuzzle her clammy forehead. The front of his shirt soaked from her tears.

The spirits, now visible to her, haunted her mercilessly. Many a time he had found his troubled angel cowered in a corner, chanting soft pleas under her breath. Her clawed hands scrapping against the walls until her fingers bled as if trying to burrow her way to a safety. How he wished there were tricks he could teach her to help her manage the torment. He viewed himself a failure for having suffered through the same curse for so long without having one shred of helpful counsel to offer. The only solace he could provide was the same he had often opted for; the occasional pull from a flash of brandy to dull the senses and provide momentary interludes of calm.

Just when Edgar resigned himself to that being their new norm, things changed in the most perplexing way. Lenore stopped cowering. Gave up sleep altogether. Would no longer humor him by even attempting to nibble at food. Instead, she spent hours staring out the picture window at the two white swans that paddled around the pond in an enchanting water ballet. No longer did a trace of melancholy mar the serenity of her stare. Curled up in the quilt he had bought her at market, she rocked in the worn wooden chair that had come with their furnished home. Hour

197

after hour, day after day, she would sit, unaffected by the world around her. At least externally. Edgar toyed with the idea that perhaps the apparitions had relented. Their power over her finally fading to nothing, allowing her to simply revel in the solitude of her restored sanity.

Then he heard the first giggle …

Penning a letter in regards to a much needed job prospect, Edgar paused. A foreboding chill skittering down his spine.

"Everything okay, dearest?" he called from the other room.

Only silence answered.

Wetting his suddenly parched lips, Edgar rose from his desk chair. As he rounded the bend into the sitting room he felt fear's icy fist plunge into his chest and clasp his pounding heart tight.

Surprisingly, her rocking chair was vacant, the door to the veranda open and swaying in the slight spring breeze. For reasons he couldn't yet explain, that creaking door held the ominous threat of a swinging noose.

He found her on the settee, her legs curled casually beneath her. His soul ached at the warm smile that brightened her face. It had become such a rarity he thought it extinct. Edgar's gaze flicked to the side in search of what had drawn out that elusive beam by his beloved. She leaned in toward … nothing …

engaged in an intimate discussion of muted chatter with an unseen force.

Catching sight of him in the doorway, Lenore shushed the vacant seat beside her and righted her posture. "Edgar, have you finished your letter?"

"Nearly." His upper body pivoted back toward the door he entered through. The woman before him was the embodiment of his very heart. Why then was he fighting the urge to bolt from the room? "I took a pause to ensure you were well."

Her head cocked as she rose from the settee. Sunlight gleaming off her alabaster skin, she closed the distance between them. Curled lashes batted over her enchanting amethyst stare, somehow made more hypnotic against their black backdrop. "You never need to fret over me. I am here because of *you*, to take care of *you*. After all you have done, and all you *can* do," she purred, her gaze wandering down to his hands. "I know now what a true treasure you are."

The curves of her body skimmed against him, her chest rising and falling in breathless anticipation.

"*Ahem*, thank you," Edgar cleared his throat and fidgeted with the suddenly constricting collar of his shirt. While he enjoyed her affections *immensely,* the transition from patient to vixen after so many months proved a hard one to accept. "I should get back to work. Our finances are tight and it has become mandatory that I secure employ."

Edgar turned on his heel, only to have Lenore catch his arm and draw him back to her with a force he could not have resisted if he tried. The chill of her fingers curled into his hair and held firm, her stare locked with his. "Tonight Winston Miller, unarguably one of the most influential men here in Brooklyn, is having a masquerade ball. The very contacts to which you were just writing will be there, their bellies full of decadence and wine. We can go! You will be your charming self. I will be your sweetly demure paramour. They will be so taken with us that you will find yourself tripping over job offers."

"H-how do you know of this?" Catching her wandering hands, he held them over his rapidly thumping heart.

"News of it is all over town; it is all anyone is talking of."

"You never leave the house, pet."

One narrow shoulder rose and fell. "True enough, however I still hear the clucking of the neighborhood hens."

"You truly believe you could handle such a gathering?" Edgar's gaze scoured her face, as if he would find the reason for this abrupt change miraculously scrawled there. "With all those people?"

Her full lips curled to the side, dimpling the thinly healed flesh of her scar. "I am not the delicate flower you think me to be,

Edgar. For the promising path before us to come to pass, our attendance at that ball is *mandatory*."

Unable to form a convincing argument to the contrary—though many plagued him—Edgar could only gulp down his trepidation and dip his chin in a nod of agreement to his beautiful lotus—flowering forth from the murky pond of death.

20

Ridley

"How could you not recognize him?" In the middle of her red-faced rant, Ireland tripped over a dip in the crumbling cement stairs that lead down into the subway. Catching herself on the wobbly handrail, she huffed an inaudible string of expletives under her breath. "He worked at the museum! You were face-to-face with him!"

Noah's hand rose to the middle of her back as she steadied herself and stomped on. "My girlfriend was turning into a homicidal killer at the time. I was a tiny bit distracted."

Ireland bounced off the bottom stair, a small dust cloud kicking up beneath her boots as she landed. The terminal was blanketed in heavy darkness, the only light offered filtering down from the stairs. In the distance she could just make out the faint silhouette of elaborate archways. Each tapered down into sturdy mosaic covered posts, some of the ornate tiles chipped away like missing teeth in a wide smile.

Her lungs constricting at the stale, stifling air, Ireland coughed into her elbow. "I was just—*ahem*—having a moment."

"A moment? That's what we're going to call it?" Noah joined her at the bottom of the stairs and squinted into the darkness. "It wasn't a sneezing fit, Ireland. There was genuine fear of bloodshed."

"Well, now you're just being overdramatic." Ireland smirked at his exaggerated eyeroll. "Remind me again why we came down here? If this is where the *obviously* fake cop—"

"Obvious only to *you*," Ridley chimed in, his arm brushing hers as he thumped off the last stair.

She paused long enough to shoot him a glare. "If *he* told us to come down here, I still think we should've run screaming in the other direction."

Their voices echoed off the walls all around them, taunting them with the extreme solitude of this abandoned abyss.

"Don' ath me," Rip snipped, drenching the back of Noah's shirt with a rain of spit from attempting to talk through two pairs of teeth. "Appawently tings happen an we awr justh suppoth tah accepth it no questhions asked. Hath a stwange pawr of teef sthuck in yawr mouf? Nofing weiwd about dat! Leth's go for a walk!"

"We couldn't find Lenore up top, maybe she went underground," Noah explained, cringing over his shoulder at his damp shirt. "And if we find her, hopefully we can find a way to get those things out of your mouth. Because they are not a redeeming new attribute, let me tell ya."

"And if not, we can go in search of that fake cop and I can threaten to give him a colonoscopy with my sword unless he tells us what he knows!" Ireland chirped with enough enthusiasm to raise eyebrows.

Rip pulled up short, his nose crinkling. "Tha's tewwifying."

Ridley skirted around behind the group, bumbling further into the darkness's enveloping cloak. His face-to-face encounter with Ireland's Hessian alter ego caused him to attempt a bit more independence from her touch. The cavernous terminal seemed as good a place as any for such a challenge—until a ghostly whistle blew. The sound resonated off the walls and whipped Ridley's head around in search of its origins. Air stirred, swirling and eddying into the wraithlike silhouettes of travelers. Dated by their period dress, the apparitions hurriedly went about their busy afterlives paying no notice to him. In the middle of it all, stood a young boy dressed in knickers and a sailor-style shirt. An over-sized bowler hat sat cockeyed on his head, shielding one eye. He scanned the crowd, an easy smile dimpling his freckled cheeks. Not a care or worry seemed to darken his spirit as he calmly waited, most likely for his mother. Every now and then he would glance up at the red balloon floating overhead, tied to his wrist, tug it down and giggle as it floated back up to full height.

Ridley expelled a relieved sigh through pursed lips. As visions went, this one wasn't too bad—*yet*. As if the earth itself hatched a maniacal plot to test that theory, the ground beneath his feet began to shake, quaking with enough force to send him stumbling to reclaim his footing. His arms stretched to the sides for balance, he pivoted back towards the others.

"Did you see his uniform? It was dated! I'm telling you, *he wasn't a real cop!*" Ireland paused to click on the flashlight app on her phone. Holding it out before her, she strode further into the terminal.

"Sorry, Crane." Noah shrugged. "I see a cop car or a man with a badge and I stop investigating. That's one of the things I take at face value."

They can't feel it, Ridley thought bitterly. Resigning himself to the need for her touch, he fought the bucking ground beneath him to get back to Ireland.

A dim blue light beamed out from the incoming subway track, accompanied by the unmistakable rumble of wheels over rails. The spectral crowd lurched forward in expectation of the ghost train's arrival. Moving as one demanding body, they pressed toward it, blocking his exit path with their unyielding urgency.

Pivoting in frustration, Ridley's breath caught in equal parts horror and revulsion. That same little boy had been caught in the midst of the mob, his slight frame being jostled dangerously close to the track and the thundering rumble of the incoming train.

Ridley's mouth creaked open, intending to call for Ireland. To beg her for a simple touch to chase away this ominous scene. Instead his own words betrayed him, "*R-red balloon!*"

Her hair framed her heart-shaped face as she glanced his way with a wry grin. "Sounds like a good time is being had in Ridley's Wonderland."

Muttering under his breath at the deficiency of his dependency on her, he acted against his better judgments by spinning on his heel and throwing himself headlong into the sea of bodies. Shivers rocked through him each time the chill of their ethereal forms brushed his skin, yet he battled through it and pushed on.

"Where'th he going?" Rip raised his chin in Ridley's direction as the darkness swallowed him whole.

"No idea." Ireland scowled and flipped her bangs from her eyes. "*Ridley?*"

"See?" Noah gestured after him. "My idea of making him a leash kid doesn't seem so crazy now, does it?"

Set on his mission, Ridley let their voices faded into nothingness behind him and stomped on through the phantom crowd. His manic stare staying zeroed in on the boy while the high beams from the incoming train grew. The first squeal of the pumped brakes threw the mass of bodies forward again, not unlike racehorses bursting through the gates after the trumpet's blast. A briefcase toting man, with a grey bushy mustache and a hurried stride, flung his overcoat over his arm and accidentally slapped the young boy with it. The boy rocked back on his heels, the first signs of fear registering on his young face as he noticed the edge of the platform precariously close behind him. Breaking into a full out sprint, Ridley cut through the vaporous forms, pumping his arms for all he was worth. His breath came in sharp pants. Would his presence matter in the afterlife of a long dead boy? He didn't let doubt of that hinder his stride.

"I'm going to get on first!" the hollow trill of a child's voice resonated off the commodious walls. Two forever-young manifestations broke through the crowd, pushing and shoving their way through the masses.

"No, I am!" the smaller of the two boys giggled, his open coat blowing behind him as he ran.

The chubby-faced boy in the lead glanced back over his shoulder, oblivious to the young boy teetering on the edge in front of him. The train materialized from its yawning tunnel. Ridley's head shook, denying what was happening even as he watched the larger boy's elbow slam into the boy with the balloon. Hurling himself forward the remaining distance, Ridley's hooked fingers swiped but caught only misty air. Slamming down on the platform edge, he could do nothing but watch the cherub-faced boy tumble back. His arms pinwheeled at his sides as he plummeted straight into the path of the inbound train. Metal screeched. Sparks lit the tunnel like tiny fireworks. Even so, the conductor's effort to stop was in vain.

Overhead, that one lone balloon drifted slowly away.

"Ridley?" Ireland, his tether, softly soothed, her voice beckoning to him like the first glimpse of home after a lengthy prison sentence.

Rolling toward her, the chipped grout edge scraped against his shoulders, snagging the fabric of what had once been an expensive shirt. His breath caught, escaping his parted lips in a throaty gasp. She sat astride the most formidable ebony stallion he'd ever seen. Its nostrils flaring with each heaved breath that exploded out in puffs of white steam. Hooves like polished onyx pawed anxiously at the ground. Impressive as the equine was, it paled in comparison to its rider.

The burnished bronze clasp of her cloak fastened in the middle of her breastbone. The black, thick-weaved fabric falling open to frame the swell of her breasts. Soft flesh strained against the beaded corset-style top of her strapless wedding gown that molded to her ample curves. What once must have been a billowing skirt of satin and crinoline had been shredded to ribbons, parting to reveal a tempting glimpse of her milky white thigh before it disappeared inside a black leather stiletto boot. Her face gleamed from beneath her drawn hood, a lunar goddess raising her proud head to honor the night.

Ridley clamped his slack jaw shut. Forcing a gulp down the arid oasis of his throat, he studied the dark shadows under her blazing topaz eyes. Somehow they added a seductive air of mystery in which he longed to lose himself.

Cerulean lips parted, murmuring his name with a breathy sigh that spoke directly to his most primal male instincts, *"Ridley."* Her clenched fist unrolled slowly, one finger at a time, to reach for him. *"Join me."*

Pushing himself up on one elbow, he let his fingers intertwine with her velvety digits. Her whispered caress setting his skin on fire in a way he never dreamed possible. Whether she pulled him up, or he floated under his own accord, he didn't know or care. Somehow he found himself seated on the saddle behind her. Scooting back, she wriggled closer between his legs. Her hood fell back as she leaned into him, giving him a stellar view of paradise. Raising one hand, she weaved nimble fingers into his hair to draw him closer still.

"Don't fight the darkness," she whispered against his lips. "Together, we can *own* it."

A growl—pure animal—tore from his throat as he grasped the rise of her hips. "How?"

"Own what's inside you." Her mouth closed around his top lip, sucking softly and sending waves of euphoria lapping through him. "Embrace it as the gift that it is."

Unable to refrain, Ridley crushed his mouth to hers; his hands expertly outlining her curves. A cold slap against his thigh jerked him from the moment. Resenting the distraction, he glanced down to find Noah's cloudy, unseeing eyes staring up at him. His mouth open wide in an eternal scream, his severed head swinging from his girlfriend's hip.

"*Son of a*—!" Ridley used more force than necessary to push himself away. The motion forced him off the horse, where the ground quickly rose to meet him.

The impact from a fall like that *should* have hurt, or at the very least rung his bell. Instead, he found himself flailing on the floor in a mad scramble to get his feet under him.

"Uh, Ridley? You all right, dude?" asked an audibly leery female voice.

His neck wrenched, throbbing its disagreement. *Ireland*. Not the *betrothed of the damned* version that collected heads of former lovers on her belt, but the flannel clad one that looked like an extra from a *Nirvana* video.

"I'm here if you need me," she gently offered, extending her hand to him.

Hissing through his teeth, Ridley recoiled as if her touch were venomous. Placing one quaking hand on the floor in front of him, he finally found is footing.

"All you have to do is take my hand," Ireland lured, casually waving her hand back and forth like she was tempting him with a Scooby snack.

"Nah!" he hollered in her face with a stern enough conviction to shoot her eyebrows straight up in to her hairline. "*Nuh-finsh-nickeny!*"

Ireland raised both hands, palms out, in hopes of slowing his crazy roll. "Okay, didn't get a word of that, yet somehow it still managed to be kind of offensive."

"It's okay, man. It's just us," Noah assured him, stepping up beside Ireland.

Ridley squeezed his eyes shut, his hands gripping his hair in white-knuckle fists. "Not real," he whispered once, his tone gaining a fiery conviction as he got stuck on repeat. "*Not. Real. Not REAL!*"

The chant became his battle cry, Ridley's shoes slipping across the tile work in his charge straight for Noah. His hell bent intention being to plow straight through what he *knew* to be the mist-formation spirit of the recently decapitated. He anticipated the momentary chill of storming through the vaporous being, *not* slamming into a muscular chest nose first. His cartilage twisted and mashed into his cheek. Noah's head snapped back as the two tumbled to the ground, tangling in each other's limbs.

Amidst Noah's pained groans, Ridley's head rose. An arm, which most definitely didn't belong to him, swung in his face. *"You're real!"*

"I could have told you that," Noah snipped, beginning the bothersome task of unknotting himself, "had you asked *before* tackling me. Thanks to you, I've now been to third base with a dude."

"I thought you were a ghost," Ridley admitted with an anxious giggle-snort.

"And here I thought this assignment would be boring," an unrecognizable voice, as smooth and decadent as melted caramel, broke through their chaotic moment.

The space around them brightened, coming alive with shimmering blue tendrils that chased away the inky blackness. Swirling in a rhythmic dance, the coiling wisps bonded together to form a wicked grinning face. Birthed in shadows, he fully emerged. A ruffled collar protruding from his tailored coat, dated him to a time period of carriages and oil-burning lamps.

Bewildered recognition settled into the lines of Ireland's face. Her head cocked in confusion, she called the newcomer by name, "*Rip?*"

21

Ridley

"Thath's not me!" Rip floundered for a more compelling argument, only to settle on the obvious, "I'm wite hewe!"

"You sure about that?" His younger counterpart floated to his side with a haunting, rolling fluidity. Positioning himself shoulder to shoulder with the aghast older version, he began a cursory comparison. "Same height, some dashingly handsome bone structure. Of course, yours is hidden beneath an excess of wrinkly skin and flea infested hair, yet if one looks hard enough they can still see it."

Ridley's head snapped from the old version to the young and back again. Pawing at the air in search of Ireland's hand, beads of sweat popped up along his hairline. "*Ghoul!*"

"Oh, I'm not a ghoul, *lieve!*" Young Rip corrected, whirling in a corkscrew of vining smoky tendrils. "That's Dutch for 'dear,' by the way."

Extending her hand to Ridley to help him up, Ireland's teeth ground to the point of pain. "I don't remember asking."

Bone rolled over bone under the pressure of Ridley's sweat soaked grip. The second his feet were under him he abandoned the laws of normal human contact by tugging her to him, intimately close.

"*Whoa*! What are we doing here?" Ireland squeaked, mentally thanking the darkness for hiding the hot rush of red flooding her cheeks.

"*He's still here*!" Ridley hissed against her ear. "*He's real*!"

"Who me?" Young Rip giggled, instantly appearing beside them. "Funny, I don't feel real, probably because I can do this." Jamming his hand through Ireland's chest, he wriggled his fingers between her shoulder blades before reaching down to slap her ass. "*Yow-za*!"

"Stop that!" Backpedalling, Ireland slapped frantically at his arm. Her efforts accomplished nothing more than churning up musty air. "We need rules about boundaries ... *and* another girl in this little group!"

A protective flare expanding his chest and tightening the tendons of his neck, Noah caught her sleeve and tugged her behind him. "Or you could go full out Hessian. Playing grab-ass is a riskier game when you throw in a broad sword."

"That's right! She *is* the beast." Young Rip's face, with its eerie transparency, bobbed before her. "Much prettier than the last one. Then again, it would be difficult to be attractive with spinal fluid pulsating from your neck stump. Even so, deep in the pools of your eyes I can see it there. Waiting. Panting for carnage."

Her lip curled in a threatening snarl. "That would be my growing dislike for the ghosts like you."

"Ghosts? Such creatures are common next to me!" A lilt of amusement trilled through his tone. Another swell of mystical haze and he was back by the older Rip's side. "I happen to be an extension of this man's essence, summoned forth when Ridley crammed those enchanted dentures in his mouth." Tipping his head to Rip, he muttered out of the corner of his mouth, "It doesn't get more intimate than wearing another person's teeth, does it? Hope that fella didn't have scurvy."

Rip's shoulders curled in, his body lurching in a dry heave.

"So, you were brought here by a set of magic *teeth*?" Ireland hitched one eyebrow in blatant disbelief.

"Not just any teeth!" Young Rip poofed from one of them to the next; leaning on their shoulders, hovering over their heads, even twining between their legs. "They are teeth belonging to a victim slaughtered by the very abomination *you* all are looking for!" *Poof.* "Her name is Lenore, by the way." *Poof.* "In case you

216

hadn't pieced that together." *Poof.* "You don't look like the 'quick to deduce' kind of bunch." *Poof. Poof. Poof.*

"Thhhop it … *me!*" Rip pulled back, stammering his frustration.

"Maybe you could just tell us why you're here." Noah cocked his head, allowing a mask of intimidation to sharpen his features. "And how we get rid of you."

The entity manifested in the dead center of the group. Clicking the heels of his shoes together, he bent in a formal bow. "I am here only to serve you. To guide you in your pursuit of that known killer, that you may stop her. Then, we shall *all* get what it is we are after."

"And what ith it you're afther?" Rip folded his arms over his chest and scowled down his nose at him.

"When you're around? A towel." Young Rip drifted to him like a fast moving storm cloud, pantomiming wiping his mouth with the ruffles of his collar.

"The truth." Ireland glared.

"Maybe I'll get my wings." One translucent shoulder rose and fell in an almost taunting shrug. "Maybe they'll turn me into a real boy. Of what concern is it to you? Either way you'll get to slay your monster."

Noah cast a sideways glance her way, his expression a question mark. "He's really the only lead we have to find her."

Silence as heavy as a lead weight fell over the group, all of them contemplating their nonexistent list of alternative options.

The hush was shattered by Ridley's manic giggle. "I can't tell you how happy I am you can all see him!"

22

EDGAR

Even as a reanimated corpse Lenore was still the most stunningly beautiful woman in the room. The bodice of her black gown hugged her curves to the rise of her hips, where it belled out. Ebony fabric split in the front of the full skirt to reveal layer after layer of snow white taffeta beneath. Her cap sleeves and sweetheart neckline exhibited enough of her luminescent skin to tempt every red-blooded man that glanced her way with hungry eyes. Onyx raven feathers swooped from the side of her black lace masquerade mask to hide her scars—the *only* flaws in her otherwise polished appearance.

Catching her elbow, Edgar steered her around the torch in the middle of the room. It burned behind blue stained glass panes that filled the foyer with an aquatic flair. "While I appreciate that you knew the names of the influential men that would be at this event, I cannot help but wonder how we will recognize them since neither of us have ever laid eyes on them and everyone's face is covered?"

"Make no mistake, my darling, I will know them."

Edgar would've questioned her bold statement further had it not been for the loud gasps and smatterings of applause that filtered through the room at the reaper-masked performer on stilts that meandered in.

"Follow me, oh, sinners and saints! To a world free from restraints!" The entertainer's body moved with a practiced grace, undulating in tempo with his rehearsed dialogue. "Each room a glimpse of a new realm of pleasure. Step inside, explore each at your leisure."

With a grand wave of his arm, he motioned for the crowd to follow. Edgar and Lenore found themselves caught in a demanding current of bodies, being forced down the narrow hall. Around each sharp bend, spaced out every twenty or thirty yards, they would encounter another chamber. Edgar craned his neck, eager to see the spectacle held within each. The color scheme bestowed on each boxy apartment was cast by a flame behind various colors of glass; blue from the foyer, followed by green, orange, and violet. The costumes of the writhing dancers perfectly matched the chamber that housed them. Through each door lay a whole new world Edgar longed to explore, yet Lenore held firm to his arm and marched on. Her amethyst gaze narrowed with single-minded intent. The crowd thinned around them, partygoers peeling off to mingle in the setting that best suited them.

Out of the corner of his eye Edgar observed the firm set of Lenore's jaw, the anxious flare of her nostrils. His brows knit together tight at how thoughtless he had been. So many people, clearly his beloved was overwhelmed at her first outing. "The spirits are flowing free this night, my flower," he said, clearing his throat and attempting a casual façade. "Any business discussions held here will not be remembered come the morrow. Perhaps we should take our leave?"

If Lenore heard him, and there was little doubt that she had, she failed to even bat an eye in response. Her strides became more determined as they rounded the last bend, where a gigantic ebony clock swelled before them. Its pendulum swung to and fro with a monotonous clang, as if keeping time with the drumming pulse of the party. The room that housed it was noticeably absent of the whimsical flare of its predecessors. Black velvet tapestries shrouded the ceiling and walls. The gothic arched panes of this chamber had been stained a bleeding scarlet. The light streaming through those fire-lit panes casted a ghastly ambiance few would be brave enough to endure. Five men fit that bill. They stood huddled in the center of the room, their thick bellies and broad chests puffed with self-importance. Lewd smiles curled across their lips as they spoke in hushed whispers.

A hiss, more animal than human, escaped Lenore's clenched jaw. Seizing Edgar's wrist hard enough to bruise the skin, she yanked him further into the shadows where they could hide.

"That man in the white coat with the heavy beard is Augustus Fantaine. *He* is the reason we are here."

Shivers of ice prickled down Edgar's spine at the unmistakable threat dripping from her tone. "You lured me here under the pretenses this involved a vocation. I have the unmistakable feeling that is not the case."

Her head snapped his way, silver specks swirling through her violet eyes like a warning flare. "You *have* a vocation, Edgar. A very important one you have been ignoring since the moment you watched Dougie die."

A hot rush of color filled Edgar's cheeks, straight up to his earlobes. "How do you know that name?"

"You are *not* a simpleton," Lenore snipped, flipping her blonde curls over her shoulder to glance back at Augustus. "Do yourself a favor and do not pretend to be. You know very well how I know Douglas. You have known since the night you brought me back."

And there it was. The secret he had been keeping for fear of upsetting his delicate flower, splayed out naked and exposed. Even so, the guilt he expected did not come. Mainly because the woman before him now could be called many things, but delicate was not one of them.

"Enough of this." Edgar's hand closed around her upper arm as he spun her away from Augustus and toward the exit. "We are leaving."

He pretended not to notice the smirk of amusement that tugged at her lips, or the fact that she wasn't even trying to resist. What he could *not* ignore was her singsong chant that echoed off the hallway walls. "Where are the angels? I counted off three: Pamela, Suzanne, and Natalie. Where are the angels? I counted off three: Pamela, Suzanne, and Natalie."

Resolve building, Edgar marched on. All around them the partygoers fell silent, turning their shocked gawks toward the ruckus. The moment they reached the foyer, with its blue light lapping over the walls like soft waves, Lenore yanked her arm back with a sharp snap and broke free from his hold.

Pirouetting to the center of the room with her skirt fanning out around her, she continued her mantra. "Where are the angels? I counted off three; Pamela, Suzanne, and Natalie." Mid-spin she paused, her hand fluttering to her mouth in a mock gasp as she feigned innocence to the curious onlookers. "This was their home. Is it taboo for me to utter their names?"

The commotion lured forth the men from the black room. Lenore turned to welcome them with a wide, villainous grin that injected an acidic burning dread straight in Edgar's veins.

"Who are you to come into my home and speak the names of those who I have lost?" Augustus snarled, spittle foaming at the corners of his thick lips.

A respectful woman would have bowed her head in apology and taken a demure step back. Not Lenore. Squaring her shoulders, she tipped her head and allowed her hair to wave behind her like a silk curtain being drawn. "Who am I? *I* am justice for those that have had their voices stolen from them, and tonight I come for *you.*"

Fighting to maintain his composure in front of his guests, Augustus's face bloomed from red to purple. "I will *not* be spoken to in such a fashion in my own home, by a *woman* no less!" His beady-eyed gaze flicked to the well-dressed men that flanked him. "Escort her out. Be quiet about it, lest we ruin the party."

Lenore shifted her weight from one foot to the other, cocking each hip in the direction of her sway. Her blatant nonchalance caused warning bells to chime a deafening chorus in Edgar's mind. *This* was the very reason she wanted to come here. The thought of what could possibly come next in her plan caused streams of sweat to streak down his back. Not for fear of *her* safety, but for that of every bystander in the ostentatious home.

"Lenore," he rasped, his voice deep with emotion. "Let us take our leave. Clearly, coming here was a mistake."

"Lenore, is it?" A building of a man with bushy auburn sideburns leered, taking a threatening step closer. "Pretty name for a pretty lass. Unfortunately, sometimes ugly things happen to even the prettiest of women."

Her narrow shoulder's shaking with a half-heart chuckle, Lenore plucked the mask from her face and tossed it aside. A collective gasp from the onlookers sucked the air from the room. Raising her chin, she seemed to revel in the ghastly pallor the blue light bestowed on her pale skin; sharpening the jagged edges of her scars and filling the hollows beneath her eyes with the shadows of looming fatality.

"Do your worst, sir," Lenore openly taunted, a devilish gleam brightening her ethereal eyes. "For I shall do mine."

Nine simple words. That was all it took for panic to erupt in the manor. Shrieking guests dashed for the door, fearing the wrath they believed to be the mistress of the damned. A skirmish of shoving bodies, frantic shouts, and overturned furniture followed, all with Edgar's dark angel as the cause. Silently, those with a vested interest—Edgar, Augustus and his crew—watched the spectacle ... and waited.

When the last of the footfalls faded into the night, Augustus fixed his murderous stare on Lenore. "You made a mistake the second you stepped foot in my home. Now, you shall learn what becomes of little girls that do not have the sense to respect their station." His double chin wobbled as he dipped his head in a brief nod to his men.

The towering redhead was the first to heed the call, his broad chest swelling with enthusiasm for the charge. Lenore feigned demure, watching his advance through wide, innocent eyes. His face ripened to the hue of his hair in the thunder of his attack. Only when he bore down, merely an arm distance away, did she act. She plucked the torch from its tripod with the ease of freeing a wilted rose from its stem. Hot air whooshed, sparks flew, as she swung at her would-be attacker. The torch connected with his jaw in a bone-crushing crunch, the sickening smell of burning hair immediately filling the space. He didn't emit so much as a peep when his head snapped back at a grossly unnatural angle.

The muscles of his arms twitched involuntarily.

His eyes rolled back.

In a heap of lifeless flesh, he thudded to the ground.

Edgar crouched behind a table that had been overturned in the mass exodus, peering up at his heaving beauty as if seeing her for the first time. Grasping the fabric of her full skirt with her free hand, she hoisted it up just enough to step over the body. One wide stride, with no outward signs of regret for the life she had taken.

"Get the torch!" Augustus boomed, purposely hanging back while the three remaining men moved in.

"Is this the torch to which you are referring?" Lenore asked in a tone as smooth as velvet, before coolly casting her weapon aside. The hand woven rug ignited in an eager blaze, causing the two men moving in from the right to pull up short.

The heavier set of the three ducked to the left, out of the range of the licking flames. Lowering his shoulder, he prepared to plow right through Lenore's slim frame. Achieving the same practiced grace of a trained matador, she spun clear of his assault, somehow managing to snake an arm over his shoulder in the process to seize him by the chest. She heaved him off his feet with a jerk and twist, the result audibly fatal. He drew his last gurgled breath, staring into the vacant eyes of his friend who had gone before him on the great journey into the beyond.

Smoke and flames filled the room, a ravenous beast lapping up substance wherever it could be found. Covering his mouth and nose with his sleeve, Edgar crept around the outskirts of the foyer in search of an opportunity to whisk Lenore from the growing inferno. Regrettably, he wasn't the only one looking for such a chance. A grey-haired man, with his scraggly pony-tail knotted at the nape of his neck, dodged his way between the flames.

His thin lips curled back, to reveal a front tooth missing from his snarl. "Let us see how you fair against a real ma—"

Lenore's hand darted out, her clamped digits catching his throat and cutting off his attempted threat. "I think I am fairing quite well, thank you."

Motion to the right whipped her head around. Augustus had pivoted on his heel and was retreating back down the hall. Grinding her teeth in frustration, Lenore administered one quick pulse of her hand that crushed her captor's windpipe.

"Lenore!" Edgar's scream morphed into a coughing fit, the smoke chaffing his throat raw. "Please, my flower, stop this! Let us take our leave now before the opportunity escapes us!"

"*Nothing* will escape me this night." An icy chill of determination turned her bold statement into an open threat.

Seemingly oblivious to the sweltering blaze around her, Lenore stalked after Augustus. The last, and gangliest, member of his crew positioned himself directly in her path. His quaking hands rose—as if it was possible to stop a rampant freight train with a stick. Amethyst eyes bored right through him. Lenore's slender fingers curled into the fabric of his coat, casual as an afterthought, and flung him headlong into the sea of flames crackling behind her. Ignoring his agonized shrieks, she continued on in her pursuit.

Edgar longed to offer the man aid, yet found himself helpless to do anything more than watch in horror as the flames

228

quickly stilled his writhing. Placing one hand against the wall, Edgar forced himself to stumble on, the heat of the room scorching his skin like brisket on a spit. Three bends in the hall and the air become more breathable—a reprieve he knew would be fleeting.

Blinking hard to clear his tearing eyes, Edgar called out once more, "Lenore?"

The only response he received came in the form of a loud crash from around the next bend that shook the floor beneath his feet. The high-pitched scream that followed could have easily belonged to a slightly deranged woman, or a man terrified to his very core. Pushing himself off the wall, Edgar raced on, his shoes clacking over the wood floors.

The black room—with its lapping and rolling shimmers of crimson—provided a fitting backdrop for the deadly showdown. Augustus had somehow produced a pearl-handled dagger with which he lashed out wildly to keep the glowering Lenore at bay.

"Keep her away from me!" the quivering man pleaded, his gaze risking a momentary flick to Edgar. "I can reward you generously!"

"And there we find the motivating force behind Augustus Fantaine." Lenore prowled the length of the room, back and forth like a caged animal. "Monetary gain, even if it is acquired in the most bloody and barbaric of ways. Tell me, did Pamela, Suzanne, and Natalie *pay* for this party? Did their pounds of flesh allow for this elaborate show?"

"I have no idea to what you are referring," Augustus stammered, his panicked gaze searching the room for an escape route. "My family was lost to the plague. It was a horrid, unspeakable tragedy."

Lenore paused, her slender arms folding in front of her. "The plague in your own home, yet *you* survived? If lies could swell the tongue you would be choking on your own deceit."

"I speak the truth! They were everything to me and I lost them!" He rendered his argument invalid by lunging for Lenore's mid-section with his readied blade.

Her face devoid of emotion, Lenore caught his wrist and squeezed in a white-knuckle grasp that stole a yelp from his lips. "You did not *lose* them. You knew right where they were ... *and* who you were turning them over to."

Sweat dripping from his brow, Augustus frantically shook his head. "No ... *no!* You are mistaken! I would never—"

Placing one finger to his lips, Lenore quietly shushed him, "*Shhhh,* free the burdens from your soul while you still can. *Admit* that you never thought of them, at all, after the bounty changed hands. After you saw the betrayal and hurt on their faces. After you handed over *your own wife and children*, you never gave them a second thought. Did you?"

Edgar's head volleyed from Lenore, to Augustus, and back again, his pulse pounding in his ears. Bile burned the back of his throat in disgust over this revelation. "Is *this* why you brought me here? Lenore, are they speaking to you?"

Augustus's eyes widened. Desperately he tried to pull away, but could gain no ground. "*I knew it*! You are some sort of *witch*!"

Slowly, Lenore turned his wrist. Angling the blade still clasped in his hand, she forced it to his throat with enough pressure to dimple the skin. Taking a brazen step forward, she wet her lips and let her voice drop to a seductive murmur. "Witches work their magicks from afar. What I plan to do will be done at the most *intimate* of proximities."

Edgar's mouth opened and shut, his deficient mind searching for some approach that would sway her from this quest. "Lenore," he pleaded, "you do not have to do this—"

"Oh, but I do." Both her hands closed around Augustus's, securing the dagger from slipping free from his fingers. "Did you think they made it quick for them, Augustus?"

At a loss for what else to do, the red-faced man nodded emphatically.

She leaned in, her voice caressing his ear. "The plague would have given them a more humane end. Those men tortured them for *weeks*, making Pamela—the woman you swore before

God to love, honor, and obey—watch as they did unspeakable things to *your* daughters. Her own children suffered before her eyes while she was powerless to stop it. Eventually, their bodies gave out—God's mercy in that moment being all that finally ended their suffering."

"I did not know. I di—" Tears spilled over his cheeks in torrents, his legs threatening to fail.

Lenore slammed his back against the ebony clock, forcing him to remain upright. "Do *not* use ignorance as your excuse! Greed and opportunity were your motivators here, nothing more!" Her iron-like grip applied steady pressure, until crimson burst from beneath the blade and soaked his collar. "Tonight will be *your* turn to experience what it is like for your body to be forced into acts against your will."

"Justice can be found another way, Lenore! You cannot do the bidding of the spirits!" Edgar's pleas fell on deaf ears. Lenore's stare locked with Augustus's. Guiding his hands back, she held his gaze as she forced him to bury his own blade in his gut.

Blood spurt from his lips, a set of false teeth slipping passed his gums as his body toppled forward. Still Lenore's rage would not be sated. When his hands fell limp, Lenore took the task upon herself. An enraged scream tore from her throat as she rammed the blade into him over and over again. His body reduced to little more than battered meat, Augustus collapsed at her feet, his blood splattering over the ivory folds of her gown. His lifeless collapse failed to register through Lenore's red fury. Once more her hand plunged forward, this time smashing into the base of the ebony clock.

Blinking once, twice, and again she focused her gaze. The twisted devil's mask she wore fading back to his lovely, serene beauty. "Edgar? Edgar wh-what's happened? Help me, please!" Tugging to free her hand from the glossy back wood only knocked more chunks of the broken kindling free and trapped her further.

Smoke rolled in from the hall, stinging Edgar's eyes and tightening his lungs with each breath. "Looks to be dogwood," he pointed out, removing some of the loose pieces holding her, "the same wood legend claims Jesus's cross was made of."

Lenore's eyebrows snapped up with an indignant flare made all the more terrifying by the blood that speckled her face. "What are you saying, Edgar? That God himself has forsaken me? Shall I remind you who made me this way?"

"No, I am making no claims," he corrected, pulling a rather long shard out and casting it aside. "I was merely pointing out your hand is stuck in a dogwood clock."

Despite his argument to the contrary, Edgar noted with great interest that if so much as a small splinter of the dogwood was touching her skin she was powerless to move it. Only when every last bit had been removed could she pull her hand free. By then the flames had reached the door, the heat rising to a level that made Edgar's skin feel as if it were melting from the bones.

"We cannot get out that way," he nodded toward the door, pulling her protectively to him. "Pull down the tapestries! Perhaps they cover a window!"

Together they grabbed the bottoms of each tapestry and ripped them free from the wall. Their urgency growing frenzied as one after the other revealed solid wall beneath. With one remaining, Edgar said a silent prayer—then yanked. Freedom stared back at waist-level.

Wasting no time, Edgar unhooked the lock and swung the panes out free. "You first, my flower," he yelled over the snapping and hissing flames that crept into the room behind him.

Her hand, still chilled by death's cold touch, closed around his. Clasping her waist, he heaved her onto the window ledge, and lowered her down as far as he could to ensure her safety. Only when her feet hit the ground with a soft thump did he turn back to the scene. For reasons he couldn't yet explain, he felt compelled to gather a piece of the broken dogwood, and Augustus's spewed teeth, and stow them deep in his pockets. Then, bracing himself against the frame, Edgar climbed onto the window ledge and threaded his legs out into the night. Seated there, he took one glance back at the body on the floor, the growing pool of blood, and the fire burning away any and all

234

traces of what had occurred. So much death and destruction, yet he blamed not Lenore for what she had become, nor Augustus for his vile acts. Guilt's dagger bore deeper than any manmade weapon could, puncturing Edgar's very soul. For he knew *himself* to be the true monster here—with the hell that was spawned by his simple touch.

23

Ridley

Small, rodent-sized feet scampered in the darkness, sending a shiver of unease skittering down Ireland's spine. Water dripped incessantly from somewhere in the tunnel, creating the foreboding mental image of Death itself tapping one bone finger in eager expectation.

"For all we know, Lenore could be down here," Ireland grumbled, mostly to break the deafening silence, "watching, waiting for the perfect moment to finish what she started in the alley."

"Maybe this time you'll get at least one good shot in before she clobbers you," Ridley smirked, his obnoxious jab contradicted by the comforting squeeze he gave her hand linked with his.

"Ugh! A vacation in purgatory would be livelier than this funeral precession bunch!" Young Rip threw himself back, his head lulling back in pantomimed exasperation while his smoke and mist form continued to float forward. A sudden idea caused his lips to twist in a wicked grin, his transparent gaze locking on Ireland in a way that made a knot of dread coil in her gut.

"Except in *this* corner of the group." In a wave of cresting and flowing tendrils the incorporeal nuisance manifested between Ireland and Ridley, his air-light form perched cross-legged on their linked arms. "Over here we have sexual tension so thick and palpable I could gobble it up with a spoon."

Ireland immediately dropped Ridley's hand, and edged closer to Noah's side. "*What*? That's crazy talk. There's no tension of the sexy kind, except maybe between me and this guy." Pivoting on the ball of her foot, she playfully punched Noah in the arm. Pausing, she stared up at him, stunned by her own awkwardness. "Why did I just do that?"

Judging by his eyebrow hitched up in bewilderment, Noah was wondering the same thing. Yet, he still came to her defense before thinking to question it. "She's holding his hand because I don't feel like chasing him down or getting tackled again." His chin jerked in Ridley's direction. "Hey Rid, are the walls talking to you?"

Ridley's head slowly turned their way, his eyes wide and glassy. "The fat little piggies found a delectable sandwich, and now they're orchestrating an elaborate masquerade ball."

"See? Would you get him, please?" Bumping her with his elbow, Noah's stern tone left little room for debate.

Filling her lungs and expelling what tension she could through pursed lips, Ireland wiped her clammy palm on the leg of her jeans and caught Ridley's hand with hers.

The change was instantaneous. His cornflower blue eyes—made a gleaming sapphire by Young Rip's haunting light—blinked into focus. The deep creases between his brow easing.

Swallowing hard, he realigned his fingers with hers and secured a firm hold. "Thank you."

Her head dipped in a modest nod.

Dropping his legs, Young Rip mimed walking even though his form hovered a couple feet from the ground. "Say what you want. I can *smell* it in the air!" His hand twirled with an extravagant flare. "*Someone* over here wants to put the F-U-N in fornication!"

"There is no U in fornication," Ireland scoffed.

In a blink his ghostly face appeared in front of her, his eyebrows wiggling suggestively. "But there could be."

"Ugh!" Ireland cringed, shooting scowls to all *three* of her male cohorts that had the audacity to snicker.

"Even in the spirit form the libido lives on," Ridley's tongue flicked over his lower lip as he chuckled. "Men everywhere can rest easy."

"Were you really *that* skeevy when you were younger?" Spinning on original recipe Rip, judgment dripped from Ireland's tone.

His mouth opened, most likely to argue, then quickly clamped shut again. His beard twitched at the corners of his mouth, fighting off a grin. "What can I thay? We din't hath the In'ernet back then."

While Ireland shook her head, her disparaging smirk planted firm, Young Rip pushed on as if no one had countered his original claim. Pacing from one side of the tunnel to the other, his legs moved in wide strides while his feet dissolved into a rolling surf that pushed him along. "Still, two beings bound to such darkness and mayhem? Imagine the pull. The raw, magnetic attraction."

"Trust me, mate," Ridley said, his gaze pointedly cast to the floor. "After the vision I had of her all vamped out, Queen of the Underworld style, I'd be terrified to even *think* of her in *that* way."

Visibly bristling, Noah stopped short. "You had some sort of morbid little fantasy about my girlfriend?" He attempted a lighthearted chuckle that somehow landed closer to an inquisitive Rottweiler ready to show fang if provoked.

Realizing his faux pas, Ridley did a quick about-face. "Yes, I did. But you should know the sexy stuff stopped the *second* I realized she was wearing your head as an accessory."

"*Wha-?*" His mouth falling slack, Noah spun Ireland's way for an explanation she couldn't even begin to offer. "*What?*"

"It was *his* subconscious! How should I know! Plus, isn't this a moot point? Because, in case you hadn't noticed," palm raised, Ireland jabbed one hand in the direction of his face, "*you still have a head!*"

"Onwy in dis cwowd ith who haths a head a wegular topic of dithcuthion," Rip pointed out, scratching his chin beneath his beard.

"A guy that *talks* to spirits," Noah stabbed an accusing finger at Ridley, "had a vision about my girlfriend, who's *possessed* by a spirit," the finger of blame swung to her, "in which she changed my hat size in the most brutal of ways! I think a slight freak out is justified!"

Ireland wanted to argue that she would never hurt him. Even so, the emptiness of that claim caused it to swell on her tongue, cutting off her air way. A hot wash of helpless tears flooded her eyes. *Twice.* Her control had slipped *twice.* Any reassuring claim she tried to make would ring as the hollow lie it was. All she had left was the paltry truth, whatever that was worth.

"I would *never* intentional hurt you," her trembling voice cracked with emotion, "And you still have my talisman. You know that."

"Yeah, I know. You're right. It was just another one of his stupid dreams. No worries," Noah attempted to reassure her, while his strained half-smile and slightly flaring nostrils attested otherwise.

Ireland's brow puckered, her head tilting to consider him. "You sure? 'Cause your heaving chest seems to say otherwise."

"I'm not heaving," Noah puffed. Noticing the odd tremor of his own voice he cleared his throat and attempted normalcy, landing closer to asthmatic mid-attack. "See? Definitely not heaving."

"You're heathing a li'le," Rip countered.

"No. *No.* I mean, yeah." Noah's shoulders rose and fell in a series of twitchy shrugs. "Do I think there's a chance her monster has the hots for his monster? Absolutely."

"My *monster*," Ridley snorted. "That's funny, that's what I call my..."

Ireland halted him with a finger raised in warning. "I have a sword. Do *not* finish that sentence."

"Noted."

Dropping all but Ridley's pinkie, Ireland dragged him along as she closed the distance between herself and Noah. "You have to know that the *only* thing between Ridley and me is the boot stomping fate has given both of us."

Wordlessly, Ridley shifted from one foot to the other behind her.

"I know that," Noah's stern gaze softened as he peered down at her. "I do."

"He lays on the guilt so heavily," Young Rip moved in a snaking cloud to whisper his poisonous ideas directly into Ireland's ear. The cool chill of his essence triggered a rash of goosebumps up and down her arms. "Yet you *know* he has his own little secrets. Why does he *really* stay? Who would voluntarily delve into such darkness?"

Simple words uttered by an undeniably conniving presence *should* have been easy to cast aside. And yet … they had poked at the outwardly calm surface of her insecurities, producing a ripple effect of self-doubt.

"Why are you here, Noah?" Young Rip clasped his hands behind his back, circling Noah he wore the glare of a protective father. "What would drive a person to choose this life?"

Retreating into herself, Ireland felt familiar prickles dance down her spine. The Hessian had stirred, clawing and lashing his way to the forefront of her mind. Blinking hard, she fought to clear away the murderous red haze creeping around the edges of her vision—to no avail.

"Not that it's any of your business," Noah responded tightly, his chest expanding as he hooked his thumbs in his belt loops. "But, I was under the assumption she and I had chosen *each other*."

Skin stretched, bones pushing outward. The abyss was racing in to claim her, leaving Ireland time only to gasp, "*Noah!*"

One glance spurred him into action, sending him scrambling to dig the talisman from his pocket.

"*Again with this?*" Ridley exclaimed and yanked his hand free.

Blue lips curled back in a cheeky grin, a demonic tremor rattling from her throat. "Beguiled by a sweet smile and sashaying hips, no doubt. Even so, the willingness to overlook the truth, that hell itself lies in wait within her soul, is cause for question. Only a saint or a fool would make such a choice."

Claiming his sought after prize, Noah pulled the talisman into view and weighed it in his palm in an open thread. "I've been called one of those things and it sure as hell wasn't a saint. Ireland, if you're in there, *now* would be a great time to take the reins. Otherwise, I'm gonna have to put bonehead down for the count, and take you with him."

"The girl *might* fight to resurface," the Horseman made Ireland's shoulders rise and fall in a casual shrug. "*If* I was speaking any words she was not too cowardice to risk herself."

Subtle as he could, Ridley inched his way back by Rip. "Talks like this are exactly why I never stick around for long term commitments," he muttered behind his hand.

"I'm pretty sure never before in the history of relationships has *anyone* ever had the 'can you love me even though I'm the Headless Horseman' conversation," Young Rip tittered with giddy eagerness, winding himself around the two men in a trail of luminescent azure.

Ireland prowled closer with the fluidity of a jungle cat. Her head tipped, she glowered up at him from under her vein scrawled brow. "Sneaky little glances at your phone. Did you think she didn't see those? A life you left so willing and never speak of. Admit it, boy, she is nothing more than entertainment to you. A dangerous thrill you think to indulge yourself with for a bit before running back to your *real* life."

"Is that what *Ireland* is worried about?" Noah practically growled, taking a threatening step forward. "Because I'd really like to hear that from *her*."

"Correct me if I am wrong," Young Rip purred, solidifying enough to steeple his fingers under his chin. "However, that did *not* sound like a denial to me."

Noah's head snapped toward the mouthy apparition, his lip twitching into a snarl. *"Are you trying to get me killed?"*

Metal hissed free from leather. Raising her sword chest level, Ireland spun, her elbow slamming into Noah's solar plexus. A choked gasp lodged in his throat as the ground rose to meet him. Frantically wheezing to regain his stolen breath, Noah's eyes widened as the edge of her blade pressed a valley of pressure against his neck.

"Answer me, boy," dropping to one knee, the Hessian leaned in to hiss in his face, "or shake hands with Death this very day. *Why are you here*?"

"That's ... enough ... of the couple ... counseling ... from the undead." Gritting his teeth, Noah wormed one hand between them and slapped the talisman flat against Ireland's forehead.

Her lips peeling from her teeth, Ireland recoiled. The smell of burning flesh permeated through the dank tunnel. Noah moved with her without hesitating, keeping the metal coin firmly planted. As she stumbled back, Noah seized the opportunity to shift the dynamic and pinned her to the ground. Writhing in pain, the monster finally rescinded, allowing the veil of obscurity to lift from Ireland's wide and startled eyes.

"Noah," she rasped, "it's me."

While he was courteous enough to shift his weight *slightly* off of her, he made no move to let her up. "I think we're going to have a little talk right here while you've got your listening ears on."

"Could you at least move the talisman? It's only a few layers of skin away from melting the part of my brain that knows the alphabet." Her attempt at humor was sullied by her tone, tight with barely concealed anguish.

Lips, as full and tempting as ripe wild berries, pursed as Noah shook his head. The tips of his hair tickled across her forehead. "I'm thinking no. Not after learning from a *demon* that we have some issues to resolve. Now, I have a few things to say and need to make sure your head is completely your own, so you can really *hear* me."

One eye twitched shut, the other rolling back to retreat under a fluttering eyelid. "Talk fast," Ireland gasped.

Rip showered Ridley with spit in his attempted to whisper, "Thith would be thweet if wathn't for the known killer athpect."

Despite his threatening façade, Noah eased up on the talisman, keeping it in place with only the pad of his thumb. "You wanna know why I check my phone all the time? It's because I *thought* I was important back in Sleepy Hollow. I was busy everyday—handling this, running there—and in my mind that meant people *needed* me. Then, I left town with you. Wanna know what I figured out?"

"*Mmmmhmmm,*" Ireland squeaked with a meager nod.

"That my entire life back there could be wiped away with one simple phone call. Turns out I was filling my days with busy work that my family could easily hand over to someone else." The tendons of his jaw tightened at the audible sorrow that crept into his voice. "So, yes, I was bummed about that, but not bad enough to bother my girlfriend with it. Especially since *she* was dealing with having a killer poltergeist squatting somewhere in her subconscious."

Ireland forced both watering eyes open, the angry red skin of her forehead creasing with concern. "You could have—"

"Pretty sure I wasn't done talking." The extra thump Noah gave the talisman acted as a none-too-subtle reminder of their situation. "You just had a sword to my jugular. I think you can let me have the floor for a minute."

Pressing her lips together in a firm white line, Ireland hitched one eyebrow in an invitation for him to continue.

"I *was* upset about all of this, until I had to carry your limp and lifeless body into the emergency room," staring deep into her eyes, where there was no room for anything but the bitter truth, his voice grew husky with emotion. "I thought I lost you, Ireland. And in that moment everything became crystal clear to me. Everything that occupied my time before was just filler to distract me until *you* came along. With you I'm needed ... and hopefully wanted?" His tone rose at the end just enough to make it a question.

Keeping her lips clamped, Ireland jerked her chin down in a brief nod of absolute confirmation.

"You're my true north. Where I belong and where I was always meant to be." A bit of the tension melted from his handsome face, that half-smile she adored tugged back the corner of his mouth. "You see where I'm going with this?"

Purposely blanking her face of all emotion, Ireland stared … and blinked. "You're frying my frontal lobe. I'm pretty sure I'm going to need it spelled out to me using small words."

Noah dipped his head closer, the warmth of his breath causing a naughty little rush to fill her chest that seemed insanely inappropriate considering their circumstances. "I'm trying to tell you that I'm in love with you, ya beautiful dumbass."

A hot blush rushed up her neck, filled her cheeks, and tiptoed its way to her ear lobes. "I'd really want to say it back, but not while my forehead smells like bacon."

"That's fair." He nodded. "If I take the talisman off, will you sheath your sword?"

"You have my exceedingly grateful word."

Slapping his hand against the grimy tile floor, Noah retracted the talisman and shoved himself away, backing away with his hands raised. Ireland rolled to her side, panting to steady her breathing, the edge of her sword scrapping against the floor. Slowly she rose to her feet, her overly cautious posture mirroring

Noah's. The tunnel around them darkened to midnight's navy shroud as if reflecting the dark moods of its collective inhabitants.

"Now's your chance Horseman!" Curling around her neck like a scarf, Young Rip blew the hair from her neck and prompted a potent shiver to shudder through her. "All those lies and secrets. You can't believe a word he utters! Seize this moment. *Finish him.*"

Ireland's neck snapped in his direction, her bothersome bangs falling into her eyes. "*What*? This isn't *Mortal Kombat*! There will be no finishing of anyone."

"Enough!" Ridley barked, his adamant outburst *demanding* their attention. His narrowed, blazing glare lassoed Young Rip and drew the essence toward him. "You're playing us like puppets. For what? Your own amusement?" Young Rip opened his mouth to answer, yet was silenced by a sharp shake of Ridley's head. "The reason doesn't matter. It ends *now!*"

Without a word of argument, Young Rip came to rest beside Ridley. His hands folded respectfully in front of him.

Rip's head cocked in appreciation. "You contwoled him. Tha'th a nifthy trick."

"We're gonna put a pin in *that* new development and discuss it in one second," Ireland said, then caught Noah's equally perplexed stare and turned her hip to show him her sword disappearing back into its sheath.

"I believe there was something you wanted to say?" he murmured, his features sharpening in a truly delectable come-hither invitation.

Her boots squeaked across the tile, making it one tentative stride before she pulled up short. "Uh … not until you put the talisman away."

Noah's gaze flicked up to her red and blistered forehead. "Oh, yeah! Sorry."

Following her lead, he held the talisman up by its chain, letting the heavy medallion sway beneath his palm before depositing it into the front pocket of his jeans. Both hands rose and he spun in a small circle to assure her it was well hidden. "We good?"

A slow smile dawned on her face, brightening it like a thousand sunrises. The pair closed the gap between them with matched urgency. Her arms weaved around his neck as he caught her by the waist and swept her up in his arms.

"I love you, too," she breathed the words into him, delving into the sweet surrender of his kiss.

"Cautious romance," Ridley forced a chuckle. His attempt slightly tarnished by the tight set of his jaw an outsider may have guessed to be jealousy. "That's what we just witnessed here."

"I had no doubths they would work it out," Rip gazed on like a proud papa. "A bond like theirths is w'itten in dah sarths.

Madda Fa'e thmiling on dem with her sarindpths gith. It may ha'e tharted wif Ikabah and Kathfrina, but dah hath thurpad dat wif deir own thpechul fercumthanths."

"Didn't get a word of that, buddy," Ridley admitted, clapping a comforting hand on Rip's shoulder that sagged with frustration.

24

EDGAR

"I did not expect events to unfold in the manner they did." Lenore smoothed the ruffles of her skirt with her hands, as if such an act could erase the gore or singe marks from the fabric. "Not to say *any* were innocent. Those in his employ openly jested with him about the *opportunity* presented by the plague. Can you imagine? How gruesomely vulgar!"

Edgar tore his gaze from the rocking carriage wall in front of him and glanced her way. All emotion noticeably absent from his tone. "There are tiny bits of flesh tangled in your hair."

If blood still pumped through her veins she may have blushed as she dipped her head to self-consciously brush it away. "I truly *am* sorry you saw me like that, Edgar. I lost myself. I am aware of that. Even so, I am confident that if you had heard all the horrible things those poor girls had to endure, you would have done just as I did."

Edgar could manage nothing more than a weak nod. His stare returning to the carriage wall before him, as he did his best to emulate it.

Think nothing.

Feel nothing.

Be ... *nothing*.

He fought off his blinks, spacing them out as far as his dry, tired eyes would allow. For tonight, death and mayhem lived behind his lids. Each blink bringing another horrifying flash of memory.

In the oddest of ways he missed Dougie and the other spirits that had long tormented him. In comparison to this, those seemed fleeting moments of horrific fancy that passed to reveal themselves as nothing more than illusions. This? There was no waking from this threshold of hell. The smell of burning flesh that still filled his nose acted as proof of that.

Lenore chattered away the entire voyage home, the anxious lilt in her voice audible. As the carriage lulled them side-to-side, her hand sought out his, seeking the reassurance of his touch. Without hesitation he offered her that. His fingers closing around hers, cold and smooth as marble. Still, he rode in silence, refusing to let himself feel, for the emotions swirling within him were too dreadful and heart wrenching to entertain.

The carriage horses eased to a stop in front of their bungalow, gravel crunching under the back wheels. The driver, whose services they rented for the night, hopped down and opened the door for them.

His friendly face folded in an expression of sincere empathy. "Can you get her inside sufficiently, sir? Such an ordeal you went through! Barely escaping that fire!"

"We will be fine, thank you," Edgar said with a dismissive nod and took Lenore's elbow to guide her inside. Courtesy was a trait for another night.

The moment they stepped inside the cottage Lenore fell against the door, securing them in their private sanctuary. "I made a mistake removing my mask. If I dare step into town people could recognize me. It may become mandatory for us to move on. First, we should let things settle. Perhaps stay out of sight for a while?" Pushing herself off the doorframe she reached for Edgar. Catching his hand, she brought it to her cheek and dotted his palm with a kiss. "Would you like that, Edgar? We could have a holiday here at home and spend an entire week in bed."

"No truer Heaven on Earth could exist," he rasped. Patting her hand, he pulled away, needing a bit of distance to collect himself. "I desire a spot of chamomile tea. Can I brew you some as well, my flower?"

"That sounds wonderful. I will go change into my night clothes and meet you on the veranda. Such a beautiful night, it would be a shame not to enjoy it." Lenore paused by the bedroom door and glanced back, her hair parting to offer a glimpse of the elegant curve of her shoulder. "Edgar?" she called as he turned for the kitchen.

Praying his face remained a neutral, he turned back. His eyebrows raised in expectation.

So many meaningless words fell from her lips that night, yet finally she found the *only* three that would crack the solid wall forming around his heart. "I love you."

"And I you. Until my very last breath, I shall belong to you alone."

Contentment softened her exquisite features, adding a sparkle to her otherworldly amethyst eyes. She held his stare long enough to blow him a kiss before leaving him to his task.

Edgar moved through a fog of tumultuous thoughts. His body carried out motions purely on well-practiced habit: filling the teapot, digging her favorite chamomile blend from the cupboard, retrieving the sugar bowl. Across the house he heard the boudoir door click shut. Only then did he expel a shaky breath and extract the broken chunk of dogwood from his pocket. Breaking off one small sliver, he dropped it into the brewing teapot then pocketed the remaining shard. He carried on preparing the tea to suit her—

two sugar cubes and a splash of cream. After loading a platter with cups for them both, he carried it out to the veranda.

Lenore joined him just as he set the tray on the table, her white lace dressing gown flitting around her ankles. Her hair, brushed free from its curls, danced in the night breeze. Having snatched her favorite quilt from her rocking chair, she flung it around her shoulders as she walked. She settled onto the settee, padding the seat beside her for Edgar to join her. Gathering both cups from the tray, he did just that.

Edgar handed Lenore her tea, his eyes never leaving her face as he tentatively sipped his own. Flicking his tongue over his lips, he searched the flavor for even a hint of taste variance. He found none. Would she?

Lenore's shoulders curled around her cup as she inhaled the aroma, a soft sigh escaping her lips. Indulging herself in a sip, her brow momentarily creased. Edgar's heart lurched in a stutter-start, before thudding against his ribs in a rampant rhythm.

"Mmmm, I do love this blend." She smiled appreciatively and tipped her cup for a second sip.

Edgar drained his cup in silence, watching and waiting with bated breath to see if his suspicions were true. Confirmation came before the clock chimed a new hour. Lenore's lashes brushed the tops of her cheeks, each blink longer than her last. Then, for the first time in months, she slept.

Only then did Edgar allow his true emotions to pour out. His shoulders shook, his quaking body folding to the ground, as sorrow streaked his face in torrents.

What followed were six days of bliss, and six nights of anguish.

A yin and yang of emotional torment.

Days tangled in the sheets, exploring new realms of pleasure with his beautiful flower.

Nights locked in his work shed, tear drops falling like rain on his loathsome dogwood project.

Days seeing God in the euphoria of her touch.

Nights fearing His wrath for what had become.

Days reveling in the seductive oasis of her mouth.

Nights lost in a desolate desert of loneliness.

Days whispering vows against moist and eager lips.

Nights screaming anguished cries at the ceiling.

Days spoon feeding each other desserts, licking away any crumbs that fell.

Nights heaving and purging from the rotting guilt within.

Days watching her sip the tainted tea and longing to slap it from her hands,

Nights rejoicing in the moments of peace he'd brought to her troubled soul.

On the seventh day, everything changed.

Ridley

The dynamic in the space had changed. How? Ireland wasn't sure. Yet the anxious knot in her gut told her something was … off. At first she thought her uttering the L word to Noah had induced a mini-panic attack. While her inner commitment-phobe was screaming like a skydiver whose chute wouldn't open, that wasn't the cause of the prickly sensation setting her nerves on edge.

"And it happened the second you realized the Younger Rip was playing us against each other?" Ireland asked Ridley, with a tone as stern as a pounded gavel. She glanced back over her shoulder, unable to shake the feeling someone was following them.

"That very instant. It was as if something inside me just clicked," Ridley snapped his fingers in demonstration, relief coating him like a much needed rain after the most desolate of droughts. "I felt my … *will*—for lack of a better word—stretch. I flicked it out, and jerked the mouthy essence into submission."

Ireland chewed on her lower lip, the fingers of her free hand tapping the hilt of her sword. "What about the other spirits? If I let go of you right now could you still see them?"

Ridley's hand slid from hers, leaving it chilled in the vacancy. He took his time, glancing around and studying the tunnel.

"They're still here," he nodded, his fingers lacing with hers once more. A strand of ebony hair, gleaming blue in the mystically enhanced light, fell across his forehead as he shot her a victorious grin. "Some have slunk back into the shadows. Others are bowing their heads in a show of respect. I think they're afraid of me."

Ireland's head twitched like a confused puppy. "Then why are we still holding hands?"

"Seeing you make out with Noah left me feeling forlorn and dejected," Ridley attempted a mock pout that veered far from convincing thanks to the mischievous crinkles of amusement at the corners of his eyes. "I just needed to feel I was still … you know … your special little guy."

"Why do I bother talking to you?" Ireland asked herself, yanking her hand free from his.

"Because I'm devilishly handsome and positively ooze charisma? *Or*, because I'm the only other cursed misfit you know?" Ridley shrugged, his lips twisting to the side. "I'm inclined to go with the first option."

Ignoring his wisecrack, Ireland kept her steely gaze locked on the silhouettes of Noah, Rip, and their spectral guide in front of her. "Can you tell if Lenore is close by? I've got a bad feeling I can't shake."

"Sorry, no." Ridley wiped at the beads of sweat on his brow with his forearm, caused by the stuffy air deep within the abandoned tunnel. "But that does bring up an imperative question. Do you have any idea how to stop Lenore? Death didn't seem to take the first time she tried it out."

Ireland drew her chin to her shoulder, listening to a soft hum somewhere in the distance. "I plan to put the pointy end of this into her and repeat as necessary," she said off-handedly, pushing down on the hilt to flip the tip of her sword up.

"Not too complex, I like that part." Ridley followed her stare, glancing behind them, his expression a question mark. "That said, do you think it will actually work?"

The hum grew unmistakably louder. Roaring in like an aircraft propeller. "Not sure. That said, here comes plan b. Heads up." Curling her hand around the back of his neck, Ireland shoved Ridley toward the ground.

"Wha-?" he stammered, but didn't fight her attempt to bend him in half.

Raising one hand, she caught her axe mid-flight. "There you are! Were you stuck in that brick wall this whole time? Poor little guy!"

Ridley corrected his posture. His eyebrows disappeared into his hairline as he tried unsuccessfully to fend off a judgmental smirk.

"To clarify, I've never talked to my weapons before." Ireland sheepishly flipped her axe in her palm and returned it to the leather loop on her belt. "And now that I see how creepy it is I won't be doing it again."

Ridley's lips moved, forming a response that Ireland suddenly couldn't decipher a syllable of over the gruff boom echoing through her mind.

Surround yourself with people and you will *be betrayed*, the Hessian hissed.

The severity of his tone seeped through her marrow like liquid Adamantium, solidifying her spine into impenetrable steel like a certain surely *X-Men* character.

"Hey, Ire?"

Jerking in surprise at Noah's voice in her ear, Ireland spun and drew. The point of her blade landing mere centimeters from giving him a brutally close shave.

His hands dropped to his sides in frustration, a wad of black fabric clutched in one fist. "Seriously? Again? I'm going to start taking this personally."

"Sorry, reflex." Ireland squinted to counter the sudden twitch beneath her right eye. Coppery warmth tainted the air. Blood, free flowing crimson, rushing, flowing, pulsating over the very walls around her. Recognizing it as a vision, Ireland sheathed her sword with a trembling hand.

Feel that, lass? the Horseman growled from his dark cavity within her. *Death is coming, and the hand he requests for tonight's promenade might be your own.*

"What's going on?" she gulped, searching for a tone that somewhat resembled normal.

Noah's narrowed gaze scoured her face, catching every one of her anxious tells as if they were glowing neon. "Young Rip said the exit up ahead will take us to where Lenore is hiding. He suggested you throw your cloak on and get ready." His hand rose in offering. One edge of the heavy wool fabric slipped past his fingers, unfurling in sensual, curling waves that beckoned to the most sinister side of her character.

Her fingers itched to close around the course wool, a hypnotic longing throbbing through her to lose herself in the tantalizing rush that came with fastening the cloak around her shoulders. For that very reason, she hesitated. She was acting like a junky in need of a fix, only this particular addiction was wasting no time spiraling out of control.

"Ireland?" Ridley stared hard at the vacant space beside him. Leaning away from it, his muscles seemed set on a hairpin trigger to bolt. "Your friend is back."

"*The Horseman*? You can see him?" Ireland's hand instinctively rose to her face, feeling for the telling protruding bones.

"Different friend," he corrected, flinching away as if she'd tried to touch him. "Same panache for being unperturbed by the binding restrictions of death. Namely, the incredibly pushy Eleanora. She wants me to give you a message. Which I will deliver so she doesn't *requisition my body again*!" He shouted the last part of his proclamation over his shoulder for the benefit of an entity only he could see.

Ireland and Noah exchanged strikingly similar looks of apprehension. "What is she saying?"

"A change in hue, a shift of light." Ridley said each word in the broken cadence of someone reading back a transcript verbatim. "Enemies conspiring their deadly plight.

"A shift in light?" Ireland repeated. Spinning in a slow circle, her brow furrowed. The change was subtle. So much so that she almost glossed over it. Yet the minute it registered she sucked in a shocked gasped. Unleashing the steel viper at her hip, it hissed free with venomous intent. *"The wrong Rip is glowing!* You were just with them, Noah. You didn't think to mention that?"

Noah turned with a jerk, his stare bouncing from Ireland to Rip and back again. "Okay, I never claimed to be the most observant person, but I *swear* that was not the case a minute ago."

Ridley stepped closer, knitting their huddle in tight. "What were they talking about before he sent you over here?"

"Nothing important," Noah shrugged, blinking rapidly in confusion. "Sleepy Hollow, mostly. The way it *used* to be."

Looking more villainous than friend, *their* Rip peered over his hunched shoulder. Fast moving fronts of animosity and uncertainty collided in a storm cloud of emotion that ravaged the lines of his face.

"The way it was when they first met the *Horseman*?" While Ireland posed her words as a question, she needed no confirmation. The air around them was charged with conspiracy, crackling with glee at the prospect of claiming one of their own out from under them.

She didn't wait for his response. Her boots slapped the ground with determined strides, her heavy footfalls echoing off the cavernous walls like an unseen army.

Young Rip turned at the sound of her trudges, his face a convincing mask of innocence. "You see how she comes with her weapon readied? That is the monster using her as his marionette. Think back to the girl she was when you first met. Would that once innocent soul have been so quick with the sword?"

Rip shook his head, struggling to clear his foggy head from the apparition's trance. "The firsth time we met she whacked me with a Magwite. So, yeth, I bewieve had there been a sword handy she would have utiwized that as well."

Blind rage flashed across Young Rip's face that he quickly squelched with a sharp twitch of his head. "Then the beast had already taken up residence within her! Either way is of little consequence. You *know* she has been slipping as of late, losing control of her monstrous tendencies. The very same beast that killed our dear friend Ichabod is chained within her, and you have seen with your own eyes that those chains are weakening!"

Flipping the hilt over the back of her hand, Ireland caught it and readjusted her hold to bring the blade up alongside her face. Her other arm stretched out before her in a battle ready stance. "Funny, I don't remember signing up for the celebrity roast. What's the play here, Astro Rip? What are you after?"

Young Rip hooked a hand around the older man's neck and pulled him closer in a conspiratorial embrace. "You—nay, *we*—failed Ichabod once before! Do not let his death be in vain by allowing her to claim even one more life!"

Crossing her back leg over her front in a cautious side-step, Ireland prowled around them in a slow, deliberate circle. "Rip, you know me. Don't buy into the Hessian hate propaganda. Remember when I explained to you the modern day meaning of the term 'dick?' Well, consider this guy exhibit A."

Young Rip's jaw tightened as he watched his counterpart's expression soften at the memory. Using more force than necessary, he yanked Rip forward and snaked his arm around his neck. The embroidered sleeve of his coat became a tight noose that streaked the older man's gasping face with plumes of red and purple.

"I know the dreams of that horrifying headless corpse hunched over Ichabod's sprawled form haunt you," he snarled against Rip's ear, "as they do me."

Rip's watering eyes locked on Ireland, shouting an unspoken plea that she answered with a resolute nod.

"We fought with all we had." Pressing his face to Rip's cheek, Young Rip seemed oblivious to the tears that streaked the wheezing man's face. "As if broken fence posts were any sort of weapon against hell's favorite pet. Yet *she* claimed him. Stole his head while we were powerless to do anything except watch in abject horror!"

"He's rewriting history." Ducking her head to catch his eye, Ireland purposely ignored the ranting essence and addressed Rip directly. "*You* guided me. For that I am so *very* appreciative, because I know I couldn't have survived this without you. Please, don't let him cloud the truth we worked so hard for."

"Enough of this!" Young Rip released his older counterpart, casting him into the circle of space between them.

His beard clinging to his sweat soaked skin, Rip eagerly filled his lungs by the gulp.

"I extended this proposition to you only because we share blood. In my mind that made you my brother. However ..." Young Rip turned to Ireland with a murderous gaze, the pupils of his eyes dilating to thick pits of tar hungry to consume. "I offered only as a courtesy. I have fulfilled the mission binding me to deliver you here—wherever this is. In exchange I have been granted corporeal form." Throwing his arms out, he turned to address each of them one by one. "All can join me, or burn alongside her. The choice lies with each man."

"Congrats on the new legs, Lieutenant Dan." Noah ducked his head, casually rubbing the back of his neck beneath his hairline. "But where the redhead goes, I follow."

"Me too." Ridley let one shoulder rise and fall. "If for no other reason than the fantastic view."

Noah's head lulled to the side, shooting him a glare of annoyance. "Think you can agree with me in a way that *doesn't* make me wanna punch you in the face?"

"It's doubtful," Ridley admitted, his face reading genuine apology.

"Have it your way!" Young Rip sneered. A geyser of black smoke festered beneath his feet, elevating him on its ominous pedestal. "You *all* deserve to die by the very hand you clamor to kiss. Fortunately, I will grant mercy enough to spare you that fate!"

His arms rose with the swell of darkness. Hoisting. Coaxing. Encouraging it to new heights before his head tipped in Ireland's direction, a lethal smile lacing across his face.

"How does that thing do against smoke?" The first traces of unease snuck into Noah's tone as he nodded at her sword.

"We're about to find out!" Ireland barely got the words out before man and mist arced back in a reptilian roll ... and struck.

Throwing his shoulder in, Young Rip slammed into her mid-section, forcing the air from her lungs. Her sword clanked to the ground, stolen from her grasp the moment her head cracked against the unyielding tile floor. Spots popped and swirled before her eyes, pain blooming at the base of her skull where her wound from Lenore reopened. Desperate to reclaim her breath, she forced air into her lungs only to choke on the dust cloud they had kicked up.

"Ireland! Take your cloak!" Noah's cry came muffled and warbled, as if he was shouting through water.

Young Rip's full weight bore down against her. His face contorted with rage, lips peeling back to expose rotted teeth set in a ravenous snarl. "*I know what you are*! I have seen your true face! You are the Mistress of Death, bringing despair to all the lives you touch! If you *truly* care for any of these men, lay down your life now and spare them all your shroud of misery!"

Wedging her forearms between them, Ireland strained with all she had. The tendons of her neck bulged, the veins of her face threatening to pop. Strength, which could only be described as demonically charged, allowed the enraged being to press in harder still. Turning her face from the rancid breath assaulting her, Ireland caught a glimpse of Noah creeping in. Her cloak clutched firmly in his hand.

"*Noah, stay back*!" she screamed to be heard over the roaring in her mind. "I can't trust myself to unleash him here! It's too risky for *all* of you!"

"A noble monster is it?" Craning his neck, Young Rip forced her to meet his stare. "I wonder if that boy you murdered thought so. Did he call for his mommy? Beg to be spared before you embedded your axe in his spine?"

Noah ignored her warning and lunged, snapping her cloak open and ready. Ridley dove to stop him, snatching a corner of the fabric and yanking it back. Voices rose; their debate quickly becoming heated. Above her came a jolting shudder as Rip launched himself onto the back of Young Rip. Wrapping his wiry arms around his youthful doppelganger's neck, he thrashed and twisted in his best attempt to free her from his clutches.

Unfortunately, none of this mayhem reached Ireland. She was already gone; transported by a simple look. The pits of hell awaited in Young Rip's irises. One direct glance and she was sucked through their scorching ring of fire and plunged into the depths of madness.

26

EDGAR

The porcelain teacups were unusually heavy on the tray. Their burden weighed them down like a loaded pistol cocked and ready to fire. Desire to fling his entire cargo against the wall rose, Edgar only managing to squelch it by biting the inside of his cheek hard enough to taste the coppery rush of blood. He had poured the amber liquid with trembling hands, all the while praying for another alternative to reveal itself. None did. Instead Edgar found himself peering into the unknown, fearing and doubting his own motivations while anguish seized his heart in a crushing grip.

"Edgar!" Lenore called from the veranda. "The sun is setting in the most gorgeous display! Come watch it with me!"

Tray in hand, he trudged across the house. His lead feet dragged him forward as if bound for the hangman's noose. His spirit lifted, in the most bittersweet of ways, the moment his gaze fell upon her. Gilded light from the low resting sun illuminated the room, adorning Lenore with a haloed radiance. Hair like spun gold, danced over her shoulders in the faint breeze. Sleep had worked its healing magic over the last week. Only a trace of the gouge over her eye could be seen. The scar on her cheek reduced to a mere shadow. The fractional bit of beauty death had stolen from her had been restored—at least externally.

"Hurry, sit!" Taking the tray from his hands and easing it down on the table, she bubbled her enthusiasm like a giddy child.

Edgar took a step toward the spot reserved for him, only to have his gelatin legs fold beneath him. Splayed on his knees before his queen, he gathered her hands in his and pressed them to his face as if in prayer.

"From the second my gaze first fell upon thee, you claimed my heart." Barely contained emotion clipped his words to a raspy tremor. "Even in my grave, all will not be lost. For my soul will still ache for you."

Retracting one icy hand from his grasp, Lenore brushed her fingers across his jaw line in a delicate caress. "I would never doubt otherwise, nor do I believe there is a force on this earth strong enough to tear us apart. Even so, why do such dark thoughts plague you, my darling?"

"My own inadequacies make me a failure unworthy of you and—" his voice breaking, Edgar swallowed hard and tried again, "—for that I am forever sorry."

Bronze light from the sinking sun reflected off Lenore's pale skin in an enchanting illusion that she glowed from within. With one finger under his chin, she tipped his face to hers. "You have *never* failed me, Edgar. You love me with every fiber of your being and I beg you not to apologize for that. In your eyes I see the depth of your devotion and it renders the meager word 'love' insignificant."

Edgar squeezed his eyes shut and leaned in to her touch, nuzzling into the palm of her hand.

Too soon for his liking, Lenore retracted both her hands and rested them daintily atop her knees. "Now then, the sky is a lovely painted canvas. I wish to enjoy it with a strong arm holding me tight and I have found yours to be a perfect fit for the task, n'est-ce pas?"

"How could I deny such a request?" Edgar attempted a smile despite the ache of his crippled heart. Arranging himself onto the settee, he draped an arm around her and guided her head to his shoulder. Reveling in the sweet torment of her body pressed to his, he gazed out at the haphazard brush strokes of pink, purple, orange, and yellow that zigzagged across the sky.

Beside him, Lenore reached for her cup … and the world slowed. No longer could Edgar linger in the moment's perfection. Hell's reign was about to descend upon his life. The dainty cup met her lips in a tender kiss, russet liquid spilling into her mouth.

He forced himself to look away, the urge to slap the cup away and suck the tainted liquid from those red, supple lips growing too strong to bear. He clasped his hand down on his knee to steady his leg that began to shake with anxious jitters. With slow, leisurely sips she drained the cup. Each one taking a blink—or a lifetime. Then, flicking her tongue across her top lip to relish the lingering sweetness, she returned the empty cup to the table.

The effects of the dogwood did not take long. They never did. Yawns hidden behind the back of her hand; blinks made long by heavy lids. Like a contented cat she curled against him, her rhythmic breathing purring from parted lips.

Burying his face in her hair, Edgar breathed in her mingling floral scent and let his tears slip free. Twilight's brisk breath slapped against him, sending icy prickles through his hollowed core. The time had come, he knew by the atmosphere of sorrow he breathed in. Extracting himself from beneath Lenore's sleeping frame, he allowed his body to be ravaged by one more anguished sob. Then, wiping his face on the back of his hand, he capped his emotions tight and forced himself to task.

The chirp of the crickets pounded into Edgar's already throbbing head with the potency of driven railroad spikes as he crossed the yard to his work shed to retrieve his pry bar. With each step he prayed for divine intervention. Yet, the sky did not open allowing an angel to descend. The shrubberies remained silent and devoid of guiding flames. Perhaps God had indeed forsaken him for utilizing a curse that went against the natural order of things.

Or, Edgar contemplated as his hand closed around the cold, iron bar, *perchance religion had simply evolved out of fraud, fear, greed, imagination, and poetry.*

Meaning he truly *was* alone.

Weighing the bar in his sweat dampened hands, Edgar spun on his heel and marched back to the house, leaving the shed door open and creaking on the hinges behind him. He could hear his father's gruff voice in the back of his mind, clear as if he stood beside him, belittling him for taking the coward's way out. That may have been true, yet he could see no other way.

Stalking through the veranda to the main living quarters, Edgar purposely averted his gaze from Lenore's slumped silhouette. His waning conviction could afford no further distraction. Wood scuffed over wood as he hooked his forearm under the back of her rocking chair to scoot it aside. The floor boards were loosened, the nails removed in preparation. Wiggling the pry bar between the planks, it took little more than the flick of his wrist to pop them free. Palming each section, he stacked them in a neat pile behind him.

The fruits of his labor appeared in the gaping hole beneath him. A hand built coffin, assembled with fresh dogwood, lay in wait that he had toiled over night after night. He drained the last of his savings to buy the lumber and have it delivered in the late evening hours. Forgoing sleep, he had ignored aching muscles and extreme exhaustion, and pushed on: building the box and lid, digging the hole, preparing her tomb, then hiding all his labors as the sun rose and her soft snores grew light before her wake. Now, the time had come to put his efforts to use and he could not loathe them more. He knew he was doing the right thing. The spirits had manipulated her once and they *would* do it again. Even so, he dubbed himself a heinous weakling for not being able to protect the one being whose life he treasured more than his own.

Far too soon, he was gathering his beauty in his arms. Her long, luxurious hair tickled over his arm in a cascade of yellow waves, her face falling toward his chest. Staring down at her, he ached for her eyes to flutter open that he may dive into those pools of violet paradise once more. Unfortunately, such a fantastical plunge would not be granted. He had ensured that by doubling the dose of dogwood in her evening cup of tea. Experience taught him that under its effects she would not rouse for a full night, no matter what kind of ruckus he made—and tearing up the floor to dig the enormous hole had not been a quiet endeavor.

Cradling her like a delicate newborn, Edgar eased her slight frame down into the dogwood box. Tears snuck from his lids in an unstoppable current, dotting the front of her dressing gown. Carefully, he arranged her hair around her shoulders and folded her arms over her chest in the same fashion she had been positioned in her first casket. The one she never should have risen from.

Stealing her pillow from their bed, he claimed the pillowcase that held her scent, and respectfully slid the pillow under her head. A quick shake snapped the wrinkles from her favorite quilt before he draped it over her and lovingly tucked it in around her legs. As he worked, her soft breath warmed his cheek—chipping away at his resolution. His weak and trembling arms gave, sending the broken shell of a man crumbling down on top of his sleeping love. Clinging to her, he let her heart beat a steady chorus in his ear as he soaked her gown with his gushing emotion.

"Forgive me," he wept. "I am a weak man. I-I cannot live in a world without you in it." Tipping his head to gaze upon her, he indulged himself by brushing the back of his hand across her velvet cheek. "It is the monster that *I* planted within you that must be stopped. If I can find a way to reverse what I have done without harming your sweet soul, I *will* be back. I promise you that."

Bending his face to hers, he let his lips meet hers in one last, tender kiss.

"I love you, Lenore Reynolds, my beautiful flower," he breathed the sentiment into her.

Numb from the ache of his shattered heart, Edgar pulled himself from the coffin. Never to suffer this loss would never to have been blessed by her in his life at all, and that he could not fathom. His last look at his golden angel came as the coffin lid slid into place ... and he hammered the first nail in.

Every swing of the hammer. Every shovelful of dirt that rained down on her tomb. Every floorboard replaced, Edgar felt with crippling anguish. His heart had been ripped from its cavity and buried alongside her. The villainous hand responsible? His own.

When the last plank of wood flooring had been returned to its rightful place, Edgar collapsed in a quivering heap. Tears puddled beneath his head and seeped between those same boards.

"B-b-buried her deep, didn't ya, Eddie?" Edgar didn't have the energy to flinch at the familiar sound of Dougie's voice, he simply tilted his head toward him. "With her covered by Earth it seems you and I are free to play again and I have got some *wonderful* games in store! Buck up, Edgar! It's time for you to shake off that horrible infliction of sanity and join me in madness—by choice or force. Either way the end result will be the same!"

Edgar's forehead thudded back against the floor, a faint noise beneath him causing a fresh shiver to creep down his spine. Muffled by the boards came the unmistakable *thump, thump, thump* of Lenore's beating heart.

27

Ridley

Spiraling in an endless free fall, cast there by Young Rip's hypnotic gaze. The earth itself swallowed Ireland whole, with the impending threat to belch her out at Lucifer's door. Tortured wails trumpeted her arrival, welcoming her to the tavern of the damned. The monster within her squirmed and writhed, recognizing each and every howling voice as belonging to one of his victims. It was in that moment that Ireland fully comprehended the bitter truth; she was slotted to burn for *his* sins.

The space around her tapered in, like an enormous rabbit hole. The soil itself expanded and contracted in eager pants at the infamous, long awaited arrival. Tufts of dirt exploded from the walls, stone and debris raining down from all sides, pushed out by clawed hands that punched their way through. Ashen, decayed flesh—cracked and oozing at the knuckles—grappled for her, hungry to tear off a pound of flesh in retribution for the lives the Horseman stole from them. Fighting back or fending them off never crossed Ireland's mind. While most of the crimes that claimed their lives had *not* been hers, it was a just punishment for the fault she *did* own. Hoping for penance through martyrdom, Ireland spread her arms wide and leaned back into her free fall. Handfuls of hair, scraps of fabric, layers of skin: anything those talon-like hands could catch hold of was viciously ripped away. Raw thirst for vengeance tore away her mundane disguise, revealing the blue-lipped, veiny-faced monster beneath. She once thought herself tragically beautifully in the throes of her transformation—an intricate sugar skull come to life. The naivety of that was tragically laughable. There was no loveliness here. Only pretty petals meant to lure prey to a venomous flower.

Was it that realization, or merely a coincidence of timing, that the ground picked that moment to swell and cradle her? The shrieking abruptly stopped. The hands dissipated into nothingness, leaving behind only the memory of their volatile touch. Ireland huddled in a heap on the floor. Her trembling, blood-streaked hands rubbed the length of her shivering arms. Twitching at the faint touch of her own hair tickling across the back of her neck, she flipped her head up, her gaze traveling one direction then the other.

Blackness—as far as the eye could see. An all-consuming abyss where hope itself could not venture.

"H-hello?" she called to no one. Fear cracked her words, advertising the vulnerability she could no longer hide behind a wry smile and quippy comment.

Hot breath sizzled over her bare shoulder where her shirt had been torn away, a gruff voice whispering her name, "*Ireland.*"

Forcing herself up on wavering legs, she spun at the sound to find ... no one. Yet icy fingertips of dread, tapping up and down her spine, assured her she wasn't alone. Covering her exposed chest with the remnant fabric of her shirt, Ireland turned in a slow circle. Her steps pulled up short at the unmistakable flutter of movement in the distance. An awkward stuttering beat seized her heart before launching the palpitating muscle into a jackhammer rhythm that pounded against her ribs. Self-preservation inched her back, her weary and battered muscles tensing to bolt.

"Ireland, don't run," a familiar voice softly urged. Ireland's breath caught as her father stepped from the shadows dressed in a three piece suit she thought he'd long since burned.

"Daddy?" Instinctively she stepped closer, and paused. Her mouth opening and shutting, searching for the right question through the sea of them plaguing her. "W-where are we?"

Tipping his head, Warren Crane fixed his handsome face into the stern mask he wore only when truly disappointed. "You *know* where we are, and what we have to do." With no further explanation, he offered her his hand.

He was strength.

He was security.

He was her salvation from this dismal fate.

Believing those all to be stark facts, Ireland didn't hesitate to curl her fingers around his. Gradually, he pulled her to him, his hand tightening around hers to the point of bone crushing pain.

Wincing and recoiling, Ireland's parched lips parted in a complaint she couldn't force from her tongue. That hunk of pink, wriggly meat was rendered useless by one glance into her father's eyes. The love that had always been there—no matter what juvenile atrocity she'd committed—was gone, replaced by frosty indifference.

Noticing her hesitation, Warren closed the distance between them. His free hand grasped her upper arm, giving it a slight rub of comfort with his thumb. "My girl, once so sweet and loving. *What have you become*?" Wrenching both her arms behind her back, hatred morphed his face unrecognizable.

"Don't talk to it," a voice she would know anywhere snapped in here ear. Ireland's mother clasped her only daughter's wrists and forced her back against a tall stake.

"Mommy, please!" Tears welled behind Ireland's eyes, spilling down her cheeks and dripping from her chin. "It's me! *It's still me!*"

"My *daughter*," Diana Crane explained, tying a thick rope around Ireland's wrist and yanking it tight enough to dig valleys into her injured flesh, "died the very second that *thing* infected her."

Task complete, Diana joined her husband in front of the brush pile pedestal that slithered from the ground beneath Ireland's bare and bleeding feet. The couple clasped hands, staring up at her like a lowly insect that must be squashed. The darkness churned behind them, taking the shape of more bodies: Noah, Ridley, Rip, and her assistant Amber. All people she cared for deeply, all peering up at her with open distain.

Noah stepped to the front of the crowd, sliding a stainless steel lighter from his front pocket. Holding it beneath his chin, he sparked it to life, the orange glow casting eerie shadows over the sharp angles of his face. "Now, it's time for *you* to die along with her."

Ireland fought against the rope, rubbing her skin raw. Noah casually flicked his wrist and cast the lighter onto the brush pile. The dry wood instantly ignited. Its fervent blaze snapping and crackling, ravenous for their offering. Flames licked up her legs, shooting flares of sparking delight high into the inky darkness.

Ireland's head fell back, a guttural scream of absolute agony tearing from her chest. Smoke burned down her esophagus, scorching her lungs. Through tearing eyes she watched the faces of those she loved disappear behind a wall of smoke and flame, her flesh blistering and bubbling from her bones while they watched. Thrashing. Struggling. Begging for the mercy of the end. For peace to finally descend.

Then, her eyes snapped opened … to a fresh hell.

Heavy drops drip, drip, dripping down in a steady stream. Their unforgiving splotch of gore pooled on Ireland's shirt, soaking through the fabric to dampen her skin beneath. The second her eyes fluttered open a shocked yelp lodged in her throat. Blinking hard, she tried to change the truth staring back at her. It was no longer Young Rip that hovered over her, but Rip himself. Her guide. Her mentor. *Her friend*. With her sword buried to the hilt in his gut, its blood covered blade protruded from his back. The hand responsible for wielding such a strike? If circumstance was true … her own.

"No! Rip, no!" Ireland pushed herself up to sitting, catching Rip's head with her forearm as it lulled to the side. A trickle of blood escaped his parted lip, staining a pink stripe through his grey beard. Her sword bearing hand flitted like a nervous butterfly in desperate indecision over whether or not to attempt to pull out the blade.

"Leave it in," Noah rasped, dropping to his knee beside her. Light from the subway exit up ahead filtered in to reveal his complexion drained chalky white. "If you pull it out he'll bleed to death in seconds."

Ireland gathered Rip in the cradle of her arms, loosening her grip when he cringed at the jostling. "What happened? How did I—?"

"It wasn't you," Rip gurgled, blood splattering from his lips.

"Whatever that other Rip was doing to you, wherever he took you in your mind, it was killing you." Noah raked a hand through his hair, his tone rising and falling with audible self-loathing. "You were screaming ... choking. I-I had no choice. Before it could get any worse, I tossed the cloak over you ..."

Ireland's pulse thumped in her temples, misery squeezing her heart and puncturing it with talons of truth. "And invited the Hessian in," she finished for him, rogue tears zigzagging down her cheeks.

"Your sword slid into your hand in that way it does." Noah's brow pinched tight, his head shaking side to side as he struggled to make sense of any of this. "You moved so fast. One blink and it was buried in him."

"*Why*? Why would I *ever* stab Rip?" Ireland posed the question more to the beast within her with blood soaked hands than anyone in the room.

Rip's head twitched in a meager attempt to deny her statement. "You … didn't."

A spark of hope flared in her chest, hungry for the right bite of air to feed it into a flame. "I-I didn't?"

"No." A bothersome lock of hair fell into Noah's eyes that he moved with a flick of his head. "You stabbed the younger Rip. But, the very second the blade slipped in," swallowing hard, he forced himself to spit the bitter words out, "they merged."

And just like that Fate licked its thumb and pinched out Ireland's flickering match of hope.

"Then, this *is* on me." Grinding her teeth to the point of pain, Ireland's tear-blurred gaze wandered to the crimson soaked fabric that surrounded the base of the sword. A sudden idea snapped her head up. Pivoting her head one way then the other, she searched darkness. "Ridley! Where's Ridley? If the worst happens—"

"No!" Rip snapped with as stern a resolution as he could muster. "If it is my time, you have to let me go."

"He sent him away," Noah explained in a barely audible whisper. "Told him to go find help. All we can do now is wait."

"Like hell it is." Shifting Rip off of her left arm, Ireland reached behind her to grasp her cloak that had slipped off when she sat up. "Help me throw this around my shoulders."

"I know this is about more than a sudden chill. You don't call on *him* lightly." Scooting closer to meet her request, the thick tread of Noah's work boots scuffed across the floor. "So, what's your plan?"

"I'll go Hessian, and Regen will come," Ireland explained, adjusting the fabric as Noah swept it around her shoulders. "Then, you're going to help me get Rip onto his back. We will gallop at proverbial balls-to-the-wall speed and get him help."

"I've hung around you long enough to know there's nothing proverbial about your balls." Noah's head turned at the incoming thunder of hoofbeats. "You have a gigantic titanium set, but in this situation I don't think it's going to be enough."

Unraveling her arms from around him, Ireland examined Rip with a critical eye. "The most important element is going to be keeping his core steady."

Rip's pale lips parted to murmur, "Ireland."

If she heard him, her mind was clicking away at too many decibels per minute for it to register. "If the blade jostles too much it'll do more damage. Maybe you could take his head and shoulders, and I'll take his legs? We'll have to practically lift him over our heads to get him on Regen's back, but it could—"

"Child, *stop*. Be still." Rip's attempt at a commanding tone was chased off by a powerful coughing fit that shook his slight frame and left him grimacing in pain.

Gently, Ireland rolled him to the side to help clear his airway. Bloody phlegm bubbled from his lips, which he spat onto the ground. "I'll be still once you're up and around and weirding me out with your old guy antics."

Noah edged up beside her, the warmth of his arm brushing against hers. "He doesn't want this, Ireland. You need to listen."

His rattling cough easing to a labored rhythm, Ireland rotated Rip back with visibly shaking hands and pressed on. "We don't want to shove the blade in further—if that's possible, I buried it deep—but if you hook your hands under his pits and hoist him up …"

Her orchestrating efforts were derailed by the rise of Rip's trembling hand, and his clammy palm pressing to her cheek.

"Ireland, please stop." His dry, sandpaper tongue dragged across his lips. His words, weak and fading, seeming to act as the last granules of sand sifting through his hourglass. "I need you to know. In my eyes you … will always be … a hero."

His sentiment trailed off, the light behind his eyes slowly fading. Ireland placed both her hands over Rip's, anchoring him to her if only for a moment longer. "Stay with me, buddy. I ... can't do this without you."

Regen galloped up behind her, announcing his arrival with a snort and toss of his regel head. Rushing in with the stallion came a strong gust of wind, blustering down the tunnel. It settled over Rip's frame, tussling his beard and tossing the course hair off his forehead, as his gaze fixed on a great beyond he alone could see. A slight smile curled the corner of his lips and held. With the gentle, loving caress of a mother's touch that same wind reclaimed the surplus of years loaned to him. The peachy hue of his skin faded with his very essence, reducing him to an ash molding of himself. Not unlike the statue she'd first believed him to be.

Ireland's face crumbled, a spigot of free flowing tears gushing passed her lids. Once more the gust churned, delicately whispering to the sleeping New Englander that his journey was not yet over. The breeze caught the particles that once defined him, and swirled them up, up, up in a jovial corkscrew overhead before setting off on a voyage wherever the wind would take him.

Noah's hand curled around Ireland's shuddering shoulder. Pulling her to him, he enveloped her in the security of his arms as her body dissolved in soul crushing sobs. As if sensing his totem's sorrow, Regen nudged Ireland's back. His hot breath in her ear acted as an equine message of love. The comfort of their contact became mandatory for Ireland to draw a breath through her gutted core.

"I got a cell phone." Thudding down the stairs covered in a light sheen of sweat, Ridley brandished the little black device high over his head. "I'm pretty sure the old woman I took it from, that spoke *very* little English, thought I was robbing her. But I got it!"

Noah's hand weaved into Ireland's hair, his lips brushing the top of her head. "It's too late."

"It is?" Raven brows drew together in confusion, Ridley's gaze flicking to the pillared archway to the right of them. "Oh. I saw … and I didn't realize …"

Abruptly, Ireland pushed herself away from Noah, wiping her face with the back of her hand. "What else did you see up there? Young …" saying his name was a knife in the heart she made herself endure, "… *Rip* said that this was the place we were looking for."

"It's mostly old, residential housing occupied by overly trusting elderly people." Ridley raised the phone as a case in point. "*But* then there's the country club, currently closed for renovations."

The implied weight of that 'but' hoisted Ireland to her feet. Her spine straightened, her cloak rippling down her back and into place. Skin tightened over bone. Nerves set on edge with barely contained power. The Horseman stirred, only this time Ireland had no problem holding him back. This was *her* fight. "What about the country club?"

Noah rose with her, his lips pressed in a thin white line of unease. "Ireland, you don't have to do this right now. After everything that's happened, it's okay to give yourself a minute here."

Her hand rose to silence him, then curled into a tight fist of brewing, bubbling aggression. "What about the country club?" Each word was punched out slow and deliberate.

"I didn't see Lenore," Ridley clarified, his palms raised to halt that idea before anyone could roll with it. "But I was told she was there ... *somewhere.*"

"Who told you this?" Ireland forced the words through her clenched jaw.

Ridley's weary gaze fell to the floor. When he glanced back up it was from under his lowered brow. "The men she killed. Apparently in her heyday she tore five men apart with her bare hands at a party back when the club was still a private residence. Needless to say, while even their lingering spirits showcased what pig-headed oafs they were, they were all more than willing to have a hand in bringing her down."

Wordlessly, Ireland strode to Regen's side. The stallion eagerly pivoted to receive her. Sliding her foot into the stirr-up, she hoisted herself astride, the leather saddle creaking as she settled in. Gathering the reins in one hand, she extended the other to Ridley. "I'm going to need your help to find her."

"Gladly, m'lady." Linking his hand with hers, he bounced with her boost and heaved himself up behind her.

Ireland guided Regen's head around, the metal of his curb chain meeting with a soft clink. Before she could spur him forward even a stride, Noah positioned himself dead center between them and the exit.

"The last time you took her on she nearly killed you." His nostrils flared, his chest rising and falling with ragged breaths. "Are you just choosing to overlook that fact?"

"She didn't have *me* last time," Ridley offered, his hands sliding down to rest loosely on Ireland's hips. "Poe himself told me it will take both of us to stop her."

"See?" Ireland retreated beneath the shadows of her hood, and gathered the reins in a two-handed grip. "We have a plan."

Noah shoved his hands in his pockets, his chest puffing in a display of masculine bravado that was vastly contradicted by the fear and hurt playing across his features. "And what about us dreary mortals? Where do we fit into this 'plan'?"

Wetting her lips, Ireland forced her catching breath into the semblance of a neutral pattern. Her vision in the hospital had been true. She *was* death. And if Noah stayed, her curse would claim him, just as it had Rip. Her own feelings paled in comparison to that.

Digging deep, she imitated the Hessian's low-demonic rattle with a striking similarity. "Go back to Sleepy Hollow, Van Tassel. There's no place for you here."

A light tap to his sides and Regen lurched forward, nimbly darting around Noah to launch them up the steep exit stairs and out into the fading day sun.

28

Ridley

There was no denying it. The Hessian was crying. Ridley cleared his throat and shifted awkwardly on Regen's haunches as yet another tear dripped down onto his hand strung loose around her middle. Her openly weeping *may* have made her somewhat less intimidating if it wasn't for the blood-stained axe handle banging a painful reminder of its threat against his knee.

The sky was an expansive canvas of vibrant oranges and deep purples. Long shadows stretched across the ground as the sun bowed its head to brother moon. Adjusting his grip around the flowing folds of Ireland's cloak, Ridley gave a nod of greeting to an old man seated on his rickety porch swing.

"Damn horse better not poop in my yard!" the old man scowled in place of a greeting. Turning away with a huff, he returned to his task of acting as a broom-wielding sentry to protect his trashcans from hooligans.

In its heyday the community they galloped through must have been a sight to see with its rows of steep rooflines, gingerbread trim, and wraparound porches. Yet time had ravaged its beauty like a crumpled old crone. Still, its charm could easily be restored with a bit of elbow grease and a loving touch. Such revitalization had begun with the country club that swelled from the scenery before them. Framed in expansions jutted from each side of the once regal estate. The plywood walls were covered with white plastic *Tyvek*. Blue tarps protected the roof from the elements, their edges flapping in the light breeze. Broken stain glass windows had been boarded over, awaiting the special shards that would restore their elegance.

Wiping her nose on the back of her hand, Ireland tipped her head in Ridley's direction. "Where are we headed?"

As inconspicuously as possible, Ridley let his gaze twitched to the side. Rip's spirit easily kept pace with the galloping horse. His legs moving out of habit while he hovered about a foot off the ground. "Lenore is around the back, by the pond." Transparent grey eyes flicked from Ridley to Ireland and back again, concern furrowing his brow. "Perhaps you should avoid telling her I'm here. She doesn't seem to be coping well."

Ridley considered the hunched frame in front of him, moving in rhythm with each of the horse's wide strides. Part of him believed that learning she could still communicate with her dearly departed friend could provide her with an iota of relief in this tumultuous time. *Or*, it could push her over the edge straight into a mindless killing spree. Those were not odds he wanted to wager.

"Any day now," Ireland snapped, venom dripping from her tone. "I need a direction."

"To the left," Ridley mumbled, shoving her sheathed sword off his thigh. "She's around back."

If she cued the horse, Ridley didn't see it. The menacing beast seemed to respond to her very thought. Twigs snapped beneath his hooves as the stallion sprinted them across the overgrown landscape at a speed that had Ridley clamoring for a tighter hold around Ireland's middle. Rounding the side of the building, his exuberant gait slowed to a high-footed trot.

There she stood, the once enchanting Lenore. From their distance she appeared an ordinary girl admiring the view. Flaxen locks danced around her shoulders, the ragged lace trim of her nightgown swaying around her shins. She stared out at the small, reed infested pond. The fading sunlight warmed the water to a shimmering golden hue. Along the far edge, two playful swans alternated between ducking their heads under the water and snapping their beaks happily in the air.

Ridley's head cocked at the poetic nature of the scene. "She looks ... serene."

Flipping a leg over Regen's head, Ireland slid to the ground with a soft thump. "She turned The Bronx into a war zone. Killed *one* person we know of, most likely the body count was higher. She doesn't get a free pass."

Ridley followed her lead, stumbling into the knee-high grass with noticeably less grace. "Never suggested otherwise. I make it a point not to argue with unstable women armed to the teeth."

If Ireland heard his suicidally stupid comment, she—thankfully—ignored it. "You go no farther. The rest is up to me." The yearning for violence and mayhem emanated from her pores, vibrating the air around them. Her fingers drummed against the hilt of her sword, her chest rising and falling in eager pants. "Matter of fact, you might wanna run."

She punctuated her warning by drawing both weapons. Her sword hissed from its sheath, the axe handle flipping from its loop into the cradle of her waiting palm. Lowering her chin, Ireland disappeared into the obscurity offered by her hood. Appearing every bit the monster she struggled against, she turned on the heavy-tread heel of her boot and strode headlong toward vengeance—or death.

"You *cannot* let her go!" Rip lurched after her, turning back to Ridley only when he realized he was powerless to stop her himself. "Lenore nearly killed her last time! *Do you wish to see her finish the job?*"

"Your friend is quite right." Poe's essence glided out from behind a skeletal looking tree, its bare branches clawing toward the heavens. The manic persona history knew him for had been replaced by calm self-awareness. "By herself she lacks the capability to stop Lenore. Halt her now, or watch her die. The choice is yours."

"There is no choice! *Go!*" Rip hollered, stabbing a finger after her.

Ridley's lips disappeared in a tight, white line. "I am *so* going to end up getting stabbed tonight," he grumbled under his breath and took off after her.

Filling his lungs, he said a silent prayer not to lose any extremities and hooked his hand around Ireland's upper arm, spinning her toward him. Mid-rotation she crossed her arms, shaving his neck with the edge of her sword on one side, while her axe pressed dangerously close to his jugular on the other. One scissor-like motion and his head would roll.

Ireland stared hard at the hand holding her, her murderous glare slowly traveling to Ridley's face. "Does that seem wise?"

"About as sound a decision as French kissing a crocodile." Ridley's Adam's apple bobbed beneath the crossed weapons. "But I need you to listen."

"Well done! You got her to stop!" Rip chirped, popping into sight over Ireland's shoulder. "At least momentarily, and with her stubborn streak even *that* is quite commendable."

"I can't risk losing her again, Ridley," tight blue lips murmured from beneath Ireland's hood. "What do you want?"

"I ... uh ..." His wide, panicked eyes flicked to Rip, who offered only a bewildered shrug.

"Tell her she is death," Poe firmly stated, appearing beside Ridley in a chilling rush. "You are life. Together the two of you are unstoppable."

Opening his mouth, Ridley gave Ireland an apologetic smirk before muttering out of the corner of his mouth, "You think *now* is the best time for me to bring that first part up?"

"Ridley?" Ireland tensed up the pressure of her duo blades. Her chin rose to catch his attention. "Perhaps you and your ghostie friends could pick a less *dire* moment for this conference call?"

"*Now*, lad! Say it!" Poe bellowed, his gruff, unearthly tone causing a flock of black birds to flap into flight from their roost in a nearby tree.

"You are death. I am life. Together we are unstoppable," Ridley rambled without pausing to take a breath.

Finally, Ireland's readied arsenal wavered, her razor-sharp blades inching from his flesh. "Where did you hear that? Lenore said something similar right before she gutted me."

Ridley's cheeks puffed to expel a relieved sigh. "Poe. He's here and he wants to help. Since he knows more about Lenore than *any* of us, I think we should give him the floor for a minute."

"That's who you were talking to?" For a fraction of a second Ireland's chin betrayed her by quivering, clouds of sorrow threatening to snuff out the blaze within her stare. "Poe?"

Rip's hand raised behind her. His fingertips traced her shoulder, meaning to offer comfort. Instead his vaporous digits passed right through her. Curling his faulty hand into a tight fist, his bearded chin fell dejected to his chest.

"Yeah," Ridley nodded, the half-truth easily tumbling from his lips in the face of her bleeding emotional anguish. "It was."

Ireland retracted her weapons, metal raking over metal in a whispered shush. "And what suggestions does Mr. Poe have for convincing his beloved to embrace her afterlife with significantly *less* exuberance?"

Ridley's head turned in Poe's direction, his eyebrows raised expectantly. He listened intently, giving brief nods of understanding as the man spoke. The disturbing nature of his directions tensed Ridley's jaw, sharpening his features.

With his hands steepled under his chin, Ridley focused back to Ireland. "My touch grants life, just as Poe's did when he brought Lenore back from the dead. There's only one thing that can alter my affliction..."

Ridley's statement trailed off enough for Ireland to pick up what he was laying down and finish for him, "*My* touch. Because ... I am death."

"You touch me, I touch her, and we hold firm until she gives up this life she was never supposed to have." Raven hair, gleaming purple in twilight's descent, fell into his eyes as Ridley dropped his head to rub his palm over his forehead. "Sounds simple enough."

"Except for the fact that she's not going to let us get anywhere near her." Ireland glanced over her shoulder, to find Lenore wandering further down the bank of the pond. "Our last attempt at girl time didn't end well."

Poe's gaze fixed on Lenore, his features softening as he breathed her in. "She will not permit anyone other than myself near her. However, if you allow me enter your vessel, I can implement a glamor of sorts. She will see you as me."

Ridley raked a hand through his hair, leaving it a disheveled mess. "Didn't you tell me you're the guy that put her in the box? Seems to me she wouldn't be too thrilled to see you."

"My hope is that she will not recall that part," Poe mused, nervously running his forefinger over his mustache. "After all she *was* asleep for it."

"*Hope*?" Ridley's hands curled in the air like he wanted to grab the long dead literary genius and shake some sense into him. "Seeing as *I'm* the guy that has to go slap a hand on your ex, I'd like a little more than *that* to go on!"

Twigs snapped under Ireland's boot as she injected herself into the conversation with a bold step forward. "Time is of the essence here. What is he saying?"

Wetting his lips, Ridley did his best to keep his tone neutral—and minus any sexual undertones. "He … wants to enter me."

An almost smile tugged at one corner of her cobalt lips. "Well, you make him buy you dinner first."

"I had tickets to see *Kinky Boots* on Broadway this weekend," Ridley muttered to himself as he spun to face Poe, "and plans afterwards to meet up with one of the female leads. Yet, here I am, asking the ghost of a mad man how we do this. Do I have to chant? Open my aura? Sacrifice a small woodland animal?"

Poe didn't wait for him to finish his rant. He drifted forward, disappearing within his host. Ridley's hair wafted from his face. A cold chill settled into the very marrow of his bones, bringing with it the full body shivers of an impending bout with the flu. Fresh awareness cloaked his mind with a time he had never known, experiences he never lived. He still stood in the yard of the rundown property, of that he was sure. Ireland was still practically panting her agitation beside him—as if that would somehow speed this process along. Only now, another world was transposed over the top of this one, like a double exposed photograph. Silhouetting the dilapidated home was the ghostly image of the regal manor it had once been. Stained-glass windows, casting shimmering shades of every color imaginable, gleamed against fresh white paint. The landscaping was clipped and sheered with painstaking detail. On the street behind him, spoked carriage wheels crunched over gravel.

Surrounded by spectral loveliness, yet it all paled in comparison to ... *her*. Ridley could feel Edgar's soul reaching for Lenore, the pull she held over him magnetic. His feet shuffled forward as if compelled by a mission all their own, disregarding the overgrown weeds that lashed against his legs and snagged the fabric of what had once been expensive slacks.

"Ridley!" Ireland caught his sleeve between two pinched fingers and tugged him back. To ensure her message was received, she brushed her hood back from her face. "If this starts to go south, I'm pulling you out and handling this *my* way."

"Read that as 'with an excess of violence,'" Rip interjected, his ghostly form twirling the end of his beard with one finger.

"If that happens," Ireland continued, oblivious to the color commentary, "I want you to run like hell and *don't* look back."

Ridley's head tipped, offering her his best attempt at a supportive smile in spite of his own building trepidation. "Nothing bad is going to happen."

Loosening her death grip on the hilt of her sword, she raised her fingers to stop him. "Just … if it does."

Beside her Rip's shoulder sagged, his hands plunging deep into the pockets of the last slacks he would ever wear. "She needs this, Ridley," he muttered, each word coated with melancholy. "Please. If only to comfort her."

"Yeah, of course," Ridley said. "Whatever you need."

With a curt nod to coax him on, Ireland retreated back beneath her heavy wool hood.

Ridley watched his foot placement as he crossed the unkempt yard. Startling the homicidal ghoul would *not* be conducive to his mission to get through this with all his limbs intact. Skirting around her in a semi-circle, he approached from the far side to draw Lenore's attentions away from the direction where Ireland cautiously crept in.

With the moment of truth at hand, Ridley filled his lungs and prayed he could manage more than a high-pitched squeak. "Lenore?"

Her neck curved his way with an elegant grace the wading swans could envy.

Through Poe's spotty vision he saw momentary glimpses of the woman she had once been. One blink; a long, flowing curtain of spun gold hair. Another: filthy, matted locks.

"Edgar?" Hopeful recognition flickered across Lenore's lovely—then ghastly—face. Tentatively she took a step toward him, her tensed posture slightly easing to find a recognizable beacon in a universe of strange. "Wh-what is this place? It rings of the familiar," her angelic face turned to glance around, granting him a glimpse of the hole rotted through the grey flesh of her cheek, "yet is cloaked in chaos."

While Ridley found himself at a loss and stammering for a method of manipulation to use on the undead, Edgar's essence pushed to the forefront to speak directly to his enchanting queen. "That is because this is no longer our world. Take my hand, my flower. Together, we can leave this place."

Lenore reached for his offered hand, her flawless alabaster fingers flickering with decay. Abruptly, she paused. Confusion puckered her brow. "I woke in a box. Unable to scream. Unable to move. Was that *your* folly, Edgar? Did *you* imprison me in that tomb?"

Out of the corner of his eye, Ridley caught sight of Ireland prowling closer. Her sword swung out in wide practice arcs to one side, then the other, slicing nothing but air—for now.

"No!" Ridley regained control of his senses to scoff at the glowering ghoul. "I would never …"

"T'was I," Poe took over and finished for him. "I cannot and will not fabricate such a jarring truth to you, my darling. That heinous act was indeed committed at *my* hand."

"Son of a bitch," Ridley yelped at the lethal glare Lenore fixed on him, only to have Edgar's powerful essence stifle him back into submission.

"I could not live with myself knowing of the affliction I had bestowed upon you. I sought protection for you whilst I hunted for a way to reverse the curse and free you. Now, I have found just that. All you have to do is take my hand and we shall move on—together." In spite of her flaring nostrils and hate filled glare, Edgar offered Lenore his hand a second time.

Black storm clouds of rage eclipsed the purple moons of her irises. Grey, cracked lips curled from her teeth in a menacing snarl. "*You buried me in the ground.*"

Her body angled, Ireland neared with stealthy side-steps. The shadows of her cloak could not hide her violent intent as she crossed her weapons in front of her, poised for battle.

"I did," Edgar answered with the right combination of apologetic calm, even though his host's pulse was pounding through his veins. "It was an act of desperation, one I committed purely out of love."

"Love?" A grave rattle reverberated from the depths of Lenore's darkened soul. Her hands clenching into unforgiving claws at her sides. "*That* is your definition of love? Trapped down there, praying for death. It whispered and taunted, yet never claimed me. You profess *that* to be love?"

Bile rose in the back of Ridley's throat at the brown ooze that seeped from the flaking flesh of her cheek. "It was far more humane than what would have become of you had anyone learned of what transpired here at this very residence," Edgar continued to answer for him.

"*Mercy*, was it?" Lenore practically spat. Taking a threatening step closer, she treated Ridley to a frightening glimpse of her pupils dilating. Her eyes transformed into swells of writhing black despair. "Perhaps I should return that same gesture?"

Ireland adjusted her grip on her weapons, steadily moving into striking distance.

"You could," it was Edgar's spirit that straightened Ridley's cowering spine, "strike true and fair in a vengeance that would be just. Even so, I am confident you will not."

His bold statement was punctuated by Ridley's involuntary whimper.

Lenore cocked her head to taunt, "Bold words from a visibly trembling man."

Ridley's chest swelled with purpose granted to him by Poe's mission of redemption. "I tremble not of fear, but of joy. To see your face, to hear your voice after years of longing is a bliss the likes of which the throne of Heaven could not compare. I tremble to hold you once again. After years of solitude, left alone with thoughts of what we had, I believe that to be your desire as well. Why else would you have been tirelessly searching for me?"

"Revenge is as good a motivator as any," she sneered.

Finally positioned directly behind the glowering corpse, Ireland drew back to strike.

This time it was under Ridley's own control that his hand rose to halt her advance. Edgar quickly claimed the gesture in his attempt to plead to the softer side of Lenore, that may have been left in her dogwood coffin. "I sought you out, my flower. I am not hiding. Here I am. Do what you will, knowing I am now, and will always, be yours."

Lenore stalked closer, daggers of devilish intent radiating from her glare. Ridley's breath caught, wavering to claim a rhythm, while Poe tipped his chin skyward to offer Lenore his throat. Nails, grown to razor-sharp talons, drew alongside her face. Her fore and middle fingers wiggled back and forth, as if eagerly twitching for a kill. Ireland matched her step, her silver blade gleaming in the rising moonlight. Still, Ridley silently pleaded with her wait.

The tips of Lenore's icy fingers brushed his cheek, her clammy palm cradling his face. She moved in body skimming close. The rancid, stale air trapped in her long dead lungs assaulting his senses. Ridley jerked back as she rose up on tip-toe and pressed her putrefied lips to his.

Bony hands, covered with a thin veil of flesh, weaved into his hair, prompting an unintentional dry heave. The slab of rubbery flesh that had once been her pink, wriggly tongue forced its way between his lips, flicking over his teeth and twining with his own unresponsive counterpart. Every fiber of his being wanted to forcibly shove her away and heave the contents of his stomach into the yard. Unfortunately, Poe was goal oriented enough not to allow such a veer from their task. Taking control of Ridley's appendages, he wrapped one arm around her waist, feeling each vertebrate protruding from her back as he held her body to his.

Sweeping the other arm under Lenore's armpit, he flailed wildly for Ireland's hand.

Ireland's prepped weapons fell, her nose crinkling in disgust. "That's ... committing to a cause," she muttered under her breath.

Ridley's fingers snapped, his splayed fingers demanding hers.

"Oh, right!" Holstering both her weapons, Ireland took a deep cleansing breath and took his hand.

Lenore's eyes popped open the second their skin made contact. Her appreciative sigh of pleasure morphing into a choked gasp. Slapping her palms to Ridley's chest, she pushed and flailed against him.   Finding her monstrous strength suddenly zapped, she was helplessly at his mercy. Black veins bulged beneath the surface of her skin, her violet eyes rolling back. Her legs buckling beneath her, Ridley held her tight against him and eased her withering frame toward the ground. The fight left her body, her clawed hands curling to her chest. Gently, Ridley guided her down, oblivious to the extreme sensitivity of her skin until it brushed the thick brush beneath her and popped her like an over-filled water balloon.

Goo—reminiscent of ink mixed with raw chicken skin—sloshed over him. A bit of turpentine flavored foulness seeped between his teeth, sliding down his throat. Ridley gagged, his

312

stomach instantly revolting. Fat drops of sludge dripped from his hair, hunks of unnamable nastiness caught in his lashes. Slowly he righted his posture, trying to decide if he should vomit before or after throwing himself into the pond.

"It's over now, right?" His skin crawling, Ridley fished for the reassurance that there would *never* be a repeat performance of any of this. "Edgar's gone, I assume to escort Lenore wherever she went. So, we did it and I can go home now?"

In place of a response or the slightest acknowledgment of his plight Ireland stuck two fingers into her mouth and whistled. Regen rounded the side of the country club at a wide gait. His neck arched, his muzzle tucked tight to his broad chest as he galloped to collect her. The black mane rippling from his neck with each stride. Adjusting the weapons at her hips, Ireland stalked across the expansive grounds to meet him.

"No, my friend," Rip somberly stated, staring after her. "I fear it's just beginning."

29

EDGAR

"You are the first visitor he has received. You shall soon see why." The young physician pushed his spectacles further up the bridge of his nose and eased the door open into a darkened room. Light seeped in only through one small window well above eye level, particles of dust dancing in the lone beam it cast. "He gets agitated quite easily, and can become volatile. There is an officer stationed outside the door if any issues arise."

Huddled on the floor beside his bed, Edgar peeked up from under the shield of his arm. "Say it, if it is so! I cannot possible begin to know unless you tell me!" Bloodshot eyes bulged, frantically flicking from side-to-side. Spikes of matted hair darted from his head in every direction, a spray of disarray. "Simple rule," he muttered more to himself than his guests, "simple, yet critical."

"My apologies, Edgar," the doctor said with a slight bow of his head. "I *am* accompanied by another party today. I can assure you, he is quite real."

The newcomer's eyebrows rose at the odd statement, his facial expression registering closer to mild amusement than surprise of any kind.

The doctor's questioning gaze shifted from Edgar to his guest and back again, as if mentally placing bets on how each would fare in one another's company. "I will grant you a few moments alone with him, however I must request that you not upset him in anyway. Last night it took four orderlies and myself to restrain him long enough for me to administer a mild sedative."

The heavy set guest smoothed one hand over his mustache, seemingly fending off a grin. "From the plethora of dire warnings you have riddled me with, I can assure you that his state of peaceful serenity has become my top priority."

Bidding him good luck, the doctor showed himself out, the click of the door echoing off the barren walls.

"Edgar, Edgar, Edgar," the man tsked. Grabbing the back of the chair in the corner, he dragged it across the floor to the trembling man's side. "Of all the places for someone with your particular affliction to hide, why in God's name would you choose to join the military? I wager every floor in this hospital alone has the spirit of at least one fallen soldier wandering through it."

315

Twitching his discomfort at the unwanted attention, Edgar turned his face to the wall and traced the groves in the brick with the tip of his finger. "Limbs squirming and wriggling long after being hacked off."

"As I expected." The man nodded as if he understood that inane line of thought perfectly. "Which brings us back to the question of why you would voluntarily enlist? 'Tis no more noble a job than that of a soldier—*except* for by someone like you, Edgar."

"Someone like me?" His shoulders curled in, Edgar cast a leery glance at the presumptuous guest.

One bushy brown eyebrow rose quizzically. "Oh, I am dreadfully sorry. Am I confusing you with *another* young man that sees ghosts and can raise the dead with a simple touch?"

Edgar's mouth fell open in a wide maw, yet could manage no sound.

"Compelling argument. You should consider a career in politics. Now, let us direct this conversation back to *why* you are here." The man leaned forward, resting his elbows on his knees. "Could it be guilt that drove you head long into your own private hell?"

Edgar's eyes rolled 'round their sockets. "Guilt is a human emotion," he rasped. "*I* am the reigning King of the Dead, anointed with a crown of feather and bone."

316

"You are indeed very kingly, cowering there, reeking of your own urine, your majesty. Tell me, then," ducking to the side, the man captured Edgar's wandering stare, "where is your queen? The lovely Lenore?"

One simple word. Two meaningless syllables. String them together and they formed a name so powerful it instantly whipped Edgar's head around, his gaze sharpening. "What do you know of her?"

"I know the world has not seen the last of her." The chair creaked beneath him as the man shifted his weight. "One day she *will* rise from her makeshift grave, an unstoppable plague against mankind. Unless *you* help me prevent that."

Edgar shook his head. Slow at first, but quickly building in speed and urgency until he was frantically flinging it from side-to-side. "*No! No grave! No telltale heart beating 'neath the floorboards!* She *lives*, having left me for a man of higher station. I do not fault her that. I wish her nothing except happiness and a warm hearth."

"Is that so? *Hmm.*" Leaning back in his chair, the man smoothed out the wrinkles of his coat. "I suppose that is a far more appealing story to convince one's self of that than to have buried the woman you loved alive."

Edgar tried, and failed, to blink away the wash of tears that flooded his red-rimmed eyes. "I could never—*would* never

..." A sudden sternness overcoming him, Edgar sprang to his feet. His hands clenched into fists at his sides. *"Who are you? Why have you come here, speaking of such atrocities?"*

"My *given* name is Herbert George, however I doubt that is of any consequence to you. What I *am* is an extensive traveler, of sorts. I have witnessed a great many things on my journeys, and have gained more knowledge than any one man should possess. With that knowledge comes the resolute conviction that a crazed mayhem will be unleashed if Lenore is ever freed ... unless we handle it properly." Herbert George paused, tilting his head to consider the visibly dubious Edgar. "Is it such a farfetched concept that I could obtain such awareness considering your own circumstances? Perhaps, instead, we should trade a bit of explanation for a dash of trust?"

"Will you hush! I am handling this!" Edgar snapped to the vacant space beside him. Filling his lungs, he exhaled through flared nostrils. "What did you have in mind?"

The man's blue eyes narrowed slightly. "Have you ever wondered why Lenore *alone* was able to block the spirits from haunting you?"

His legs threatening to fail him, Edgar eased himself down on the side of his thin mattress. "Yes, of course," he croaked.

"I researched her ancestry quite extensively in search of that answer," Hebert George explained, twiddling his thick

318

thumbs. "It seems Lenore's great, grandmother was a white witch—a pure and good child of the earth. From what I can tell, she past that trait down to the unsuspecting Lenore, who, in turn, safeguarded you from the dark energy that surrounded you. It is quite fascinating really."

The rare smile that curled the corners of Edgar's chapped lips was an awkward fit, yet he allowed it to linger for a moment. He could easily picture Lenore in a white lace gown, living in a small cabin in the woods. She would kneel in her exquisite garden of wild flowers and herbs to collect ingredients in a hand-woven basket to use in healing tonics. Another life. Another world. Another chance.

"She truly was magical," he murmured to himself, his smiling fading into nothingness.

"She was." Hebert George dropped his head for a moment, his expression turning somber when he raised it once more. "And now she is shut in a little wooden box, slowly going mad. You had a very good reason for doing what you did, Edgar—
"

"The images of her spree still haunt me," Edgar interjected and attempted to run his fingers through his hair, stopping when they got tangled in the mess.

"As they would any witness to such ferocity. Which is why we must do what we can to ensure she is never allowed to hurt anyone else."

"How?" Edgar hesitantly asked. "I wish to do her no further harm."

"Nor will we." Hebert George's broad chest swelled, drawing in a deep cleansing breath. "It will not be an easy feat. In fact it will take both of us and a few trusted colleagues of mine to manage it. According to your physician, you can be discharged into capable hands due to your condition. That shall work in our favor. Rumors of her resurrection and the massacre that followed have already begun to spread. That means we need to get in front of the fast moving gossip train and derail it, so to speak. We can hide the truth in plain sight under the guise of freshly penned tales, weaving facts into works of fiction that can be easily dismissed as untruths."

"How do we accomplish such a deception?" Edgar asked, intrigue leaning him into this mysterious stranger.

Hebert George folded his arms over chest. His warm, friendly smile countered by the impish gleam in his ice blue eyes. "Tell me, Mr. Poe, what talent have you for writing?"

Epilogue

"Great work, except for the part where Ridley played tonsil hockey with the undead." Noah commented with a slight lift of his chin. Positioning himself directly in Ireland's path, he hooked his thumbs in the front pockets of his jeans.

The mere sight of him caused her heart to lurch. Unfortunately, that foolish muscle fluttering away in her chest could no longer be trusted. As ideally perfect as Noah was, with his quippy humor, sculpted jaw line, and hazel eyes that flawlessly reflected the sky's indigo hue, there was no place for him beside her. At least not one with a long life expectancy, and she'd be damned before she'd *ever* allow herself to hurt him—or anyone else—again.

He makes you weak, girl, the Horseman purred to his audience of one. *Draw your sword and—*

No! Her own resolute roar echoed off the torturous cell walls of her mind, drowning out his voice altogether. *He will not be harmed!*

To her surprise, the beast fell silent.

Squaring her shoulders, Ireland concentrated on keeping her tone ice cold and aloof. "What are you doing here?"

Biting his lower lip, Noah tried to distract from the smirk tugging at the corners of his mouth. "What because I *didn't* vanish at your blatantly obvious *White Fang* technique? You know, the one where you try to get rid of me under the guise of protecting me? I don't know. It's a mystery why that didn't work."

"Yes!" Sauntering up behind them, Ridley threw his hand in the air, fat drops of black ooze flinging from his arm. "I *knew* that whole scenario seemed oddly familiar!"

Their cavalier attitudes threw gasoline on the fire of Ireland's resolve. Her fingers drummed against the handle of her axe, in a tangible reminder of the new identity that claimed her. One she now had to draw strength from. "You both saw what I did to Rip. I tried to cling to normal, surrounding myself with people I cared about, and *he* paid the price. This is *my* curse. I will *not* allow it to become your death."

"You're right. We *were* there," Noah agreed. His one tentative step forward forced her back three paces. "We saw what happened, and *it wasn't you*! In the same situation, it could've happened to any of us."

"Any of you?" Ireland huffed a humorless laugh, her gaze momentarily drifting skyward. "So, you all have homicidal monsters living inside you, too? Fantastic, we'll set up play dates."

322

Noah opened his mouth to argue, only to snap it shut again. Pausing for a deep, calming breath, he laced his fingers behind his head, his biceps straining against the fabric of his cotton t-shirt sleeves. "You know the cloak clouds your judgment. Why don't you shrug that thing off, and we'll talk this out."

Staring him straight in the eye, Ireland thumbed her clasp free. The fabric rippled into a pool at her feet. Her lips parted, intent on informing him to run for his life, when a bucketful of icy awareness sloshed over her. She hadn't felt the swell of her skin fleshing back out. Her nerves and senses hadn't dulled down to normal levels. Her breath caught. *Nothing* had changed.

Noah's hands fell to his sides. His head and Ridley's volleyed from her, to the cloak, and back again. Their brows puckered in matching looks of confusion.

"W-why didn't you change back?" Noah directed the question to the cloak.

"Maybe it's because you didn't get to kill anyone?" Ridley offered. "We could troll by a prison, find you a truly awful specimen you could—"

"I beg you not to finish that sentence."

"Sorry," Ridley cringed to Noah. "I knew I crossed the line, but couldn't seem to stop. Oh, look, I'm still talking." Pressing his lips in a firm white line, he dropped his stare to the ground.

A hot breath warmed the back of Ireland's neck, Regen having inched up behind her as if sensing her spiraling mood. Reaching a hand over her shoulder, she sought comfort in the tender brush of his velvet soft muzzle.

The mysterious allure of night shadowed Noah's eyes, yet his anxiety was audible in the tremor of his throaty tone. "You're understandably upset by Rip's death. We all are. But if you concentrate on calming down, then maybe—"

"No amount of deep breathing or mediation is going to change facts." A quick sweeping motion and Ireland collected her cloak, fastening it back into place. Regen dipped his head, permitting her to hook her arm around his powerful neck. Once she had a firm hold, he raised up, drawing her feet from the ground. Angling her body, she kicked a leg over his mane and settled into the supple leather saddle.

"I'm almost afraid to ask what you think that fact is," Noah grumbled through grinding teeth.

Retreating into obscurity beneath the fabric of her hood, Ireland hid the pain stamped across her features. "That there *is* no separation anymore. I *am* the monster."

Yanking the reins hard to the side, Ireland coaxed Regen into a sharp turn. Breaking into a full canter, the stallion shook the ground with his thunderous strides, chunks of earth flying from his hooves.

Noah and Ridley stood powerless to do anything except watch The Horseman disappear into the night.

Whistling a merry little melody, his peach and navy necktie flapping out from beneath his black trench coat, the blue-eyed man locked the museum's backdoor behind him.

Ireland watched from her perch up high. Her ebony cloak snapped in the wind behind her, a malevolent entity crackling with its own devilish intent. Regen pawed anxiously against the liquor store roof, patience clearly not a defining characteristic of the resurrected equine. Leaning forward, she scratched his neck, her soft cluck cueing him that it was time. One flip of his mane, lashing enthusiasm against her wrists, and he launched them forward at a speed that stole the breath from her lungs. Ireland kept her stare locked on her target, who spun at the ominous drumming of hoofbeats. Regen whisked them across the roofline, precariously close to the edge, yet neither flinched at the drop-off.

Ireland listened hard, noticing the effect of their echo resounding in the alley below. The sound seemed to shift at their incoming charge, as if abruptly changing direction. Like the true phantom she'd become, the Hessian was everywhere and nowhere all at once.

Riding the shadows.

Claiming the darkness.

Regen bounded off the roof's edge without a fleck of hesitation. His taut muscles outstretched as they soared. Powerful legs bent, absorbing the shock of the fall, to deliver his precious cargo to the ground with a pillow soft landing. Tucking her chin to her chest, Ireland threw herself off his back in a tight tuck formation. She landed in a low crouch, one hand gripping the hilt of her sheathed sword. From beneath the shadows of her hood, she peered out for the man's reaction. If she was going to burn in the eternal hell fires for embodying The Horseman, she might as well enjoy the dramatics of it.

Not one gasp of dread was earned, or even a surprised jerk, nothing except a somewhat bored expression from the blue-eyed man that folded his hands beneath his doughy mid-section. "You did take your dear, sweet time getting here. Didn't you, Ireland?"

With the fluidity of predatory cat, Ireland rose to her feet. Rage bubbled through her, scorching her from the inside out.

"You know me," she rumbled in a demonic purr.

The hilt of her sword hummed with energy as she coaxed it free from the leather that enveloped it. Flipping the blade over her forearm, she caught it in an inverted grasp and lunged. The air left the heavy set man's lungs in a labored gasp, his back slamming against the red brick wall behind him. Pressing the razor sharp edge of her blade to his trachea, the lone light swinging overhead gleamed off the steel like a lone distress flare.

The fingers of her free hand curled into the fabric of his coat, pinning him where he stood. "That should save us some time."

She expected to see fear widen his eyes, for the color to drain from his ruddy complexion. Once more she was met by nonchalance.

His head merely cocked, as if she were a fascinating slide he would like to shove under a microscope and study. "In your Horseman form, no less. I wasn't anticipating that."

"What can I say?" she murmured against his ear. "I made friends with the monster in my head." Twisting the blade beneath his chin, she dimpled the wobbly flesh that hung there. "Now how about if you and I have a nice, long talk about why you've been sneaking in and out of my life, and what it is you know?"

His broad chest shook with a throaty chuckle. "Sneaking? Now that's rich." Pressing his palm against the flat of her blade, he shoved it away and took a brazen side-step around her. "My dear girl, I was *painfully* obvious in my charade. The names alone that I chose should have been a giveaway; Granger, Potter,

Mallark. *All* taken from popular literature of your time. You know, as the actual embodiment of a Washington Irving character, you might want to consider picking up a book on occasion."

With a showy bounce of her palm, Ireland readjusted to a standard grasp. "My free time has been sparse lately, thanks to a ghostly possession *you* seem to know an awful lot about."

"Yes, well." Glancing down at the leather-banded watch on his wrist, he wound it once and then paused to give it a listen. "I would be happy to tell you a bit more about all of that. However, I first must ask that you stow away the sharp and murderous objects."

Knowing it would take nothing more than a simple thought to free either weapon, Ireland showed him her blade and stored it away. Regen snorted and stamped his disapproval behind her.

"For now." A cavalier indifference dripped from the clipped edge of her words. "But if I find out you had *anything* to do with what led to my friend's death, I *will* kill you."

"I can assure you, I had nothing to do with Rip's demise. Even so, his death acted as a tragic catalyst to a necessary string of events to follow." Pulling a knit driving cap from his coat pocket, the man situated it into place on his head. "After all, it brought you here, which is *right* where you need to be."

Ireland rolled her neck, attempting to shake off the red haze of mayhem that crept in around the edges of her vision.

"What about your friend that came with you to Sleepy Hollow in the rent-a-cop Halloween costumes? Did *he* play a part in it?"

Stroking his index finger over his recently shaved lip, the man glanced down the length of the alley. Something that resembled regret flashed across his face. "No," he assured her. "He would never have hurt Rip. The bond they forged during their time in the service together was far too deep for that."

The taut skin of her forehead twitched into the closest she could get to a frown. Rip had told her the story of his time served. He developed a deep brotherhood with *two* men. The first, Ichabod Crane. The other ...

"Washington Irving? I-It can't be," Ireland rasped in a barely audible whisper.

His hands fell limp to his sides, genuine disbelief carved into his round face. "You didn't figure that out by the rant he went off on about literature verses movies? I thought for sure that had given away his true identity. Hence my decision to quickly return him to his own thread." He flippantly waved the thought away like a bothersome gnat and checked his watch yet again. "On occasion I forget that not everyone has the benefit of the panoramic time line."

The deep longing to embed her sword into his frontal lobe twisted up her spine, slithering into the very marrow of her bones. Shaking her clenched fists out at her sides prevented her from doing something she would regret—at least for the moment. "I'm sorry. Am I keeping you from an important date, White Rabbit?"

"As a matter of fact, yes," he stated, turning in an about face straight toward her. "I had hoped you would bring Ridley, but we will just have to find him later. That said, we run short on time. Shall we go?" He didn't wait for her response, before turning on his heel and marching down the alley.

"Give me one good reason I shouldn't toss my axe, pin your pant leg to the ground—a shot I am *more* than capable of by the way—and get my answers right here and now," Ireland demanded, making the threat more real by pinching the top edge of the axe and pivoting it one way then the other.

Filling his lungs, the blue-eyed man expelled an aggravated sigh and glanced back over his shoulder. "You want answers and I plan to take you to them. *That* would be why."

Ireland's tongue dragged over her top teeth, the stranger's enigmatic ways causing her pulse to throb in her temples. "You haven't told me who you are, or how you could *possibly* know so much about any of this. That doesn't breed a great deal of trust."

The man stopped short, his thick torso swiveling in her direction. "Heavens, I forgot to introduce myself? I *definitely* can't fault your hesitancy there. Well, young lady, my given name is Herbert George." Plucking a burnished bronze pocket watch from the breast pocket of his shirt, he compared the time to that of his wrist watch. Seemingly pleased with what he found, he spun the chain around his hand and offered her a warm smile. "However, history has come to know me as HG Wells."

About the Author

RONE Award Winner for Best YA Paranormal Work of 2012 for Embrace, a Gryphon Series Novel
Young Adult and Teen Reader voted Author of the Year 2012
Turning Pages Magazine Winner for Best YA book of 2013 & Best Teen Book of 2013

Stacey Rourke is the author of the young adult Gryphon Series as well as the thrilling Legends Saga. She lives in Michigan with her husband, two beautiful daughters, and two giant, dogs. She loves to travel, has an unhealthy shoe addiction and considers herself blessed to make a career out of talking to the imaginary people that live in her head. She is currently hard at work on the conclusion of the Legends Saga, as well as other literary projects.

Visit her at www.staceyrourke.com
diaryofasemi-crazyauthor.blogspot.com
Facebook at http://www.facebook.com/pages/Stacey-Rourke/
Twitter @Rourkewrites
Instagram rourkewrites

Somehow Luther's hand had made its way to my chin, and
he gripped it firmly. His lips lowered. I wanted to look away and
couldn't.

"Don't make me do this," I begged.

Luther grinned even as my lips parted. "Witch, I'm not in
your head right now. What you want now, in this moment, is all
you. There's a lot of things I'll take by force. Not that."

His lips crashed down onto mine, and I didn't fight him. I
didn't fight him because he was right. I wanted this.

His free hand went to my waist, playing with the skin just
under the hem of my t-shirt, and I plunged my fingers into his
hair. I had planned on pulling him away, but I gripped his head
instead, allowing him to deepen the kiss even as my other hand
found its way to his back, fisting the fabric of his t-shirt, the move

as desperate as the kiss. The muscles under his shirt were tight, restrained, and I knew then he was holding back.

The kiss, the moment, was so wrong, and yet that's precisely what made it so right. For *this* moment, I wasn't broken, I wasn't cursed, I wasn't a witch. I was Monroe, the vintage loving control freak kissing a man I was reasonably attracted to. Only he wasn't a man, and I wasn't just a girl.

Luther pulled me into him, and my hands moved to his face, my palms keeping his mouth trapped against mine. He growled, the sound primal as his hands gripped my hips painfully, one palm making its way slowly, *oh so slowly*, up to my ribs. I leaned into the touch.

A sound made me freeze.

Luther pulled away, his eyes trapping mine to his face even as I caught a glimpse of Belle at the edge of the clearing. My cheeks flamed.

"Sometimes," Luther whispered as Belle's figure disappeared, "being bad is better."

And with that, he released me. I almost stumbled to the ground, but caught myself, my eyes on anything but Luther.

"Tell me something really stupid or mundane about you," I said breathlessly. It seemed such a silly thing to say, and yet I needed something from him, something that made him more human than what he claimed to be.

I knelt on the lake's bank, one hand on the ground, an arm across my middle. My heart raced.

Luther knelt next to me. "I collect baseball caps."

I choked on the laugh that escaped. My eyes came back up to his. "Baseball caps?"

He shrugged. "I don't wear them. I just collect them. I like them."

I laughed, and this time I couldn't stop. It bubbled up and just kept coming.

Luther stood, his hand out. "It was just a kiss, Monroe. I didn't steal your soul."

I looked at his offered palm, my laughter turning to coughs.

I pushed myself up without taking his hand. "To be on the safe side, let's not do that again," I said.

Luther's lips twitched as I moved past him, my steps carrying me back toward the cabin.

"Oh, Witch," Luther chuckled. "I don't ever make promises like that."

82212534R00204

Made in the USA
Lexington, KY
27 February 2018